I KNOW WHAT YOU DID

A PSYCHOLOGICAL SUSPENSE THRILLER

N. L. HINKENS

Text copyright @ 2019 Norma Hinkens

Published by Dunecadia Publishing, California

ISBN: 978-1-947890-13-8

Cover by: **www.derangeddoctordesign.com**

Editing by: **www.jeanette-morris.com/first-impressions-writing**

❀ Created with Vellum

---

*J*o Murphy was losing her husband piece-by-piece. One day, one argument, one miscarriage at a time. Either that, or she was losing her mind. For the first time in her life she was at an impasse. Accomplishing whatever she applied herself to had always come easy to her, which made it that much more infuriating to be cheated out of this one thing that meant so much.

Three days earlier, a tiny heart inside her had thumped with life. Today, her womb was empty and her own heart full of a gnawing grief that her husband, Liam, couldn't fully grasp. She'd whispered to the jellybean person inside her, planned for his or her arrival just in time for Christmas, dreamed of a bright future filled with birthday cakes and playdates, and come up with a dozen different possible name combinations. The counselor side of her knew it was irrational to feel angry that Liam didn't seem overly sad about losing another baby. But he wasn't the one coping with the hormone crash that followed each miscarriage and left behind a chaotic tangle of dark emotions that devoured her reason, and consumed her soul. She would do anything to have a child—anything at all.

It was the doctor's loaded silence in the moment before he cleared his throat that shattered her dream of becoming a mother yet again. He expressed his sympathy in hushed tones, then swiftly moved on to explain her options for removing and disposing of the "clinical waste" that remained—a medical verdict reducing her child to a hazmat cleanup operation. A verdict she didn't want to accept.

"We'll keep trying, Jo," her husband whispered as he helped her to her feet.

Leaning on Liam's arm, she'd stumbled out of the gyne-cologist's pastel peach office and along the corridor of shame, as she'd come to regard it, hung with oversized canvasses of blooming flowers with babies tucked among their petals, past the front reception desk and the cork board teeming with dog-eared photos of gummy newborns, and through the waiting room full of flushed mothers-to-be exchanging congratulatory smiles as they patted and hugged the lives inside them—oblivious to the dead husk of a baby that Jo was carrying. For once, she'd managed to hold back her tears until she reached the car.

The drama had become too repetitive to recount in any great detail to her inner circle, a bomb of bad news that made everyone uncomfortable. So she opted to grieve alone this time, the haunting static noise from the fetal monitor on a continual loop in her head, while Facebook mercilessly shoved ads for maternity wear into her newsfeed at every opportunity.

Back at her desk at Emmetville High on Monday morn-ing, she exhaled a shuddering breath as she switched on her computer. Liam hadn't wanted her to return to work right away, but this was the one place where she was still in control. She was a lot better at her job as a school counselor than carrying babies as it turned out.

"Morning, Jo!" Robbie Gleeson, the AP chemistry teacher, stuck his head inside her office and wiggled his brows in an attempt at humor. "I won't assume it's a good one yet—too early to come to that conclusion. Can I grab you a coffee?"

She gave a tight, plastic smile that felt more like a portal to her pain than a cheery greeting. "Thanks, Robbie, I could use a strong one."

"You got it!" He disappeared down the corridor, whistling loudly, his footsteps echoing after him on the tile floor. Robbie, and his wife, Sarah—who taught AP studio art—had become close friends over the past year. Jo had been tempted on more than one occasion to share the agony of her miscarriages with them. But Liam, who worked as an independent computer network specialist and serviced the school's account, didn't want her work colleagues privy to their fertility struggles.

"It's emasculating, Jo. You don't understand."

"How's it emasculating?" Her tone wavered between incredulous and frustrated. "*I'm* the one who can't carry a pregnancy to term."

"Yeah, but it amounts to the same thing. I'm forty-one and still don't have kids. The thought of walking a gauntlet of pitying faces every time I show up on your campus makes me cringe."

Jo grimaced inwardly at the ominous reminder that their fertility clock was ticking. Her greatest fear was that Liam would walk away when her time ran out. She knew it was unfounded, but she couldn't shake the angst that had set in her brain like fast-curing cement. Even if Liam wasn't intentionally trying to make her feel worse than she already did, it didn't change the hard facts. She was almost thirty-nine—a combined total of eighty years between them. It didn't take a seasoned gambler to recognize that the odds against them were mounting. She was becoming increasingly desperate with each passing day.

Her archaic computer booted up just as Robbie reappeared with two paper cups of steaming black coffee. He plopped one on the desk in front of Jo and sank down in the creaky, tufted seat opposite her. "So, how was your weekend?"

Jo tried to give a nonchalant shrug. "Oh, you know, so-so."

"*So*-so?" Robbie slurped his coffee without taking his eyes off her. "Sounds more like a Monday. That can't be good."

Jo pushed her glasses up her nose and managed a wan smile. "Just got some family stuff going on. That's all."

Robbie ran a hand through his thick, dirty blond hair. "Are you and Liam all right?"

"Of course." She averted her gaze from his scrutiny. "We just … see things differently at times."

Robbie weighed this for a moment and then nodded thoughtfully. "You're intuitive, and Liam's more of a linear thinker, like me. Us left-brained types need to stick together. I swear, you creatives have psychic instincts or something."

Jo laughed despite herself. "You hold your own just fine."

"I give it my best shot. Why can't couples argue in equations or something that makes sense to me?" He let out an exaggerated groan. "All joking aside, if you want to talk about it, Sarah and I are here for you."

"Thanks, Robbie, I appreciate that, I really do. But you know Liam's a very private person, and—"

"Understood. Say no more." Robbie got to his feet and raised his half-full cup in a parting toast. "To a productive morning. I have an atomic theory quiz to put up on the board before my comatose students start rolling in. See you at lunch if they haven't gassed me out with body odors before then."

With a final wave, he strolled out of the office swinging his weathered briefcase. Jo settled back in her chair as he retreated down the corridor. Robbie was a good sort, always trying to make her laugh and lift her spirits. She hated having to lie to him, but Liam was right to be wary about sharing their problems with work colleagues. She wasn't strong enough emotionally to withstand a barrage of well-meaning questions about the infertility wasteland they seemed destined to camp out in. Besides, Robbie and Sarah were a good decade younger and wouldn't understand her all-consuming yearning to have a child.

She took a generous swig of her coffee before pulling up her daily calendar on the computer and viewing her appointments. She'd scheduled meetings with several students who were struggling in their classes. One of them in particular concerned her. She tapped the end of her pen distractedly on her desk. Mia Allen was a popular senior and varsity tennis player who was due to graduate in a couple of months. She'd been dating the football captain, Noah Tomaselli, for the past year, and, by any standards, they made a striking couple. Broody, olive-skinned, six-foot-four Noah was the campus stud. With a head of rich, dark curls and permanent five-o'clock shadow his Italian features contrasted dramatically with Mia's sleek, waist-length, blonde locks. They were both bright students, but lately, Mia's grades had slipped and several of her teachers had expressed concern.

Jo welcomed the challenge of getting to the bottom of whatever was bothering the girl. Focusing on someone else's issues would take her mind off her own troubles for a bit and, hopefully, dull the feelings of failure and despair that corroded her insides while she fought to hold it together on the outside. She drained the last of her coffee and tossed the empty paper cup in the trash can under her desk, grateful for the caffeine jolt.

A rap on the door made her look up. She smiled and slipped into her professional demeanor with practiced ease. "Come in, Mia. Sit down, please."

Mia Allen hitched up one side of her glossy, bow-shaped lips in a half-hearted greeting as she sank down in the seat Robbie had occupied moments earlier. Her big blue eyes swept the room disparagingly before settling on Jo. "You wanted to see me." She teased a hand lazily through her hair, looking as though she hadn't a care in the world.

Her tone verged on bored, but Jo was experienced enough to pick up on the strained note in her voice. Something was nagging at her.

"Yes, I did. Thanks for coming in early. I wanted to talk with you before the day gets underway."

Mia shrugged and examined an imaginary chip on her flawless fingernail.

Sensing a wall of resistance, Jo slipped into camaraderie mode. "Hard to believe the school year's almost over. Are you looking forward to graduating?"

Mia's eyes narrowed. An awkward pause ensued before she tilted a penciled brow in faux confusion. "Isn't everyone?"

Steeling herself, Jo plowed on. "Have you chosen a college yet, and a major?"

Mia's long lashes fluttered, a shrewd look in her eyes. "I'm … undecided."

"About going to university or what to study?"

"Both."

Jo frowned. "I'm disappointed to hear that. You're one of our most promising seniors, but your grades have been on a downward spiral lately."

Mia twirled a lock of hair around her finger. "Everyone's uptight about finals."

"But not everyone's grades are slipping. Is there something going on that you want to talk about?" Jo leaned across the desk, lowering her voice to a level of respectful compassion. "Maybe something at home, or between you and Noah?"

Mia scowled. "What makes you think it has anything to do with him?"

Jo leaned back in her chair, momentarily taken aback at the terse reaction. Evidently, she'd touched a sore spot.

"Anything you say to me in here is confidential," Jo went on. "I'm pretty good at helping students find solutions to their problems, especially the tough ones. There's not much I haven't encountered. Bullying, substance abuse—"

Mia exhaled a sharp breath. "I'm not a pothead, Mrs. Murphy!"

"No, I didn't think so. But obviously something's bothering you, and it's my job to help you."

Mia's eyes fluttered to catlike slits, studying Jo's face as if trying to gauge her trustworthiness. "I don't want to get in any trouble."

"Go on," Jo urged gently.

Mia wet her lips with the tip of her tongue. "I'm not sure I should be talking about it with a school counselor."

"Why, is it illegal? Did you see another student do something you're afraid to report?"

Mia snorted a laugh. "No, nothing like that. Just … an annoying problem."

"What is it then? I can't help you if you won't tell me what's wrong."

Mia darted a glance to the glass door as a shadow walked by. She lowered her voice. "The thing is, Mrs. Murphy, I'm pregnant."

"*I* can't keep it." Mia's gaze drilled into Jo. "I have to get rid of it. Will you help me?"

Goosebumps prickled along Jo's arms like maggots writhing under her skin. Her hands shook, and she hurriedly pulled them out of sight beneath the desk. She could scarcely believe what she was hearing. She'd promised to help Mia, but she hadn't expected this.

Shock detonated through her heart, but it was only a small component of what she was feeling. She was also fighting a rising tide of white-hot anger. Anger that this gorgeous girl sitting opposite her, who already had everything at her polished fingertips, now had a baby growing inside her. An *annoying problem* she didn't want. Just another bonus bestowed on her charmed existence. A triple play on the lottery of life that had also graced her with enviable looks and brains in equal measures.

A serpent-like jealousy twisted in Jo's gut, melding with the physical pain until she couldn't tell which was tormenting her more. She sucked in a tiny breath, fighting to keep her composure. Her work and her personal life weren't supposed to intersect like this. The wounds inside her were too raw, too fresh to ignore as Mia's words raked over them. Her request for help was like a trigger opening the dam, and now the emotions swirling and seething inside Jo were making her head spin, causing her mood to plummet once again to the ugly depths where her miscarriages lay buried.

"Are you all right, Mrs. Murphy?" Mia peered at her, sounding more peeved at being ignored than concerned that her counselor might be on the verge of passing out.

Jo blinked and passed a hand over her forehead. "Uh, yes. Sorry, Mia. Just a dizzy spell."

The sound of footsteps and voices in the corridor began to swell as students made their way to their first classes of the morning. Mia threw a harried look at the closed door. "So, will you help me?"

Jo cleared her throat in an effort to steady her voice. "What about Noah? Are you going to tell him?"

"No. I don't want him involved. If he tells his parents, they might try and talk me into keeping it, and that's not an option as far as I'm concerned."

Jo cringed inwardly at the words flung carelessly across the desk at her. Mia was talking about a living, growing human person as if it were a wart. Why couldn't *she* have been the one to miscarry and have the clinical waste that remained suctioned out of her? See how she liked it when she didn't have a choice in the matter. Jo should be the one still carrying her baby. She'd always been immeasurably grateful for the potential gift of a child. She settled her glasses farther down her nose and forced herself to look at Mia. "How far along are you?"

"Seven or eight weeks, I think." She twisted her lips. "I should have taken care of it by now, but I wasn't sure what to do."

"You did the right thing to ask for help." Jo leaned across

the desk and squeezed Mia's hand, her training kicking in despite the raging cauldron of emotions searing her heart. "Do your parents know you're pregnant?"

Mia shook her head. "They're separated. I live with my mom, but I can't tell her. She'd kill me, *literally*."

Jo hesitated, contemplating Mia's words. Her heart thundered in her chest as a radical idea took shape.

*J*o leaned back in her chair, her heartbeat booming inside her chest. The dark void inside her harbored a flicker of hope. What if she and Liam adopted Mia's baby? It would be the perfect solution for everyone involved. The thought of aborting a child genetically predisposed to be beautiful, smart, and talented was abhorrent. And even if the child was none of those things, Mia's and Noah's baby shouldn't be denied the chance to live. Jo would love it regardless of any defects. There was no sacrifice she wasn't willing to make to be a mother. She took a quick steadying breath and then dove in before she could second-guess herself. "There are other options, Mia. Adoption, for example. Your baby would be loved by a couple who—" Her voice caught in her throat and she coughed to cover up the emotion threatening to betray her. "Your baby would be brought up by parents who loved and wanted it, and you wouldn't have to live with any regrets."

Mia traced her slender fingertips across her brow, a perturbed frown forming on her flawless skin. "I ... don't want to do anything I might cringe over later, but I can't let anyone at school find out I'm pregnant. I feel so stupid for letting this happen."

Jo pasted on a suitably sympathetic expression. Inwardly, her resentment was building. Maybe an abortion was just a cringeworthy moment in time to Mia, but she hadn't been on the infertility side of the equation where every week in the womb was its own miracle. Beneath the desk, Jo squeezed her fingers tightly together. Her pulse fluttered as she wrestled for a moment with the idea of stepping outside of ethical boundaries. It was now or never. Everything happened for a reason. Maybe this was meant to be.

"No one in school has to know you're pregnant," she said, lowering her voice to a confidential whisper. "You'll have graduated before you're even showing."

Mia blinked her long lashes as she contemplated what Jo was saying. "So, are you saying you would help me put it up for adoption?"

"Absolutely," Jo assured her. "If that's what you want, I'll do what I can to make the process as smooth as possible."

Mia pressed whitened knuckles to her lips, a calculating look in her eyes. "I need to think it over. It's a big decision."

Jo nodded, digging her nails into her palms. She couldn't push too hard, but she couldn't give Mia too much slack either. She didn't want her walking out of here and scheduling an abortion after all. "I'm available to talk any time, so don't hesitate to come back later on this afternoon or tomorrow if you have any questions. Just don't put off the decision for too long—it's only going to get harder."

Mia stood, flicking a waterfall of silky blonde hair over one shoulder as she headed for the door. "Thanks, Mrs. Murphy. You've been very helpful."

Once Mia had left the room and closed the door behind her, Jo sank her face into her arms on the desk, trembling all over. She felt like a deflated balloon, bereft of air and sentiment, an empty sack of skin. How in any universe was it fair that Mia got to make the decision about whether her child lived or died when that decision had been made for Jo against her will? Salty tears pricked her eyes, but she forced them back as she gulped a steadying breath. She had to hold her head above the wave of emotions that threatened to drown her. Her next appointment would be here in a few minutes. She needed to get a grip and do what she did best. Tonight, she would evaluate her options and plan a reasonable course of action to steer Mia in the right direction.

BY THE TIME Jo shut down her computer for the day and pulled her car keys out of her purse, her thoughts were already gravitating back to Mia and her unborn child. The universe was holding out an olive branch to her, and she intended to take it. This baby was her ticket to saving her marriage, and her sanity in one fell swoop. She knew what she had to do and she would not allow her plan to fail. Time was of the essence. First, she had to sound out Liam. Would he be in favor of them adopting Mia's baby? They'd briefly discussed adoption in the past, but Liam hadn't wanted to give up on the dream of having their own child. The truth was, Jo was tired of the unending cycle of disappointment and defeat. Tired of the highs and lows that defined her as barren. She hated that word, so empty and purposeless. Her body had conspired against her for far too long. But now fate had thrown her a lifeline and she intended to take hold of it with both hands.

Besides, this was a chance for her and Liam to do something good while fulfilling their desire to have a child of their own at long last. Everyone would get what they wanted out of it. What was wrong with that? She deserved this child. A tiny bubble of anticipation flickered inside Jo's chest. By her calculation, they could be parents in time for Thanksgiving. A baby for the holidays. Could anything be more perfect? Surely it was a sign it was meant to be. She smiled at the framed photo of Liam on her desk. She would stop by the store on the way home and pick up some steaks to cook a romantic dinner before she presented her idea to him. Any resistance would melt in the face of her persuasive culinary efforts.

After locking up her office, Jo made her way to the parking lot and climbed into her car. She was about to turn the key in the ignition when someone pounded on the passenger side window. She glanced across to see Sarah Gleeson waving at her through the glass. She rolled down the window and grinned at her friend. "Hey you!"

"We missed you at lunch," Sarah said. "I just wanted to make sure you were okay. Robbie thought you seemed a bit down this morning."

"Just having some couple communications issues, nothing serious," Jo replied with a sheepish grin. It was even harder hiding the truth about her infertility from Sarah than it was from Robbie. She was one of those genuinely warm and caring people with an infectious smile—the kind of person you wanted to bare your soul to.

"Things aren't always what they seem. It's easy to get the wrong end of the stick—we've all been there," Sarah said, a shadow momentarily crossing her face. "But I have the perfect solution. Robbie and I are planning a getaway to Europe this summer. You and Liam should come too! It would do you good to have an adventure—experience something new. Of course, everything there's old, but that's kind of the point, isn't it?" she gushed. "Medieval castles, historical ruins. It all sounds so romantic, and it's been on my bucket list since seventh grade. It would be even better if you joined us."

"Wow, thanks, Sarah," Jo responded. "I'll run it by Liam this evening." She wouldn't of course, not now when there was a possibility of a baby on the horizon and all the added expense that went along with it. But, it was a sacrifice she was more than happy to make. Europe had been in existence for hundreds of years, and it would still be around to visit when their baby was grown.

"Awesome!" Sarah beamed at her. "Let me know what Liam says. We'd have a blast together." She blew Jo a kiss and headed off in the direction of her car.

Jo pulled out of the school parking lot and merged with the afternoon traffic, clearing her head of all thoughts of medieval Europe, her mind going instead to the sonogram of her most recent baby and the tiny heart that had inexplicably ceased to beat despite the empowering words she'd whispered to it and the love messages she had sent through the blood pumping along her own veins. She couldn't go through another miscarriage, and there would be no need to if her plan succeeded.

Inside the grocery store, Jo wheeled her cart down the dairy aisle eying the squirming babies propped up in carts as she went by. She glanced down at the two empty seats in the front of her own cart, imagining what it would be like to see tiny fingers gripping the bar, chubby legs kicking excitedly as she pretended to race the cart up and down the aisles. The anticipation inside her was building to volcanic overload. There was a real possibility she could become a mother this year if she played her cards right.

But first, she needed to persuade Liam to buy into the idea. After that, she would set her sights on Mia. The only hitch was the thorn of guilt that nagged at her about hiding Mia's pregnancy from the Tomaselli family. Noah had parents who would, no doubt, want their grandbaby to be a part of their lives if they knew of its existence. But she quickly quashed her pangs of conscience. She couldn't allow anything to come between her and the chance of becoming a mother.

When she reached the meat counter, she took her time selecting a cut of filet mignon, and then wandered over to the liquor aisle to pick up a bottle of Liam's favorite Syrah. The twenty-dollar price tag made it an indulgence for a weeknight, but it would be worth every penny if it bought her Liam's endorsement of her plan.

"Now that's my kind of dinner," the balding checker remarked as he rang her up. "All red and no green."

Jo chuckled politely. "My husband has a vegetable garden he takes great pride in, so I'm usually stuck cooking whatever has to be picked that week."

"And here I was thinking I'd found a soulmate," the checker said, shaking his head in mock sorrow as he handed her the receipt. "You have a good evening now."

Jo made it home shortly after four o'clock, which left her plenty of time to take a hot shower and set the table before she heated up the grill. Standing in front of the vanity mirror in her bathroom, she slipped off her glasses and surveyed herself with a critical eye. Her roots badly needed touching up. She kept putting it off, telling herself she needed to save her money for another round of IVF. It wasn't fair to herself or Liam to keep going on like this year after year. Deep down she suspected Liam was growing weary of it all too, working longer hours to avoid her and the empty house they had purchased with future children in mind. It was time to change tactics. If she couldn't make a baby, she would take Mia's unwanted one off her hands, one way or another.

*J*o hummed to herself as she prepped a platter of stir fry vegetables to accompany the steaks marinating in a casserole dish on the counter. Euphoria had replaced her feelings of failure. Her sense of desperation had dissipated now that she had a new target to shoot for, one that wasn't at the mercy of doctors, and monthly cycles, and fruitless procedures. She hadn't even opened the bottle of Syrah yet, but she already felt tipsy. This opportunity to adopt a baby had fallen into her lap out of the blue, a gift from God, who, up until now, had given and taken away with unrelenting consistency. She was well aware it would still require her finest negotiating skills to steer Mia toward making the right choice. Her main concern seemed to be hiding the fact that she was pregnant, although she had expressed some reluctance to make a decision she might regret later. Then there was Mia's mother to take into consideration. Would she push for an abortion? Even if she wanted her daughter to have the baby, would she be in favor of Mia's high school counselor adopting her grandchild? Jo wasn't entirely opposed to the idea of Mia's mother visiting the baby, but she had a feeling Mia wouldn't want that. If her mother began popping around to Jo's on a regular basis, it wouldn't take long for some nosy neighbor to connect the dots.

Once the vegetables were scrubbed, chopped, and diced, Jo set the glass table with an embroidered runner, silver-plated candlesticks and the Waterford crystal wine glasses that had been a wedding present but had sat in solitary confinement in a display cabinet ever since. The occasion merited risking their demise. That was the thing about euphoria, you took risks you wouldn't entertain in your normal emotional state where common sense prevailed.

Deciding the elegant decor needed a splash of color to finish it off, Jo took a pair of shears into the back yard and gathered a posy of pink, peach, and crimson roses for her favorite cut-crystal bowl centerpiece. As she stood back from the table admiring her handiwork, she heard the key turn in the front door. She hurriedly smoothed out her hair and whipped off her apron before turning to greet Liam.

"Hey honey," he said, a catch of uncertainty in his voice as he surveyed the dining table and subdued lighting. "What's going on?"

Jo slipped her arms around his neck and kissed him. "I just thought we deserved a special dinner tonight. It was a rough weekend for both of us."

Liam set his briefcase on the kitchen island and eyed the steaks. "Great."

The lingering wary note in his voice told Jo he was treading carefully, afraid to say too much, too little, or the wrong thing. Experience had proven that her post-miscarriage mood could change direction quicker than a tropical storm on steroids. Perhaps he feared she was about to proposition him with another round of IVF and all the humiliation it entailed for someone who valued his privacy as much as Liam did.

"Let me pour you a glass of wine and then I'll turn on the grill," Jo said. "I picked up a bottle of your favorite Syrah."

"Now you're talking. In that case, I'll cook the steaks," Liam replied, his tone warming to the occasion. He slipped off his jacket and hung it over the back of a bar stool before accepting the Waterford crystal wine glass Jo held out to him.

"Heavy," he said, raising the glass up and down. "Are these new?"

Jo shook her head in mock disbelief as she filled a glass for herself. "You've only been staring at them in the cabinet for the past decade. But to be fair, we never use them."

Liam carelessly clinked his glass to hers. "Well, I'm glad you changed your mind. Seems a shame not to fill them with a good vino and air them out every now and again."

A reprimand to be more careful with the crystal danced on the tip of her tongue, but Jo swallowed it back. Liam was blissfully unaware that he was drinking from a glass three times more costly than the wine they were consuming. But this wasn't the time to sidetrack him. She'd already resolved not to complain if her steak was overdone, which tended to be the case when Liam manned the grill. She would praise his efforts effusively. Tonight, she needed her husband to be receptive to what she was about to propose. Knowing Liam, he would have a hard time seeing past the potential pitfalls in adopting a student's baby. Somehow, she had to convince him they could make it work, and more importantly, that it was the right thing to do. She couldn't bear any more failures. Or heartbreak. The painful shards of her most recent miscarriage were still embedded in the darkest corners of her heart.

"Let me know when you're five minutes out and I'll throw on the vegetables," she said, handing Liam the dish with the marinated steaks. She watched as he set about firing up the grill and brushing it down. For once, she let her mind wander in the forbidden realm, imagining him tossing a hot dog on the grill next to the two steaks, and then chasing a squealing, diaper-laden little person around the backyard while their meal cooked. That was what tonight was all about. Paving the way to becoming a proper family. She needed to convey that to Liam, to counter every negative point he raised with a positive one until she broke down his resistance, and the captivating picture of their future family became lodged in his mind as firmly as it was in hers.

"Tell me about your day," she said once they were seated opposite each other at the table in the dining room. She spooned a helping of crispy vegetables onto Liam's plate and passed it to him.

"Thanks, honey. I'm upgrading a network system for some new clients—a law firm in town, nice people. They took me out to lunch at that new place that overlooks the river, The Monarch Grill. We should go there sometime." He sawed on a piece of overdone steak and chewed and swallowed before settling a circumspect gaze on her. "How was your first day back at school?"

"Really good actually. I'm glad I only took Friday off. It's better for me to be at work where I can feel useful. I don't want to hang around the house moping."

"You certainly make a difference in those kids' lives," Liam said. "I don't know how you do it, listening to them spouting about their problems week in and week out. It would do my head in."

"Speaking of making a difference," Jo said, her tone measured and deliberate. "I had a senior drop by my office this morning. She asked me to help her with something and I thought I'd run it by you to see what you thought."

"Shoot," Liam said agreeably, reaching for the bottle to

refill their wine glasses.

Jo dabbed at her lips with her linen napkin, her nerves coiled like a spring inside her. She had to bear in mind that it was unrealistic to expect instantaneous buy-in to her scheme on his part. Decision-making for Liam was a multi-step process involving copious amounts of research and analysis, whether it involved buying a new refrigerator or planning a vacation. The idea of jumping on an opportunity was foreign to him.

"Her name's Mia Allen. She's one of our most accomplished seniors," Jo said, selecting her words carefully. "She's been dating Noah Tomaselli, the football captain, for the past year or so."

"Yeah, I know his dad, Sérgio," Liam mumbled between bites. "Good guy. Big shot financial planner. I played golf with him at a charity fundraiser."

Jo took a quick sip of her wine, allowing herself a moment to digest this. It wasn't necessarily a bad thing that Liam had socialized with Noah's father. But it wasn't exactly a good thing either. It might make him push back on the idea of not telling the Tomaselli family about the baby. Jo speared a forkful of vegetables and shoved them into her mouth wrestling with how to proceed. There was too much at stake to risk Liam axing the idea before it got off the ground. There was only one way to ensure he wouldn't raise any objections about Noah's rights. She would simply tell him that Mia didn't know who the father was. Granted, it wouldn't portray Mia in a particularly good light, but Jo could live with herself telling one little white lie if it meant getting Liam on board.

"You were saying?" he prompted, reaching for the salt.

Jo set down her glass, her scalp prickling. She was about to betray a student's confidence, but, under the circumstances, it was justifiable. If this conversation went the way she hoped it would, Mia's *annoying problem*, would be resolved in the most rewarding way imaginable. "I could tell right away she was distraught about something," Jo continued. "She kept fidgeting and she looked nervous—totally out of character for her—but it took a while before I could persuade her to tell me what was wrong."

Liam blinked expectantly across at Jo.

"She finally confessed that she's pregnant."

Liam raised his brows a fraction. "By the Tomaselli kid?"

"That's the thing," Jo said, studying the stem of her glass as she twirled it between her fingers. "She doesn't know who the father is."

Liam released a low whistle and leaned back in his chair. "What a mess, and right before graduation. What does she expect you to do about it?"

"She wants me to walk her through the adoption process." Jo picked at a frayed thread on the runner before settling her gaze on Liam. "I've been thinking about it ever since. Why don't you and I offer to adopt her baby?"

"Whoa! Slow down there." Liam set down his fork with a clatter and coughed before straightening up in his chair. "You're a school counselor not a relief agent for a charity." He wiped a hand over his jaw, frowning. "You didn't say that to her, did you—about wanting to adopt her baby?"

"No, of course not. I wouldn't suggest anything like that without talking it over with you first." Jo smiled tentatively at him over the cut glass bowl of roses. "What would be wrong with us adopting her baby?"

Liam twisted his fork nervously in his hand. "She's a student in your care. Is that even ethical?"

"She won't be a student anymore by the time the baby's born. She graduates in two months, and she turns eighteen in ten days—I checked her file. It's perfectly legal for her to select whomever she wants to adopt her baby." Jo adjusted her glasses and gazed earnestly at Liam. "Mia would feel a whole lot better about her decision if her baby was placed with someone she knew and respected."

"Honey," Liam said, in a tone brimming with caution. "You're still hormonal. You're not thinking straight. We haven't even decided if we want to adopt or try another round of IVF."

Jo sighed. "I'm tired, Liam, and we're not getting any younger. And we both know how much you hate the whole IVF process. This is our chance to become parents—this year, not at some vague date in the future—and, at the same time, we'd be doing something good for a young woman about to embark on the rest of her life."

Liam shook his head slowly. "That all sounds good in theory, but what about the father? What about his rights?"

"Do you really think some teenage boy Mia had a fling with is gonna want to be a dad right out of high school? Besides, Mia's adamant she doesn't want anyone to know she's pregnant. She's not interested in finding out who the father is."

"But we'd have to lie to our friends and … our parents," Liam said, the horror of it written all over his face.

"No, we wouldn't," Jo protested. "We can tell them it was a private adoption per the mother's request."

Liam reached for his glass and took a hefty swig of wine before setting it back down with a *thunk* that made Jo cringe.

"How far along is this girl anyway?" he asked abruptly.

"Seven or eight weeks, or so."

The vintage ring tone of Liam's phone interrupted them before he could respond.

Jo gritted her teeth in frustration at the bad timing. She was certain Liam had just begun to entertain the idea of adopting Mia's baby—moving beyond throwing out objections to fact-finding.

"It's the new clients. I need to take this." He pushed out his chair and got to his feet, a relieved look flooding his face at the temporary reprieve.

Jo heard the sound of the door opening and then a murmured exchange, too low to make out. A moment later, Liam reappeared in the arched entrance from the kitchen to the dining room. "Their system's gone down. I need to go in and reboot it. Don't wait up for me."

Jo remained seated until the front door slammed behind him, and then got to her feet with a sigh. She made her way back to the kitchen and started rinsing off the plates and loading them into the dishwasher. It was painfully obvious that she and Liam had very different priorities.

Her mood plummeted as she scrubbed the wok she had cooked the vegetables in. The despair she'd felt over the weekend roared back in like a tidal wave—filling the empty hole inside her with doubt. Maybe Liam wasn't as deeply invested in becoming a parent as she was. Was he growing weary of a relationship that seemed to center around the issue of their childlessness?

She closed up the dishwasher and set it to run, then poured herself another half glass of wine before sitting down to scroll through her YouTube channel subscriptions, hoping to numb her pain with mindless consumption. Forty-five minutes went by before she caught herself and closed the app. Biting back tears of frustration, she retreated to the stairs to get ready for bed. The evening was shot. There was no point in waiting up for Liam—he'd be too cranky to discuss anything by the time he got home. She would finish her conversation with him tomorrow night. The clock was ticking, but there was still time to convince him they needed this baby.

*A*fter a restless night spent worrying about the best way to convince Liam that adopting Mia's baby was the right thing to do, Jo rolled out of bed the next morning feeling shattered and running too late for a much-needed shot of coffee. At school, she struggled through her first appointment of the morning, stifling yawns and trying to make appropriately sympathetic sounds at regular intervals as a junior with a marooned pimple in the middle of her forehead ranted bitterly about her basketball coach's bias against playing her. When the bell finally rang for morning break, Jo gratefully dismissed the student. Before she had a chance to take a bathroom break, her phone rang. She frowned at the unknown number before putting the phone to her ear. "Hello?"

"Mrs Murphy, this is Tory Allen … Mia's mother. Do you have a minute? I can call back later if this isn't a good time."

"Not at all, I just finished up an appointment," she sputtered, endeavoring to recover from her shock. "And please, call me Jo."

"I should have scheduled a meeting, but it's an emergency

and I needed to talk to you as soon as possible." Tory let out a sigh before adding. "Mia told me she met with you yesterday."

"Did she tell you what we talked about?" Jo asked, her tone polite but guarded.

"Yes." Tory let out an aggrieved breath. "I should have seen it coming. All those sleepovers at friends' houses. She must have been with him the whole time."

"By him, you mean Noah?" Jo prodded.

"Yes, they've been together for a while now."

Jo chewed on her lip for a moment. She wished she'd had more time to prepare for this conversation. If she could win Mia's mom over, it might help sway Mia's decision, but she had to be careful not to overreach too soon. She had to make it feel like it was their decision. "Did you and Mia get a chance to discuss what she wanted to do about it?"

"That's why I'm calling you. She said you offered to help her with the adoption process."

"I did, and I meant it," Jo assured her. "As her counselor, I'll support her in any way I can."

"The thing is, she doesn't want Noah to find out—about the baby. For that matter, she doesn't want anyone at school to know." Tory hesitated. "Is that legal? I don't want any of this coming back to haunt us. The Tomasellis are loaded, so if they sue me, I'm screwed."

"There's no legal requirement to notify Noah unless Mia intends to keep the baby and go after child support," Jo answered.

"She doesn't want to keep it. To be honest, I'm not in a position to help her raise a child anyway. I clean offices for a living." Tory gave a hollow laugh. "I was only sixteen when I dropped out of school to have Mia. I want something better for her."

"Then she can simply put *father unknown* on the birth

certificate," Jo explained, squirming under the prick of her conscience. Just because it was legal didn't mean it was fair to the Tomaselli family. But then, nothing was fair when it came to the roulette wheel of conception and miscarriage either.

Tory blew out a perturbed breath. "I told Mia she'll have to go and stay with her father after she graduates until the baby is born if she wants to keep the pregnancy a secret. This town's too small."

"Where does he live?" Jo asked.

"San Francisco. I imagine there are plenty of couples in a city that size who'd want to adopt a baby."

"I'm sure you're right," Jo said, her stomach writhing at the thought of strangers adopting Mia's baby. In her mind, she was already the chosen one. It was only a matter of sealing the deal. Sweat prickled beneath the bridge of her glasses and she pinched her nose between her thumb and forefinger, wiping it away. "Why don't you and Mia make an appointment to come in to my office, and we'll get the process started. I'm here from seven-thirty until four-thirty every day."

"I guess. If I can get off work early," Tory said, sounding dubious. "I work until four."

Jo scrunched her eyes shut. She sensed that Tory Allen might never darken her door if she hung up without getting a firm commitment. It was time to take a risk, just a small one to begin with. "I'm happy to see you at my home after hours if that makes it easier for you. Or at your place if you prefer. Are you free any evening this week?"

"I have to work tonight. Wednesday or Thursday would suit. It would be easier if you came to our place."

"Then let's say Wednesday at five-thirty. Is your current address in Mia's file?"

"Yes. Thank you. You've no idea how much I appreciate

your help. It's overwhelming to even think of tackling this on my own. It's bad enough being a single parent on a regular day. When something like this comes along, it feels like a tsunami bearing down."

Jo hung up the phone, flushed with success. This was going to work. She'd never been more certain of anything. Tory knew only too well the struggles of a young, unwed mother raising a baby alone. It could work in her favor if she played it right. She would put all the pieces in place and present her idea to Tory and Mia on Wednesday night, with Liam at her side. She just had to work on him before then and make sure he was fully committed. She didn't want him showing any reluctance in Tory's presence.

As she exited her office to head to the staff break room, shouts from the student locker area reached her ears. She broke into a jog in the direction of the disturbance. A group of students were waving fists and cheering someone on in their midst. Jo began elbowing her way through the crowd to get to the center of the ruckus. To her horror, a wild-eyed Mia was flailing her fists on Noah's chest, yelling insults as he tried to fend her off.

"Don't lie to me! You've been sleeping with someone else for months now," Mia screamed at him, while several onlookers laughed and egged her on.

"You're crazy," Noah responded. "I'm not seeing anyone else. Get a grip. I don't have to account for every minute of my day to you."

"I have proof you've been cheating on me!" Mia spat back. "A photo!"

"Mia!" Jo called out.

Her head spun in Jo's direction and a scowl settled on her face. "I don't need a counselor right now. This has nothing to do with you."

"Fair enough," Jo responded. "But if you don't break it up, I'm calling security."

Mia balled her hands into fists and glared at Noah again, before turning on her heel and storming through the audience of students already snap-chatting the drama out to any friends who hadn't been lucky enough to have a ringside seat.

"You all right, Noah?" Jo asked.

He opened his locker, grabbed an armful of books, and slammed the door shut before answering. "Fine. She's been acting all crazy lately."

A sliver of fear cut through Jo. Had Mia told Noah about the baby? She needed to do some damage control and find out exactly what was going on between them. She wasn't about to let this chance to become a mother slip through her fingers. "I want to see you in my office tomorrow after break, Noah."

"I wasn't fighting," he protested.

"No, you were assaulted, and several students recorded it. I need to take your statement. It'll only take a few minutes."

"I have an away game tomorrow," he said, tossing his hair to one side.

Jo pressed her lips together. "Thursday then, first period after break."

"Yeah, whatever." He turned and swaggered off down the hallway with a fellow teammate. The crowd began to disperse, laughingly recounting the highlights of the brawl.

Jo walked back down the corridor, her pulse still quivering from the encounter. When she reached the seclusion of the staff break room, she poured herself a large coffee and sank down in a sagging lounge chair nursing her mug as she mused over what she'd witnessed. Mia had come across as somewhat dispassionate in Jo's office, but she was obviously in a fragile emotional state. Jo had no idea whether or not her accusation about Noah cheating on her had any merit, but it might drive Mia to rethink the whole idea of giving up her baby for adoption. What if she decided to tell Noah she was pregnant in an effort to keep him? With the Tomaselli family involved, any hope of adopting the baby would be dashed.

"Hey you!" Sarah threw herself down in the chair next to Jo. "Why the long face?"

She gave a wry grin. "It's the counselor in me, always worrying about my students. I just broke up a scuffle between the school heart throbs."

"Mia and Noah?" Sarah arched a questioning brow.

"Yeah. Mia was really going at it, hammering on Noah with her fists. She accused him of cheating on her."

Sarah grimaced. "I noticed Noah's been rather stressed out in my class lately. And who gets stressed out in art class? I had to give him a bit of a pep talk the other day."

Jo gave a vague nod, not wanting Sarah to dig any deeper. If she found out Mia had been in to see her, she'd be curious to know why. "Graduation flutters most likely. It'll pass."

Sarah lifted her green faux-leather purse onto her lap and rummaged through it, knocking a cell phone to the floor in the process.

Jo went to reach for it, but Sarah snatched it up and tossed it into her bag. "My mother's. She left it in my car."

"How's she doing anyway?" Jo asked, seizing the opportunity to change the subject. Sarah's mom, Barb Davidson, suffered from early onset Alzheimer's and had moved into Brookdale Meadows, an expensive residential facility, several years earlier. She'd been a successful real estate investor in her day and thankfully had the funds to pay for her own care. Sarah visited her faithfully every Sunday afternoon and sometimes took her out for a short drive if Barb was up to it.

"No clue who I was, as usual." Sarah gave a rueful grin.

"She asked me if I was her doctor. Last week she thought I was the gardener, she buzzed security because she couldn't understand what I was doing in her room."

"Yikes! I'm sorry," Jo said. "That must be hard."

"Yeah, she's been there almost five years now. I think she still enjoys my visits even though she doesn't always recognize me." Sarah pulled a handful of brochures out of her purse and waved them seductively in front of Jo. "On a brighter note, I brought these for you to look through. Thought it might convince you to shake things up a bit—book a couple of tickets and join us."

Jo reached for the brochures and flipped through the top one on the pile. A smiling doll with blonde braids dressed in a black and red dirndl stared back at her from a shop window, eyes as startling blue as Mia's. In the background, a picturesque Bavarian village replete with brightly-colored window baskets buzzed with activity. Sarah and Robbie could afford to splurge on trips like these thanks to a generous annual disbursement from Barb's estate. Jo didn't begrudge them their frequent trips away, but she remained laser-focused on channeling all her and Liam's extra funds into their pursuit of parenthood. "Looks enticing," she said, with a sigh of regret as she pushed her glasses back up her nose, "but I'm afraid Europe's not in our budget this year." She tugged at her hair self-consciously. "First thing on the agenda is getting these roots redone. I'm an embarrassment to myself."

Sarah laughed. "I have an eleven o'clock at the beauty salon in the mall on Saturday for a haircut. Why don't you come along? We can do lunch afterward."

"Sounds good. But lunch is on me this time."

"It's a date. Keep the brochures in case you change your mind. I'll probably bug you about it some more before I give up." Sarah glanced at her watch. "Gotta run. I need to set up easels for my next class."

Jo finished her coffee and stood to leave just as Robbie strode through the doorway. He grinned when he caught sight of her. "Ah, the counselor with superpowers."

Jo wrinkled her brow. "What are you talking about?"

"My chem students told me you powered through a line of football players and single-handedly broke up a lover's brawl," he said with an elaborate wink.

"More like a spat," Jo replied. "But I did have to weave my way through a labyrinth of sweaty bodies, and most of them had a good six inches on me."

Robbie threw back his head and guffawed. "Wish I'd witnessed that play!"

Jo rolled her eyes. "I've been meaning to ask you, how have Mia and Noah been in chemistry class lately?"

"Noah's been a bit withdrawn to tell you the truth." A circumspect expression flitted across Robbie's face. "Did you know Mia stormed off campus after you broke up their scuffle? She must be taking it very badly that Noah's been two timing her."

"Where did you hear that?" Jo asked.

"You mean apart from the chatter on the student grapevine, Snapchat, Instagram posts, and the scrawled messages of support on Mia's locker?" Robbie chuckled. "It's the number one news item on campus."

"I'm sure it will all have blown over by tomorrow." Jo waved the stash of brochures in front of Robbie before stuffing them into her purse. "Sarah's trying to talk me and Liam into joining you on your trip to Europe. She's hawking it as a communications cure for couples."

A flicker of irritation crossed Robbie's face. "That's not a done deal yet. We're still tossing around the idea."

Jo shrugged, thrown off by his unusually cool response.

"No worries, it's not in our budget this year anyway."

AS SHE WAS PULLING out of the school parking lot at the end of the day, Liam texted to say he was working late and wouldn't make it home in time for dinner. Jo fought back her frustration as she messaged him back, telling him about the altercation between Noah and Mia, and reminding him that they needed to talk about the baby. As she drove home, she resigned herself to sitting up until whatever hour Liam came home at in order to finish their conversation. No matter how tired he was, she had to get his blessing before tomorrow.

After stashing the pork chops she'd bought for their dinner in the freezer, Jo made herself a quick sandwich and took it into the family room to catch the evening news. It occurred to her that it might be a good idea to swing by Mia's house and check up on her. After all, she felt partly responsible that she'd stormed out of school early. Tory was at work so that meant Mia would be home alone, and there was no telling what she might do if she was upset enough. Jo debated texting first but decided against it in case Mia told her not to come.

She swallowed down the last bite of her sandwich, barely tasting it, and then logged into the school website on her phone and pulled up Mia's file to get her address. She frowned at the familiar street name, *Fairview Court*, in the West Ridge district. What a coincidence. Mia and her mother lived in the same sub-division as Robbie and Sarah—they were just around the corner on Fairview Place.

As she drove across town, Jo rehearsed in her mind what she would say to Mia. Mostly, she wanted to reassure her that she was still on her side and willing to help her with the adoption process. She was worried that the argument with Noah might have pushed Mia in another direction. Obviously, the girl wasn't thinking straight, and Jo didn't want her doing anything stupid on the spur of the moment. Hormones, as she knew only too well, were couriers of confusion, buzzing your mind with so many irrational thoughts that it was impossible to tackle anything in a logical manner.

It was dusk by the time she turned onto Fairview Court. She drove slowly down the tree-lined road counting down house numbers until she arrived at Mia's place. To her surprise, Sarah's car was parked outside. Jo increased her speed and drove on by. She didn't want to barge in if Sarah had already stopped by to check up on Mia. Maybe it wasn't such a bad thing. Sarah was her neighbor, after all, and a very nurturing person. More than capable of talking Mia down off the ledge if it came to that. Jo would just have to wait until tomorrow evening to meet with her and hope for the best that she didn't make any rash decisions before then. Resigned to her course of action, she returned home and waited for Liam to get back.

It was close to midnight when she finally heard the front door open. She was wide awake on the couch, clutching the remote, her mind too revved up to sleep or to concentrate on the movie playing in the background.

"You're still up." Liam's tone conveyed surprise but also a kernel of annoyance that made Jo wonder if he'd deliberately stayed away this late in a bid to get out of talking about the adoption. Didn't he realize that she was trying to rescue them from the infertility curse that was slowly destroying their relationship?

"Are you trying to avoid me?" Jo prodded. She knew better than to put Liam on the defensive, but after waiting all this time on him she couldn't rein in her frustration.

"Of course not," he said evenly. "This has nothing to do with us. I ran into some glitches with the network system and the company has a product launch tomorrow. So, I had to make sure everything was functioning smoothly before I left."

"And you don't think a baby is a tad more important than a product launch?" Now she was stoking the fire, but she needed Liam to want this as badly as she did.

"Honey," he soothed, "this isn't a question of which is more important. The product launches tomorrow. The baby, by my reckoning, is still seven months away."

Jo blinked in surprise, a momentary flicker of elation almost taking her breath away when she realized that Liam had actually been paying attention when she'd told him that Mia was seven or eight weeks along. Maybe he was more interested than she gave him credit for. The audacious speed at which her emotions could pivot perplexed her, but for now she would embrace the direction they were taking. She patted a spot on the couch. "Sit down."

Liam threw his briefcase on the leather recliner and loosened his tie before joining her. He rubbed his eyes with his thumb and forefinger before letting out a sigh. "I've been thinking about our conversation in the few minutes I was able to snatch at work. You know there's nothing more that I want than for us to have a family, Jo. If you're sure you're ready to move on to adoption, then I'm with you. We might as well begin by exploring this opportunity that's come our way."

Jo gaped at him, her heart somersaulting. "Do you really mean that, Liam? Because I don't want you to say it just because it's past midnight and you're too exhausted to argue."

Liam put an arm around her shoulders and drew her close. He gently removed her glasses and kissed the tip of her nose. "I mean it. If anyone can make this work, it's you. I know how determined you are. You'll stop at nothing."

6

Shortly before seven the following evening, Jo and Liam pulled up outside Tory's two-story crafts-man-style house. Jo hadn't been able to stop smiling all day. Her face was physically aching from the feat. She reached over and squeezed Liam's hand before they climbed out of the car. "Let me do the talking. I know Mia reasonably well, and I have a good understanding of where Tory's coming from after speaking with her on the phone the other day. The fact that you're here with me is more than enough to show them that you support our decision."

Liam gave a mock salute. "Yes, Counselor Jo, happy to take a backseat and watch you wield your masterful powers of negotiation."

Jo leaned over and kissed him softly on the lips. Why had she ever doubted that Liam was in this with her? He'd always been her staunchest supporter and ally in everything she'd embarked upon—guiding her to shore each time she lost her way on a sea of despair.

They walked hand-in-hand up the cracked concrete pathway to the wraparound front porch. The house itself had good bones, and this was a great neighborhood, but the dingy facade was in sore need of a paint job. Liam rang the doorbell and, after a moment or two, the door scraped open. A willowy, blonde woman dressed in a loose-fitting black top, black leggings and Vans peered out at them. She glanced uncertainly from Jo to Liam and then back to Jo, her high ponytail flipping back and forth. "Oh, hi. I'm Tory. I … wasn't expecting both of you."

Jo flashed her a disarming smile, taking in her high cheekbones, porcelain skin, and wide, blue eyes so reminiscent of Mia's. She must have been a very young mom or else she'd had some quality work done. "My husband, Liam, is going to be an integral part of the process, so I brought him along in case you have any questions for him."

Tory raised her sculpted brows, but she stepped aside and gestured for them to come in. She led them past the stairs and into a low-ceilinged kitchen with dated appliances and older cabinetry that someone had repainted a shade of moss green in a misguided attempt to spruce things up. It only served to lend a moldy ambience to the room. A stack of dirty dishes peeked out over the lip of a stainless-steel sink, and a long, fluorescent beam light that barely lit the recesses of the room buzzed overhead. Tory grabbed a tea towel and hurriedly wiped down a spot on the table before pulling out a couple of chairs. Jo slid into one, eying the mountain of paperwork and school text books that covered the other end of the table.

Tory stuck her head around the kitchen door and yelled up the stairs, "Mia! Your counselor's here."

She beamed awkwardly at Jo and Liam as she joined them at the table. "She'll be down in just a minute."

"Not a problem," Jo said. "Have you two had a chance to talk any more about what you want to do?"

"Mia was all for giving the baby up for adoption, but after

yesterday's fiasco at school she changed her mind and said she wasn't sure what she wanted to do." Tory twisted her lips. "She's all over the place. Crying one minute, raging at Noah the next." She jerked her head up as Mia's form darkened the doorway. "There you are!"

Mia stared brazenly at Liam, arms folded across her chest. "What's he doing here?"

"This is Liam Murphy, Mrs. Murphy's husband," Tory answered. "He's here to help with the adoption process. Your counselor was about to explain to us how it all works."

Scowling, Mia slumped into a chair at the far end of the table half-hidden behind the huge pile of books.

Jo took a quick breath and turned to face her. "I told you I would help you with the adoption process, and I will, Mia. The reason I brought my husband along tonight is because, after talking things over with him, we'd like to do more than just help facilitate the adoption." She threw a quick glance at Liam and reached for his hand before turning back to Mia. "Liam and I would like to adopt your baby."

Tory gasped out loud, her hand shooting to her mouth.

Mia puckered her forehead, as she picked an imaginary fleck from the sleeve of her sweater. "Why?"

"It's because—" Jo began but Mia cut her off.

"Not you." Her eyes darted to Liam. "I want him to answer."

Liam cleared his throat and rubbed the back of his neck with his free hand. "Well, Jo and I have been trying to have a baby of our own for the past ten years. It's been a painful journey filled with disappointment and more miscarriages than I want to remember. We've discussed adoption in the past, and when you met with Jo on Monday and told her you were pregnant, she came home and talked it over with me." Liam paused briefly before continuing. "I want to be a dad more than anything in the world."

Tory stared at Liam, her whitened knuckles pressed tight to her face. She shot a curious look in Mia's direction as if waiting for her to respond.

Mia trailed her long fingernails slowly through her hair, studying Liam with a catlike stare that Jo found somewhat unnerving. Finally, her lips curved into a cool smile. "Not all men make good fathers. You might, though."

Jo and Liam exchanged cautiously optimistic looks, not daring to speak.

"So, now what happens?" Tory piped up.

"Well," Jo began, trying not to sound flustered at the abrupt transition. "If you want to proceed, we'll need to start by hiring a lawyer to ensure the adoption is legal. Naturally Liam and I will cover all the legal fees."

"And we're happy to help with medical and miscellaneous expenses too," Liam added.

"That's very generous," Tory said. "It's tough to keep up with the bills as it is. This has thrown me for a loop." She threw a loaded look at Mia who narrowed her eyes in return. A tiny shiver ran down Jo's spine. What was that all about?

"We'll go ahead and contact an adoption lawyer to draw up the paperwork to make sure we comply with any adoption laws," Jo continued. "In the meantime, Mia, you'll need to make an appointment with your OBGYN, if you haven't already."

Mia gave a disgruntled shrug. "Whatever."

An awkward pause ensued during which Tory mouthed an apology to Jo.

"Well, we should probably get going," Jo said, looping the strap of her purse over her shoulder. "I'll bring the paperwork over for you to sign as soon as it's drawn up. You both have my number if you have any questions." She glanced at Mia who was staring fixedly at a spot on the table in front of her. "If you need some extra time to catch up on the work you missed yesterday, I can have a word with your teachers for you—unless Mrs. Gleeson already offered to talk to them for you?"

Mia regarded her with a bemused look. "What?"

"When she stopped by last night," Jo hastened to explain. "I was worried about you being alone when you were so upset, so I drove over here to check up on you. I felt better once I saw Mrs. Gleeson's car outside, so I went on home."

A flicker of annoyance crossed Mia's features. She waved a hand vaguely. "Oh, that's right. She dropped my chemistry homework off."

"Great, well let me know if I can help you with anything else," Jo reiterated. "And thank you, Mia. I can't even begin to tell you what a gift you're giving Liam and me." She hesitated for a moment, debating whether or not to give Mia a hug, but it felt like forced intimacy. There was bound to be a more opportune moment further down the line when Mia would be more receptive to such a gesture.

"Good to meet you both," Liam said with a smile and a nod as he got to his feet. Tory accompanied them to the door and then threw a quick glance over her shoulder in the direction of the kitchen before lowering her voice. "I'm sorry Mia's acting so prickly tonight. I think she's taking it real bad about Noah. She's convinced he's seeing someone else."

"That's totally understandable," Jo assured her. "She's under a lot of stress. Don't worry, I promise I'll keep a close eye on her at school."

"Thanks. I'll make sure she sets up that doctor appointment." Tory extended her hand and Jo shook it firmly, a shiver of anticipation tingling down her spine at the touch of the woman's slender fingers. She was shaking hands with her baby's grandmother. It felt right, a handshake to secure the mutually beneficial deal that was in the making.

Back in the privacy of their car, Liam exhaled loudly as he

turned the key in the ignition. "Well, the offer's on the table. Looks like we're going to be parents."

Jo grinned at him, blinking back tears. "Mia had her defenses up, but on the whole, it went a lot more smoothly than I expected."

"She was throwing poison-tipped daggers my way at first," Liam said with a chuckle.

"She wasn't expecting you to be there. To be fair, we sprang this whole thing on her. But I think hearing you share your heart convinced her."

"I meant every word," Liam responded. "Although I was sweating so much, I can't remember half of what I said. All I can tell you is that I'll put every effort into being the best dad ever."

Jo traced the back of her finger down his cheek. "The best dad and the best husband. Thanks for sticking with me through all of this. I know it hasn't been easy at times, but you're finally going to experience fatherhood. What do you say we celebrate and go catch that new action movie you've been wanting to see?" She glanced at the clock in the car. "It starts in fifteen minutes. We can still make it."

Her phone rang before Liam had a chance to respond. She fished it out of her purse and stared at the screen. "It's Sarah. She's probably gonna try and talk me into that European trip again."

She swiped a finger across the screen. "Hey there!"

"Hi, Jo," Sarah replied. "I was just talking to Robbie about our trip to Europe and—"

Jo stifled a laugh and hit the speaker button so Liam could listen in.

"—I thought I'd ask if you'd run the idea by Liam yet. I know you said it wasn't in the budget, but if you wanted to go, Robbie and I could spring for the rental car and VRBO's.

I've been browsing some really reasonable ticket prices. What do you say?"

"That's more than generous of you, Sarah. To be honest, I haven't had a chance to talk to Liam about it yet. We're on our way to catch a movie. But maybe over the weekend we'll take a look at the brochures." Jo rolled her eyes at Liam and he gave a knowing smile.

"Which movie?" Sarah asked.

"Some new thriller Liam wants to see." Jo raised her brows questioningly at him.

"*Manhattan Mystery*," he said.

"Oh, I saw it last night. It's good! We went to dinner first and then caught the seven-fifteen show."

Jo frowned. That was odd. Sarah's car had been parked outside Tory's house when she'd driven by around seven-thirty.

"What did Robbie think of it?" Liam asked.

Sarah laughed. "He was too tired to go. I went with a neighbor. Anyway, enjoy! I'll catch you tomorrow."

Jo slipped her phone back into her purse trying to figure out why Sarah had left her car parked outside Mia's house. She must have got a ride to the movies from there with her neighbor.

"We can't afford Europe and a baby in the same year," Liam said. "We need to find a way to extricate ourselves before Sarah gets too carried away plugging us into their vacation plans."

Jo gave a thoughtful nod. "You're right, I think it's time to tell them we're looking into adoption."

---

7

*O*n Thursday morning, Jo drove to work rehearsing how to tell Sarah and Robbie about her and Liam's decision. She would have to say they were pursuing a closed adoption—that way her friends wouldn't press the issue of who the parents were. She chuckled when she pictured their reactions. No doubt, Sarah would envelop her in one of her hearty hugs and Robbie would crack a few parenthood jokes. In reality, they would be delighted for her.

She parked in one of the staff parking spots and gathered up her paperwork and purse. She'd arrived early in the hope of catching Robbie and Sarah before class started. She wasn't sure she'd be able to contain her good news until break time. To her disappointment, neither of them were in their classrooms when she walked by, and their doors were locked. She checked the staff break room to make sure they hadn't slipped in for a quick coffee, and then headed to her office, resigned to wait until later in the day to talk to them. Time seemed to stretch as she had no early morning appointments to distract herself with. For once, she wished the chair opposite her was occupied by a needy teenager she could give her full attention to. She began cleaning out her file drawers, but her thoughts kept drifting to the delicious secret burning inside her, warming that barren part of her with renewed hope.

When the bell finally rang, she made her way to the staff break room and chatted with several other teachers while keeping an eye out for Sarah and Robbie. When there was still no sign of them halfway through the break, she made a beeline over to Marshall Harrington, the AP math teacher whose classroom adjoined Robbie's.

"Hi, Marshall," Jo said. "Have you seen Robbie this morning?"

He scratched his chin, clutching a travel mug in one hand, his bald head glistening under the artificial light in the break room. "Don't think he's in today. I saw a sub in his classroom this morning."

Jo thanked him and moved off to find out if anyone had seen Sarah. She was surprised to learn there was also a substitute teacher in the art classroom. Growing concerned, she pulled out her phone and texted them both as she walked back to her office. It seemed odd that neither of them had shown up. Sarah had sounded in good spirits last night when she spoke with her, and she hadn't mentioned anything about Robbie feeling unwell either. Maybe something had happened to Sarah's mother.

Neither of them responded to her texts. Frustrated, she sat back down at her desk to prepare for her appointment with Noah Tomaselli. She really did need to take his statement about the altercation in the hallway to make sure there were no repercussions for Mia, but more importantly, she wanted to fish around and see if Noah had any idea that he was an expectant father at seventeen. She had to be certain there were no glitches on the road to adoption. As the minutes rolled by, she grew increasingly annoyed when it became obvious Noah was a no show. He might have forgotten about it, but she suspected he'd deliberately blown it off. He'd only reluctantly agreed to the meeting in the first place. She could send a note to his class and request that he be excused, but it was already well into the class period now. It would be better to try and catch him at lunchtime and have him reschedule. She glanced at her phone screen again, drumming her fingers on her desk, willing it to ping with a message from either Robbie or Sarah. Eventually, she turned it upside down and tried to ignore it. Staring at it was accomplishing nothing, she might as well get to work on something else, like the adoption.

She straightened her keyboard in front of her and did a quick Google search for adoption lawyers. After perusing the reviews, she picked up her phone and called to make an appointment with a Derek Parsons. After she hung up, she downloaded the forms from the website that the receptionist had requested her to fill out and bring with her the following Tuesday.

Absorbed in the task, she was shocked when the bell rang for lunch. She hurriedly checked Noah's schedule and then grabbed her purse and walked over to the science lab to try and catch him. She waited for several minutes as students filed out. Catching sight of one of his teammates, she called out to him, "Greg! Where's Noah?"

He shrugged his burly shoulders without missing a step. "Dunno. He skipped class."

Jo seethed with frustration as Greg disappeared around the corner before she could pepper him with any follow-up questions. There was nothing more she could do for now. She turned and made her way to the staff break room. As she pushed open the door, a frown settled on her forehead. None of the usual chatter infused the room. Instead, a somber silence hung in the air. The teachers stood around in twos and threes, their faces drawn, as the principal, Ed McMillan, addressed them. He stopped mid-sentence and turned to look at Jo. "Come in, close the door. I just told the rest of the staff I received some bad news."

Jo's eyes darted around the room, searching in vain for Robbie and Sarah. A foreboding feeling came over her. Her throat began to close over. Ed wouldn't be addressing the teachers if something had happened to Sarah's mom. It must be worse than that. She closed the door quietly behind her and padded over the industrial carpet to join the other teachers.

Ed twitched his nose to adjust his glasses and then continued, "I got a call from Robbie Gleeson this morning."

Jo's legs began to shake beneath her. She leaned against the cabinet behind her for support, sensing something terrible was about to fall from his lips.

"Sarah's gone missing."

Muted gasps of horror rumbled around the room.

"We don't know any details other than that she wasn't in the house when he woke up this morning. The sheets on her side of the bed were cold, so he thinks she must have been gone for some time. Her car's missing too. It appears she took her purse and phone with her. Robbie's been trying to reach her all morning, but he's had no luck. He called the police about half an hour ago. As far as he knows, she had no plans to go anywhere today other than to school. I'm going to ask all of you to keep this on the QT for now. I don't want the students getting upset until we know more." He paused and looked directly at Jo. "Naturally, this will leak out at some point if Sarah doesn't show up soon, so I need you to be prepared to counsel any students who need it."

Jo opened her mouth to respond, the words sticking in her throat. "Of course," she croaked. "Is there anything we can do for Robbie in the meantime?"

Ed shook his head. "I asked him that. Not much we can do at the moment other than pray for Sarah's safe return. This is really out of character for her to disappear without letting Robbie know where she was going." He exhaled a heavy breath and glanced at his watch. "Please be discreet, and don't discuss the situation anyplace you could be overheard by students. I'll keep you posted if there are developments during the afternoon." With a curt nod he strode across the room and disappeared out the door.

For a long moment, a sobering silence reigned as the teachers exchanged apprehensive looks with one another before breaking into subdued conversation.

"Poor Robbie," the teacher standing next to Jo said to no one in particular. "I can't imagine anything more frightening than waking up to find your spouse has disappeared during the night. It's like something out of a movie."

While the teachers swapped thoughts and theories, Jo quietly slipped out of the break room and dialed Liam's number. The phone rang several times before he picked up.

"What's up, honey? I'm right in the middle of something."

"Sarah's missing." The words tumbled out in a frightened bleat of sorts. Jo felt tears welling up and she screwed her eyes shut in an attempt to keep them at bay.

"What do you mean *missing?*" Liam's tone was a careful blend of patient and wary, the same way he spoke to her when she was on the verge of having a meltdown.

"Robbie woke up this morning and Sarah wasn't in the bed." Jo let out a gurgling sob. "He's been trying to call her all morning but she's not picking up. He contacted the police about a half hour ago."

"Jo, that's awful. How'd you find out?"

"Ed McMillan came into the break room and addressed all the teachers. What should we do, Liam? There must be something we can do for Robbie. I don't understand it. I mean, we just talked to Sarah last night."

"I know, it's crazy."

"I think I'll go by his place after school. They don't have any family in the area, other than Barb, so I feel like I should be there to support Robbie."

"Good idea," Liam replied. "Text me and let me know if he wants me to swing by after work. Otherwise, I'm going to stay late again and try and nail down this job. If the police are there, they might not want us all piling into the house anyway."

"Okay, I'll keep you posted." Jo ended the call and went back to her office in a daze. She slumped down in her chair, still trying to get her head around the news, the erratic beat of fear in her chest growing more insistent. Where could Sarah have gone so early in the morning? And why had she not returned? If there had been some kind of emergency with Barb, she would have left a note for Robbie or texted him by now.

Jo pulled her chair into her desk and typed in her password to log into the school system. She couldn't sit and stare at her phone all day waiting to hear if Sarah had turned up safe and sound. She needed to do something to distract herself until three o'clock. She pulled up the attendance record for the day and scrolled through to Noah's name. Absent. *Great*! He hadn't bothered to cancel. She would give him the benefit of the doubt and assume he was sick. She rested her chin on her hand, her thoughts drifting back to Sarah. She might have been involved in a car accident. Jo wondered if Robbie had called the hospital, or if the police were even looking into any angles like that yet. She had a hunch from the crime shows she'd watched that the police didn't kick into gear right away, unless of course it was a child who was missing. But Sarah was an adult and entitled to drive her car wherever she wanted.

Her phone buzzed with a text notification. She jolted upright when she saw it was from Robbie.

You probably already heard. Sarah's missing. Police came around but no sign of forced entry. They think she left of her own free will so not making it a priority yet. I'm freaking out!!! Called Brookdale Meadows to see if something happened with Barb but they haven't heard from Sarah either. Any idea where she might be?

Jo took a deep breath and began to type a response, her fingers shaking so much she had to backspace every second letter.

I'm so sorry, Robbie. She didn't mention anything to me. I'll come by after school. Let me know if there's anything I can do in the meantime.

After a few minutes, Robbie wrote back.

Thanks, I've driven all over the neighborhood looking for her car. Nothing we can do but wait. Police on the lookout for her license plate so that's something.

After typing and deleting several unsatisfactory responses, Jo settled on sending back a sad face emoji before slipping her phone back into her purse. What was she supposed to say—that everything would be all right, that the police would find Sarah? Platitudes were the worst kind of wound dressings, as she knew only too well.

The rest of the afternoon dragged on as she racked her brain, trying to figure out where Sarah might have gone or what she could possibly be doing. By the time three o'clock rolled around, her emotions were jangling almost as loudly as the bell signaling the end of another school day. She hurried out to her car and pulled out of the parking lot, only half paying attention, and forcing another driver to swerve and lean on their horn. She mouthed an apology through the windscreen, both hands gripping the steering wheel tightly to stop from shaking as she merged with the traffic.

By the time she turned onto Fairview Place, her chest felt like she was encased in a straight jacket, and she was hyperventilating. Two cop cars were parked outside Robbie's and Sarah's house. She parked a few doors down, not wanting to take up essential space for emergency vehicles.

An ominous feeling of being watched came over her as she climbed out and locked her vehicle. Instinctively, she glanced across the street. Mia Allen was standing at the curb staring intently at her, a small dog on a leash at her side. Jo raised her hand uncertainly and gave a shaky wave. Mia must have heard by now that Sarah was missing. Without acknowledging her, Mia turned away and walked around the corner. Jo frowned as she made her way to the front door and jabbed at the doorbell. What exactly was that expression on Mia's face? It wasn't sympathy, or even curiosity, if she had to name it, she would say it was something akin to enjoyment.

8

A female police officer with frizzy red bangs and a short ponytail opened the door, her alert green eyes flicking appraisingly over Jo.

"Hi, uh … I'm Jo Murphy, a colleague of Robbie's and Sarah's from Emmetville High. I told Robbie I would come by after work and check up on him."

The officer nodded wordlessly, her stoic expression unchanging as she led Jo inside and through to the family room. The pleated, stone-colored drapes were drawn, presumably for privacy from curious passersby, like Mia. Robbie was slumped on the sage green couch with his head resting in his hands. A crew cut police officer sat on a chair just inside the door scrolling through the phone in his hand with intermittent flicks of his thumb. He looked up questioningly at Jo.

"She's a colleague of Mr. Gleeson's," the female police officer explained before exiting the room.

Robbie glanced up, confusion flooding his face. "Jo?" He half rose out of his seat, the muscles in his jaw taut with a sense of urgency. "Have you heard from Sarah?"

Jo shook her head, sucking in a ragged breath at the crest-fallen look on his face. "No. I said I'd stop by, remember? Oh, Robbie," she began, taking a step toward him, "I'm so sorry. It's unbelievable."

He got to his feet unsteadily and they hugged for a long moment, Robbie clinging to her as though she were the only rock left in his world. When he finally released her, they sat down next to one another on the couch. Jo darted a quick glance at the policeman seated by the door, still toying with his phone. Her stomach churned at the disquieting thought that he might have been assigned to keep an eye on Robbie. They always suspected the partner first when someone went missing.

As if reading her thoughts, Robbie muttered. "They won't let me leave the house. I think they suspect me of having something to do with it."

"I doubt it," Jo protested. "They're probably here to make sure you don't fall apart under the strain of it all. Have the police found out anything more?"

Robbie made a disgruntled sound at the back of his throat. "Nothing. No sign of a struggle and no evidence of a break-in. Their theory is that she went somewhere, well, just on her own accord. The worst thing about it is—I took a sleeping pill and went to bed right after dinner. I was feeling like crap. Sarah went shopping after school. I don't know where. I don't even know for sure if she ever came home last night." He groaned, dragging a hand through his hair. "Of course, the police don't believe me. They're reviewing CCTV footage from stores in the area."

"This isn't like Sarah at all," Jo said, wringing her hands. "Something must have happened to her. Did the police try tracking her phone?"

"Yeah, nothing. It must be turned off."

"Any leads on her license plate?"

Robbie shook his head. "No, it's just like she disappeared."

Jo shot him a pitying look. "Is there anything at all Liam and I can do to help? Put up posters, hand out flyers?"

Robbie gave a despairing shrug. "You'll have to ask the police. I overheard them talking about some kind of community outreach, but my head's buzzing and I don't know who's organizing what."

Jo patted his arm. "Don't worry. I'll find out what we can do and make sure to help any way we can."

Robbie rubbed his hands over his face and sighed. "Thanks, Jo, I appreciate it."

"Have you eaten today? I'm happy to bring you over some dinner."

He gave a mirthless laugh. "I don't think my freezer can hold all the meals the neighbors are dropping off. They don't know what else to do to help."

"I'm glad they're taking care of you at least. Do you want Liam to swing by after work?"

Robbie sighed. "No, don't bother him. There's been a steady stream of people in and out of here all day. I could use a little space this evening—to clear my head."

"Of course," Jo said, getting to her feet. "Call or text us anytime, day or night."

Robbie reached out and squeezed her hand gratefully. "You're a good friend, Jo. I know they'll find Sarah soon, and there will be a simple explanation for all of this."

Jo nodded her agreement, not wanting to voice any doubt that would add to Robbie's distress. She exited the room and followed the sound of voices coming from the kitchen. The female police officer who had opened the door to her was deep in conversation with another officer.

"I'm just leaving," Jo said. "Is there anything I can do to help? I'm sure the teachers at school will pitch in—putting flyers in mailboxes or whatever it is you normally do in these situations."

The female police officer picked up a small stack of flyers from the table and handed them to her. "If the teachers want to start distributing these in their neighborhoods, that would be a help."

Jo took the flyers and studied the photograph of Sarah beaming at her from the page. The joy she always exuded reflected in the light dancing in her eyes. The picture had been taken at the Botanic Gardens on a school field trip. Jo swallowed a hard lump in her throat. Up until now it had been impossible for her to grasp the fact that Sarah was actually missing, but she was holding the proof right here in her hands. She nodded to the officer. "I'll pass these out tomorrow. If you think of anything else, Robbie has my number."

Back in her car, Jo exhaled a heavy breath and set the stack of flyers on the passenger seat next to her. She stared at them for a moment and then leaned across and flipped them upside down. The idea of driving all the way home with Sarah's smiling face watching her was unnerving, a nagging reminder that something was terribly wrong, that this was no ordinary day. She started up the engine, and then pulled out her phone and sent Liam a quick text to let him know not to stop by. On a whim, she decided to drive past Mia's house on her way out of the subdivision. She wasn't sure what she would say to her if she saw her again, but for some reason she felt compelled to check up on her.

She cruised through the neighborhood, keeping a sharp eye out for any dog walkers along the way, but there was no sign of Mia anywhere. As she approached her house she slowed down even more. Driving by, she thought she caught a glimpse of the curtain in the family room twitching. That same foreboding feeling of being watched came over her again. Unnerved, she accelerated and pulled out of the subdivision, suddenly eager to be on her way before Mia appeared in the doorway.

BACK HOME, Jo decided to turn in early after tossing and turning the previous night. Liam might work until midnight again for all she knew, so there wasn't much point in waiting up for him. When her alarm went off the following morning, she stirred from a deep sleep, disoriented as her mind yanked her out of a vivid dream. She reached for her phone on the bedside locker and stared bleary-eyed at the indecipherable text on the screen. As she scrabbled for her glasses, Liam yawned loudly and threw back the covers, swinging his feet to the ground. "Morning, honey," he said, stifling another yawn. "You were sleeping hard when I got back, and I wasn't even that late—nine or so."

"I crashed as soon as I hit the pillow." Jo slid her glasses on and peered at the text on her phone again. She let out a moan. "Ed wants the staff to come in half an hour early this morning. He must be going to make an announcement about Sarah to the students."

"Don't be surprised if you see police officers on campus," Liam warned her. "If Sarah's still missing, they'll likely want to start interviewing all her colleagues."

Jo scraped her hair back from her face and climbed out of bed. "You're right. They'll probably ramp up the investigation now that she's been missing over twenty-four hours."

"Man, I feel bad for Robbie," Liam said as he pulled open a drawer and rummaged around for some socks. "I can't even imagine what he's going through."

"He was pretty broken when I talked to him yesterday. He's normally always the one cracking jokes and making everyone else feel better."

Liam walked into the adjoining bathroom and turned on

the shower. "I'll swing by this morning on my way to work and check up on him."

"Good idea. He'll be glad to see you. I'm going to hand out some flyers to the teachers at school and ask them to pass them out. Apart from that, there's not much we can do other than be there for him."

"I'll let you know how he is," Liam called, before disappearing into the shower.

Jo hurriedly pulled on her clothes and tied her hair back before slapping on some lip gloss and smacking her lips together to set it. That was about all she had time for. She wasn't hungry for breakfast anyway, not with her stomach roiling at the thought of Ed briefing a sobbing assembly of kids on their beloved teacher's disappearance. She would be flat out today counseling distraught students.

By the time she arrived at the school at seven-fifteen, over half the teachers were already there, in addition to several police cruisers. They gathered in the staff break room, whispering among themselves in hushed tones until seven-thirty when Ed appeared, flanked by the police officers. He inhaled a deep breath before addressing the staff. "Good morning. As you're all aware by now, Robbie Gleeson reported Sarah missing yesterday. Her status remains unchanged." He traced his fingers across his forehead in an agitated fashion before continuing, "Unfortunately, it seems that I have *another* missing persons' report on my desk this morning."

The oxygen seemed to leave the room as everyone sucked in a breath. The teachers stood silent and unmoving, as if Ed's words had cast a spell over them, freezing them in place. Their expressions ranged from incredulous to petrified. Jo could almost hear the tick-tocking heartbeat in her chest accelerate as adrenaline flooded through her. There must be some mistake. This couldn't be happening. These kinds of things didn't happen in a small-town high school. And then an awful thought struck her. What if it was Robbie? Maybe he'd taken it upon himself to go off looking for Sarah. Or worse, what if he'd harmed himself? Her eyes darted over the wooden expressions of the police officers, a silent platoon bolstering the veracity of Ed's shocking disclosure that a second person from the school had gone missing.

"Sérgio Tomaselli called me this morning," Ed continued. "He reported his son, Noah, missing around ten o'clock last night." He paused as another ripple of shock coursed through the room.

Once again, Jo felt her legs about to buckle beneath her. She was still weak after the miscarriage, and the trauma of this second announcement wasn't helping. She grabbed the back of a chair for support, loathe to draw attention to herself by taking a seat.

Ed cleared his throat and began again. "Apparently, Noah told his family he was staying at a friend's house on Wednesday night, so they were unaware of the fact that he didn't go to school yesterday until he failed to show up at home following football practice. After talking to some of Noah's teammates, Mr. Tomaselli learned that Noah skipped both school and practice." Ed turned hesitantly toward the police officers. "Did one of you want to elaborate?"

A burly plainclothes detective stepped forward. "I'm Detective Saunders, lead investigator on this case. As Mr. McMillan has stated, Noah Tomaselli, a seventeen-year-old minor, is now officially a missing person. Currently, we have no leads on where he went on Wednesday night or his whereabouts after that. We're extremely concerned for his safety, and for that of the missing teacher, Sarah Gleeson. At the moment, we have no reason to believe there is any connection between the two cases, although we haven't ruled anything out yet. That being said, I would ask you to do your best to quell any rumors students might generate about serial kidnappers and such." He stepped back and nodded to Ed to continue.

"Naturally, this is going to be an extremely difficult day for all of us at school," Ed said, his tone grave. "I'll be making an announcement about Noah at a special student assembly this morning. Furthermore, the police have requested permission to question his teachers and friends, and also his girlfriend, Mia Allen. I apologize in advance for any disruption to your classes and ask that you make facilitating Detective Saunders' interview requests a priority."

Jo's stomach curdled as Ed's voice droned on. The room seemed to spin around her, Ed's jaw moving up-and-down like a shredder slicing and dicing her dreams and hopes yet again. She had to do something to make sure Mia didn't tell the police about Noah's baby.

9

Sequestered in her office, Jo picked at her fingers beneath her desk as she waited for Detective Saunders to join her. She had intended to look for Mia immediately after the staff meeting, but Ed had intercepted her and told her the detective wanted to interview her first. The roller coaster of emotions she'd been forced to endure over the past few days was beginning to catch up with her. The devastation of another miscarriage that always left her feeling like a war zone inside, the short-lived joy of anticipating parenthood with Liam that had briefly lit her spirits, the blinding terror of finding out that Sarah was missing, and now—the shattering of her dreams in the most random way possible. Her baby's biological father was missing. Mia would be questioned. The truth would all come tumbling out. Fate had conspired against her, denying her a baby yet again. Indignation brewed inside her, but she fought to keep her anger at bay, reminding herself that this was not about her, no matter how much she wanted it to be. This was about two missing people, and she needed to act like the professional she was and rise above her personal heartache.

A knock on the glass door made her look up. Detective Saunders strolled into the room and sat down in the chair opposite her. He inspected his surroundings in one efficient sweep, his trained eye cataloging, assessing, and observing, no doubt already drawing conclusions about her from the contents of her office. Jo smiled weakly across the desk at him, for once feeling oddly displaced and out of control in her own space. Did he sense she was hiding something?

"Thanks for taking the time to see me, Mrs. Murphy," he began, pulling out his notebook."

"Of course," Jo replied, grimacing inwardly. As if she had a choice in the matter. "Please, call me Jo."

He gave a slight tilt of his head in acknowledgment. "I'll try to keep this brief as I know you'll have your work cut out for you once the student assembly disperses, which is why I wanted to interview you first."

"Yes, I expect that will be the case," Jo agreed, wary of the friendly overtures she recognized were designed to soften her defenses.

"I understand you broke up a fight on Tuesday between Noah Tomaselli and his girlfriend, Mia Allen?"

Jo gave a small shrug of acknowledgement. "I would hardly call it a fight. They were arguing. Mia was upset and beating Noah on the chest."

Detective Saunders frowned. "Did he hit her back?"

"No, he didn't touch her. He's a big kid, a football player. He stood there and took it. Mia was more flailing her arms around than punching. I doubt she hurt him."

"What were they arguing about?"

"She accused him of cheating on her."

"Did she mention any names?"

"None that I heard." Jo hesitated. "She mentioned something to the effect that it had been going on for a while."

Detective Saunders made a few notes and then looked up again. "What happened after you broke up the argument?"

"Mia stormed off after I threatened to call security. I asked Noah if he was all right. He seemed more embarrassed that the other students had witnessed it than anything else. I told him to come see me in my office Thursday morning after break. I needed to take a statement from him, it's school protocol."

Detective Saunders gave an approving nod. "Did you also make an appointment with Mia Allen? From everything I've heard, she was the one who instigated the fight."

Jo squirmed uncomfortably in her seat under the detective's eagle eye. She didn't want to mention the fact that she'd already counseled Mia earlier in the week. Detective Saunders would want to know why. "Not yet, I wanted to talk to Noah first of all to get his take on it."

"I see."

Jo could tell from his tone that he didn't see at all. It struck him as odd. She cringed when he scribbled something in his notebook and underlined it.

"And Noah didn't turn up for his appointment yesterday?" Detective Saunders went on.

"That's correct. I logged into the school system and saw that he'd been marked absent for the day. I figured he was sick and forgot to cancel."

Detective Saunders tapped a forefinger on the desk for a moment looking pensive. When he spoke again, he switched gears. "I understand you and your husband are friendly with Robbie and Sarah Gleeson?"

"Yes, we socialize with them on a regular basis. My husband takes care of the school's computer network."

"Can you tell me what Sarah's mood was like in the days before she disappeared?"

Jo blinked, disconcerted by the question. "Fine, I mean she's a very happy person by nature."

"So, you don't think there's any chance she might have harmed herself?"

"No, absolutely not! Not Sarah. That's not possible. We had plans to get our hair done and go to lunch on Saturday." Jo frowned down at her desk, shaking her head, considering this angle for the first time. "No, Sarah enjoys every minute of life. All you have to do is take a look around her art room at all her paintings and inspirational quotes to know she was a very upbeat person."

Detective Saunders took a few more notes and then twisted his pen between two fingers as though considering how to frame his next question. "How was her relationship with her husband, in your opinion?"

Jo stared aghast at the detective, not liking the direction the interview was taking. "They have a great relationship. Robbie's a very funny guy and Sarah's the kind of woman everyone wants to be around, a ray of sunshine."

"So you never saw any hints of unhappiness between them?"

Jo averted her gaze as she contemplated the question. They appeared to be happy, as far as she could tell. They certainly didn't argue in front of her. Sarah had mentioned recently that things weren't always what they seemed, that spouses sometimes got the wrong end of the stick, but she'd just been trying to cheer Jo up, make her feel like all couples had their struggles. Granted, Robbie had acted a bit put out about Sarah's plans for Europe, but that was typical couple stuff too. Liam would probably react the same way if she planned a big overseas trip and then tried to talk him into it. She wasn't about to throw Robbie under the bus for no good reason. "They're extremely compatible. I think they're very happy together."

Detective Saunders pressed his lips together and gave a terse nod. "I appreciate your time. I have one more favor to ask. I need to interview Mia Allen, Noah's girlfriend. Unfortunately, her mother has to work this morning, but she gave me permission to interview her daughter provided you were present."

Jo wet her lips, her heart knocking against her ribs. Would she have to sit here and listen to Mia tell the detective that she was expecting Noah's baby, twisting the knife in her wound? Or could she find a way to warn her not to bring it up—some subtle signal? "That's fine," she croaked. "A verbal permission from a parent will suffice."

Detective Saunders nodded and got to his feet. "Thanks, I'll fetch her. It's probably easiest to conduct the interview in your office if you have no objections. Maybe you can round up another chair while I'm gone."

Once the detective's footsteps faded into the distance, Jo sank her face into her hands. She couldn't force Mia to conceal the truth from Detective Saunders. She had to prepare herself for the worst. If Mia broke down and told him everything, Jo's chance to adopt her baby would be gone. Once the Tomaselli family found out that Mia was carrying their grandchild, they would almost certainly move to adopt it, especially now if, God forbid, something had happened to Noah. Jo groaned. She pulled out her phone and started typing a quick text to Liam but thought better of it and deleted it. There was nothing he could do to help her through this interview, and there was no point in burdening him until it was over and she knew where they stood. It broke her heart to think he might not become a father this year after all, but she needed to focus on the more pressing issue. Two people were now missing from the school, one of them a minor. It was her job to assist the police in whatever way she could, no matter the pain it caused her in the process.

With a sigh of resignation, she opened the drawer on her desk and lifted out some Advil. She swallowed two pills with a swig of water just as Detective Saunders and Mia appeared in the doorway. Jo looked up, startled. "Oh, I didn't expect you back so soon. Let me run next door and grab a chair."

She returned a moment later with a plastic stacking chair and placed it next to the padded chair opposite hers. Detective Saunders gestured to Mia to take a seat. She slumped down and immediately folded her arms across her chest avoiding meeting Jo's eyes.

Detective Saunders sat down next to Mia and nodded at Jo. "Mrs. Murphy, why don't you begin by explaining to Mia what we're trying to accomplish here today."

Jo raised her brows, taken aback at being called upon. She'd envisioned her role as an observer, but not to smooth the way for the interrogation with an uncooperative student. She wondered briefly if Detective Saunders was testing her in some way.

"Mia," she began in a subdued tone. "I know you must be really worried about Noah. Rest assured, the police are here to do everything in their power to help find—"

"I don't need your sympathy," Mia snapped back.

Ignoring the outburst, Jo continued, "You're not in any kind of trouble. Detective Saunders just needs to ask you a few questions."

Mia pulled down the corners of her lips but offered nothing that indicated she would cooperate.

Jo nodded to Detective Saunders. "Over to you."

He turned to Mia. "I understand you and Noah argued the day before he went missing. Can you tell me what that was about?"

Mia rolled her eyes. "I'm sure you've already heard the gory details. It was all over campus five seconds later."

Detective Saunders fixed a placid smile on his lips. "I'd like to hear your account of what happened."

Mia let out an aggrieved sigh. "He's cheating on me. It's been going on for months. The scumbag wouldn't admit to it."

Jo flinched at Mia's tone. Her voice was hard as steel. She sounded a whole lot more angry than hurt, but then pain could make you react in strange ways sometimes.

Detective Saunders wrote down some things on his notepad. After a moment or two, he glanced up again. "Do you have any idea where Noah went after school on Wednesday?"

Mia shrugged. "I don't know and I don't care."

"So, you didn't try and contact him—text him or call him at all on Wednesday evening?"

Mia's eyes darted from Detective Saunders to Jo. "I don't remember."

Jo shifted uneasily in her seat. She and Liam had been at Mia's house until around six-thirty that night. Hopefully Mia wouldn't bring up their visit.

"You don't remember?" Detective Saunders set down his pen and fixed a stern gaze on her. "This is important, Mia. I'm trying to find your missing boyfriend. If you lie about any of the details in this investigation, you could get into serious trouble. You know we only have to look at your phone to see who you texted and when."

Mia let out a huff of annoyance. "I might have texted him to meet me at the skate park."

Jo's eyes widened.

"What time was that at?" Detective Saunders asked, no hint of surprise in his voice.

"Nine, I guess."

"Why did you want to meet him?"

"I wanted him to tell me the truth. I wanted to know who he was seeing."

"And did he tell you?"

Mia fixed a granite-like stare on the detective. "Not at first." She fluttered her eyelashes and gave Jo a crooked grin. "We were drinking vodka. Eventually, he loosened up and admitted he was sleeping with someone else. But he still wouldn't tell me who."

Jo gritted her teeth, suppressing an exasperated scream. *Vodka!* So much for good pre-natal care. She was going to have to have a serious talk with Mia first chance she got.

Detective Saunders made another note. "And how did you react to Noah's admission?"

"How do you think?" Mia scoffed, firing a challenging look in Jo's direction. "I told him I never wanted to see him again, and drove off."

Jo winced at the thought of Mia drinking and driving with her precious cargo on board. She had a sick feeling Mia was enjoying making her squirm at her reckless behavior.

"Did he seem upset at all that you were breaking it off with him?" Detective Saunders asked.

Mia cut a hard laugh. "Not in the least. He said I was doing him a favor."

"I see." Detective Saunders scanned through his notes quickly before continuing. "Did you have any other communication with Noah after that?"

Mia shook her head. "It's over. I'm done with him. I'm moving on." She caught Jo's eye and a small triumphant smile tugged at her lips before she whisked it away.

"Mia," Detective Saunders said in a measured tone. "Can you think of any other reason why Noah might have been upset enough to take off on Wednesday night?"

"I told you, he wasn't upset. He was laughing at me!" Mia retorted.

"Got it." Detective Saunders snapped his notebook closed. "Thanks for your help. You can return to your classroom now. We'll be in touch if we have any more questions."

Without another word, Mia rose and exited the room.

Jo waited for Detective Saunders to say something, but an awkward silence ensued as he rubbed his jaw, frowning.

Finally, Jo spoke up. "Did you need anything else from me?"

He peered at her from beneath his brows. "Not at the moment. But I'll keep you on standby. I have a feeling I'll need to interview Mia Allen again before this is over. She wasn't exactly forthcoming."

Jo swallowed, her voice scratching at the back of her throat. "You don't think she knows anything about Noah's disappearance, do you?"

Detective Saunders grimaced. "I'm not ruling out the possibility. She's hiding something, and I intend to find out what it is."

10

The rest of Friday passed in a blur of activity as Jo divided her time between consoling sobbing Noah Tomaselli groupies, and urging his stunned teammates to tell the police anything about his activities, even potentially illegal ones, that might be helpful. In the rare moments between appointments, she found herself fielding a bevy of phone calls from frantic parents demanding everything from increased security for their kids, to answers on whether or not a kidnapping ring was targeting the school, neither of which Jo was in a position to deliver on.

When she finally put her key in the front door of her house that evening, she barely had the strength to propel herself to the couch and collapse. It was all such an unbelievable nightmare. Why hadn't Sarah or any trace of her car shown up yet? Jo was beginning to resign herself to the idea that Sarah must have had a car accident. There was no other explanation for her disappearance. It was beyond frustrating that the police weren't sending out search parties to comb highways and climb down embankments to search for her vehicle. She couldn't survive more than a few days without water. Even if she had a water bottle in her car, she might not be able to reach it if she was trapped in her seat. Or she could be unconscious for all anyone knew.

Jo pressed her fingers to her temples. Her headache was back with a vengeance. Reluctantly, she eased herself into a sitting position and made her way to the downstairs bathroom to look for some more Advil. After she'd thrown back a couple of tablets, she returned to the family room and switched on the television. She turned the volume down low and then lay back down on the couch to rest until her headache abated.

She wakened with a start to find Liam shaking her. "Jo! Check this out!" She sat up abruptly at his urgent tone, her heart lurching painfully in her chest as everything came flooding back. "What is it? Did they find Sarah?"

Liam pointed the remote at the television and turned up the volume. "Not yet, but it's all over the local news."

"Did you go by Robbie's?"

"Yeah, he's hanging in there, barely."

Jo shivered and hugged her knees to her chest as Liam joined her on the couch to listen to the report. The newscaster began by describing the circumstances surrounding Sarah's disappearance as the camera zoomed in on a picture of her in the background. "In another twist to the disappearance of Emmetville High School art teacher, Sarah Gleeson," the newscaster continued, "a seventeen-year-old male student from the same school was reported missing by his parents last night."

Jo swallowed hard as a picture of Noah in his football uniform came up on the screen.

"At this time, it is not believed that the two incidents are connected, but the local community is extremely concerned that the disappearances might point to something sinister. For more on this developing story we go to Anna Kotosky."

The camera panned to a reporter standing outside the school, flanked by a small somber-faced crowd. "Thank you, Karen," Anna said, holding a mic to her mouth. "Tonight, parents and locals alike are deeply concerned about the troubling events of the past few days. People in this neighborhood are locking their doors and there is talk of a possible serial killer on the loose, despite the fact that no bodies have been discovered—"

Jo snatched the remote from Liam's hand and switched off the television. "I can't watch this circus. Sarah's not dead. How can they put Robbie through this just for ratings? And the Tomaselli family too. It's flat wrong."

"I know, it's awful." Liam sighed as he put an arm around her. "I have to admit I'm worried about you though. If someone is targeting the school, you could be next."

"That's a far-fetched theory. Noah was probably mad after Mia broke up with him and took off to cool his jets."

Liam raised his brows. "They broke up?"

Jo nodded. "A detective interviewed Mia in my office today. Tory wanted me to sit in on the interview as she had to work. Turns out Mia met Noah on Wednesday night at the skate park. She wanted to have it out with him. They were both drinking. He admitted to seeing someone else, but he wouldn't tell her who. She told him she never wanted to see him again and took off in her car. That was the last anyone saw of him. I just hope he didn't get into a wreck."

Liam drew his brow into a frown. "So Mia was the last person to see him?"

"Yes." Jo stared at him. "What are you insinuating?"

"Nothing, it's just … did anyone see them there? How do we know Mia's telling the truth? Noah told you he wasn't seeing anyone else, and she's been acting crazy."

"She seemed pretty convinced he was cheating on her. But I suppose she could have been overly-emotional because of the pregnancy." Jo bit her lip. "What if the Tomaselli family finds out about the baby because of all this? What if they try and seek custody? They have the money to hire the best lawyers in the state if they choose to."

Liam shrugged. "We'll cross that bridge when we come to it. No sense speculating what Mia will or won't do."

Jo let out a small sob. "You probably think I'm being selfish thinking about the baby now that Sarah and Noah are missing."

Liam kissed the top of her head gently. "It's not selfish to care about what happens to the baby. All we can do is take one day at a time. Hopefully, Noah and Sarah will both show up unharmed over the course of the weekend and we can put all this behind us. In the meantime, we can help hand out flyers around the subdivision."

SATURDAY PASSED in a flurry of activity as Jo and Liam canvassed their neighborhood distributing flyers and stapling posters to power poles and community boards. Sunday morning they were reading in bed and enjoying coffee when Jo's phone pinged. She lifted it off the bedside table and glanced at it, almost knocking over her coffee mug as she scrambled to get out of bed. "They've found Sarah!"

"What?" Liam threw back the covers and jumped to his feet. "Is she ... okay?"

"I don't know. Robbie just said they found her, and he wants us to come over."

Jo locked eyes with Liam for a moment searching for reassurance in his face but finding none.

"It doesn't sound good, does it?" she ventured. "I mean, he knows we're worried sick. He would have said if she was all right. Maybe she's injured." Jo's voice wavered. "Oh, Liam. What if something's happened—"

"Don't! Let's get dressed and go over there. I'm not going to speculate."

"But we need to prepare ourselves. What are we going to say if it's bad news? Robbie will be inconsolable."

"You can't prepare for something like this. You know better than that. Nothing we say will fix it. We just have to be raw and honest and comfort him as best we can."

Jo chewed on her lip as she messaged Robbie that they were on their way.

They finished dressing in silence and hurried out to the car. As they drove, Jo's stomach roiled with a carousel of emotions ranging from hope that Sarah had been found alive —at worst, injured—to fear that the police had discovered her body in her wrecked car. And she couldn't entirely rid her mind of the reporter's words on the news last night. What if something horrific had happened? What if Sarah had been killed by a serial murderer?

Twenty minutes later, they pulled up along the curb near to Robbie's house. Five squad cars were parked along the road, in addition to several other unidentified vehicles. The front door was ajar, and Jo could see a police officer inside talking on her radio. She climbed out with a quaking heart, praying she would find Sarah sitting wrapped in a heat blanket on the couch next to Robbie, safe and sound, if a little shaken by her ordeal.

Liam reached for her hand and together they walked along the sidewalk and up the path to Robbie's front door. The red-haired police officer who had escorted her in on her last visit blocked the entry.

"Robbie texted us and asked us to come over," Jo explained.

The officer gestured for them to go inside, an impassive expression on her face. "He's in the kitchen."

Pulse throbbing erratically, Jo led the way down the

hallway to the sleek, modern kitchen Sarah and Robbie had remodeled only the previous summer. Two officers stood next to the window engaged in a muted conversation. Robbie sat alone at the table, dry-eyed but with a dazed look on his face. A flicker of hope darted through Jo. He hadn't fallen apart completely, surely that was a good sign. She slid into the seat next to him and gazed at him earnestly. "Robbie, we got your text. Where's Sarah?"

He blinked as if reorienting himself. "She's ... they found her ... in her car."

The blood in Jo's veins chilled. She threw Liam an anguished look as he pulled out another chair and sat down next to her, waiting on Robbie to continue.

Instead, he let out a long shuddering sigh and buried his face in his hands.

Tears welled up in Jo's eyes. She clapped a hand over her mouth to trap the scream halfway up her throat. It was just as she'd feared. She knew what Robbie was going to say the minute he removed his hands from his face. She could feel it in her bones—in the tension in the air. Why else were the police standing around with no sense of urgency and deadpan expressions on their faces? Sarah was dead. Her friend was gone. A sob escaped her despite her best efforts and she bowed her head, her shoulders shaking as Liam laid a soothing hand on her back.

After a lengthy silence, Liam cleared his throat. "Robbie, is she dead?"

"Yes." His voice was thick, a dense ball of wound-up emotions he was fighting to keep under control.

"Oh Robbie, I'm so sorry," Jo choked out in a faint whisper. She wiped the tears off her cheeks with her hands. "I ... I just can't believe it! She was so full of life."

Robbie scratched at his cheek, peering at her as if evaluating the comment. "Yes," he said flatly. "She certainly was."

Jo pulled a puzzled frown, thrown off by the odd tone in his voice. It wasn't fitting. It seemed … almost resentful. Although it was hardly surprising he might feel that way. After all, his beautiful, vibrant wife was dead. He was in shock—they all were.

"Where did it happen—the crash?" Liam asked.

Robbie shook his head slowly. He took a few short breaths and opened his mouth but then closed it again.

"It's all right, man. You don't have to talk about it if you don't want to. Just know, we're here for you."

Robbie smoothed a shaking hand over his hair. "There was … there was someone else … "

A cold fear sliced through Jo. *Someone else.* Had Sarah killed another driver?

"You mean, she hit another car?" Liam prompted.

"No." Robbie's eyes were wide and frantic. "There was someone else in the car with her!"

Jo gasped, her mind reeling. A passenger had died along with Sarah. No wonder Robbie looked so shell-shocked.

He ran a hand through his hair, staring down at the table. When he lifted his head again, his expression was tortured. "She was with Noah Tomaselli."

11

Shock decimated Jo's mind. Her thoughts ran helter-skelter as she tried to make sense of Robbie's words. Noah Tomaselli was in the car—with Sarah. How had he ended up there? Had he been driving around attempting to come to terms with the breakup with Mia and run out of gas or something? Maybe Sarah saw him walking in the early hours of the morning and offered him a ride. How horribly ironic that in trying to help him out, she had inadvertently been responsible for his death.

"Robbie, it was an accident," Jo began. "You mustn't blame her. Sarah would never do—"

He cut her off with a wave of his hand. "It wasn't an accident, Jo. That's the worst part about it." His eyes roved over her face and then he turned to Liam, his throat bobbing as he swallowed.

Liam frowned. "I don't understand. What are you saying?"

"It was deliberate. They … they killed themselves."

Liam recoiled, shock spreading across his face. "How do you know that?"

"Sarah left a suicide note," Robbie rasped, gesturing with

his chin to the police officers. "They're doing some kind of handwriting analysis on it." He rubbed a hand over his stubble. "They showed it to me. It looks like her writing, as far as I can tell."

Jo shook her head. "No, that can't be right. It doesn't make any sense. Sarah wasn't even remotely suicidal. I would have noticed something."

Robbie shrugged helplessly. "I don't know what to tell you. That's what the police are saying."

"What did the note say?" Liam asked.

"Not much. Something about regret and shame, and never looking back."

"Regret about what?" Jo asked quietly. A foreboding feeling crept through her as she recalled Mia's accusation that Noah had been seeing someone. Surely it couldn't have been Sarah.

Robbie heaved an uneven breath before responding. "I don't know." His voice broke. "I'm not sure I want to know."

"What about Noah?" Liam asked. "Did he leave a note?"

"Not that I know of," Robbie responded.

"I just don't believe it." Jo said. "How do they know for sure the crash was deliberate?"

"There was no crash," Robbie wheezed. "It was carbon monoxide poisoning. The car was parked in an empty garage. The homeowners are on vacation. Their gardener found the bodies."

Jo clapped a hand to her mouth and scrunched her eyes shut, pain ripping through her. *No! No! No!* None of this was making any sense. Sarah wouldn't kill herself. And Noah Tomaselli wouldn't have ended his life over a breakup either. Granted, he was a teenager with raging hormones, but he seemed like a level-headed young man with everything going for him, from a well-to-do family, with college prospects. Robbie seemed to be insinuating they'd been having an affair, but that was ridiculous. Sarah would never betray a student's trust like that. Granted, she was only a decade older than Noah, but he could have had his pick of any girl in the school.

"The suicide note sounds pretty vague," Liam said. "It doesn't prove anything."

Robbie sighed, a detached look in his eyes. "The police are still gathering evidence, but they said so far everything points to some kind of double suicide pact." His voice wavered as he continued, "They ran a hose pipe from the exhaust in through the car window, and Sarah stuffed her sweater in the crack. They're going to do autopsies, but as it stands, they're treating it as suicide."

"It's just unbelievable," Liam said in a hushed voice.

"Things weren't perfect between us," Robbie added, so softly that Jo had to lean in to hear him, "But, I never imagined Sarah would do something like this." He rested his face in his hands again. "How can I ever look the Tomaselli family in the face again?"

"Whatever happened, this wasn't your fault, Robbie," Jo assured him." You're just as much a victim as Noah's family. You can't blame yourself."

"The Tomasellis aren't going to see it that way. Sarah was a teacher at Noah's school—he was her student, a minor. They're going to say I must have known about it. How can I go back to school after this? I might even lose my job."

"You can't think about stuff like that right now," Liam said. "You haven't had time to take in the shock or grieve your loss."

Robbie pressed his fingertips to his scalp. "I don't know how to grieve. I don't know how I feel. Angry and confused, for sure."

One of the officers walked up to the table before Jo or Liam could respond. "Mr. Gleeson, we're going to need you to come with us to identify your wife's body. The crime scene has been processed and we're moving her to the morgue."

Robbie gave a hesitant nod and struggled to his feet, his face paler than Jo had ever seen it before.

"Want me to come with you?" Liam asked.

Robbie shook his head. "There's nothing you can do. I'll keep you posted on the ... the funeral arrangements and stuff."

Jo and Liam hugged Robbie good-bye and made their way back outside. They walked in silence to their car, and then waited until the squad car with Robbie aboard pulled away.

Liam started up the engine and let out a heavy breath. "Poor guy. This is gonna be a huge news story. If it turns out Sarah and Noah were having an affair, Robbie will be hounded by the media. I don't envy him finding out all at once that his wife is dead and that she was carrying on with a student."

"How can you say that?" Jo retorted. "None of it's been proven yet."

"I don't want to believe it either, Jo, but the evidence speaks for itself."

She turned away and leaned her head against the car door, watching the houses zoom by. She'd been afraid all along that Sarah had died in a car wreck. But this was so much worse. If it was true what the police were saying, this was a betrayal of Robbie, her friends, her school, her students, her whole community. Was it possible the Sarah she'd known was not the real Sarah at all?

WHEN THEY PULLED into their driveway, Liam pointed out a police cruiser parked along the curb a little farther down the street. As soon as they stepped out of their car, two police officers approached them.

Jo gritted her teeth. It was the red-haired officer again and her partner.

"I'm Officer Bowman," the red-haired woman said by way of introduction. "This is my partner, Officer Ferguson. Do you mind if we come in for a few minutes?"

"Uh, sure," Jo mumbled, shooting Liam an apprehensive look. She led the officers up the pathway to the front door. As she turned the key in the lock, her hand trembled a little— partly from shock, partly because she was afraid the officers had found out about Mia's and Noah's baby. Maybe she was in trouble for not disclosing it. She tried to keep her breathing even. The last thing she wanted to do was get dragged into this whole mess. But she wasn't about to give up on her dream if she didn't have to. She'd have to be careful not to say too much until she found out exactly what the police knew.

They sat down on the couch in the family room while the officers remained in the hallway talking on their walkie-talkies. A moment later, they stepped into the room and took their seats.

"I just have a few follow-up questions for you from your interview with Detective Saunders," Officer Bowman said with a tight smile aimed at Jo.

"Of course," she replied, reaching for Liam's hand.

"Detective Saunders mentioned that you were adamant Sarah was not the type to commit suicide. As you know, we found a suicide note which seems to contradict that."

"Robbie said it was vague," Liam interjected.

The officer nodded. "Suicide notes aren't always detailed explanations of the deceased's state of mind. Some are more generic, talking about not wanting to live, wiping out the past, that kind of thing."

"Couldn't someone else have written it?" Jo suggested.

"We're trying to establish that. We're having it analyzed."

"Where did you find the note?" Jo asked. "Robbie never mentioned seeing anything in the house."

Officer Bowman pressed her lips together. "Sarah was clutching it in her hand."

Liam frowned. "If the handwriting expert confirms she wrote it, that seems pretty cut and dried, doesn't it?"

"Yes and no," Officer Bowman replied. "The suicide note was mostly illegible. The ink had run—either from tears or some kind of liquid that was spilled on it. Unfortunately, we can only make out a couple of lines. It's not conclusive, although it does seem to hint at suicide."

"So if Sarah didn't write it, is it possible someone might have set it up to look like a suicide?" Jo persisted.

"The only prints on the hosepipe are Noah's." Officer Bowman grimaced. "It's possible he killed Mrs. Gleeson first and then committed suicide himself. We'll need to wait on the autopsy results to find out exactly how she died."

Jo shook her head. "I can't believe Noah Tomaselli was capable of murder. He was a good kid." Even as the words fell from her lips, doubt niggled at her. Did she know him well enough to make that judgement? What if he'd found out about the baby and was afraid Sarah would leave him once she knew? He'd been drinking vodka that night. Maybe he'd been doing drugs too. Could he have killed Sarah and then himself in a drug-induced rage?

Officer Bowman flashed her a sympathetic smile that seemed to say she'd seen too much in her career to rule anything out. "I understand you set up a counseling appointment to see Noah on Thursday but he never showed up. What was the appointment for?"

Jo shifted uncomfortably on the couch. Liam seemed to sense her discomfort and squeezed her hand softly. "I needed to make sure he was okay after the altercation with Mia, and to take his statement about what happened. Technically, I witnessed an assault and staff members are obligated to document any such incidents."

"Did you attempt to contact him when he didn't show up for the meeting?"

"No, he was absent that day. I figured he'd forgotten all about it."

Officer Bowman consulted her notebook. "Mrs. Murphy, were you aware of any strain at all in the relationship between Sarah Gleeson and her husband, Robbie?"

"Nooo..." Jo hesitated. She'd dodged that question when Detective Saunders had asked it, but now was not the time for pat answers. Sarah was dead, and Jo needed to do whatever she could to assist the police in finding out what had happened. "Well, she did mention a couple of days ago that things weren't always as they seemed between her and Robbie, something about spouses getting the wrong end of the stick at times. I thought she was just trying to make me feel better because I told her ..." She broke off and shot Liam an apologetic glance. "I told her I was having communications issues with my husband."

Liam raised his brows but said nothing.

"And now, after what's happened?" Officer Bowman pressed. "Do you think it's possible Sarah could have been hinting at something else?"

Jo squirmed beneath the officer's penetrating gaze. "I suppose so. But there's nothing to suggest that Sarah and Noah were having an affair, other than the fact that they were found together."

Officer Bowman exchanged a quick glance with her partner. "I'm afraid that's not entirely true. They'd been texting each other over the past several months. It's clear from the texts they were involved in an illicit relationship."

Jo's jaw dropped. "But, how's that possible? Robbie would have found out about it. He and Sarah knew each other's passwords."

"They used burner phones." Officer Bowman tightened her lips. "Mrs. Murphy, this is important. Do you ever remember seeing Sarah with a second phone?"

---

12

*J*o sat at the kitchen table, fingers clamped around a mug of hot tea that Liam had set in front of her after the officers left.

"I shouldn't have told them about her mother's cell phone," Jo groaned. "It had nothing to do with anything, and now the police are going to think she was trying to cover up the fact that she had a second phone."

"You did the right thing, honey," Liam countered. "You can't hide anything from the police that might turn out to be important later."

"Barb has Alzheimer's, Liam. How is her phone important?"

Liam averted his gaze looking uncomfortable. "We don't know anything for sure. Let's face it, Jo, you've no way of knowing if that was Barb's phone or if Sarah was lying to you."

Jo stared down at the steaming liquid in her mug as if she could somehow discern the truth in the curling, white tendrils that rose from it. Had Sarah lied to her? Had her free-spirited friend been living a double life all along that no one else knew about? And had she talked a vulnerable seventeen-year-old into committing suicide with her?

"Will the school be closed tomorrow?" Liam asked, stirring her from her thoughts.

Jo pushed her mug aside. "No, the police need to conduct more interviews. Ed sent out a text saying we'll be closed the day of the funerals."

Liam frowned. "I'll have to get time off work for Sarah's funeral. Will you be okay going to Noah's service by yourself?"

"I think you should go too. Didn't you say you knew his father?"

Liam shrugged. "I met him once at a charity event. I'd hardly call that knowing him. But, if you want me to be there with you, I'll find a way to make it happen."

Jo pulled off her glasses and rubbed her eyes. "I know you're super busy at work. Let me find out if the other teachers' spouses are going first."

"What about the appointment with the adoption lawyer on Tuesday afternoon. Do you need me to go with you to that?" Liam asked.

Jo squinted at him, aghast. "I totally forgot about it in the middle of all this." She scrubbed her hands over her face. "I feel so guilty pursuing the adoption after what's happened. It seems … almost disrespectful. Maybe I should postpone the appointment."

Liam placed a hand on her shoulder. "We can't forget about the baby in the midst of everything that's happened. We made a promise to Mia and her mother. We can't let them down. And now that the father of Mia's baby is dead, there's no chance of them reconciling, sad as that is. The baby needs us now more than ever."

"Yeah, you're right." Jo drew in a deep breath. "I don't

think you need to be at the appointment. I can bring all the paperwork home for you to sign."

Liam shot her a grateful look. "Great, it's gonna be tough enough to get off work for the funerals with everything else I have going on."

Jo got to her feet. "Not as tough as it's going to be for me to get through school tomorrow. I should get an early night." She kissed Liam on the cheek and dumped the remnants of her tea in the sink before making her way to bed.

MONDAY MORNING WENT EXACTLY as Jo had predicted. The female students who flooded her office were inconsolable, and even some of the tougher guys on the football team had tears in their eyes when they came to see her. They all had questions about why Noah and Sarah had been discovered in the same car, but Jo's standard response was always, "It's an ongoing investigation. They need to conduct autopsies first to establish the cause of death. The police will keep us informed."

At lunchtime, Jo remained in her office to catch up on her reports, which were rapidly falling behind. As she took the first bite of her sandwich, Ed McMillan stuck his head around her door. "Mr. and Mrs. Tomaselli want to see you this afternoon."

Jo swallowed without chewing, almost choking in the process. "Me?" She flinched at the high-pitched tone to her voice. "What about?"

"They're trying to piece together Noah's last days to determine exactly what happened leading up to his death. I think they'd like to hear from you directly what transpired during that blowup on campus between Noah and Mia."

"I can't tell them anything other than what I already told the police."

Ed waved a dismissive hand. "Just be empathetic. It's understandable that they want to talk to everyone who interacted with their son in his last days."

"Yes, of course," Jo said, flustered. After Ed exited the room, she wrapped her sandwich back up with shaking fingers. Her appetite was gone, her stomach churning with apprehension. How could she look Noah's parents in the eye knowing she was planning to take the grandchild they didn't know existed? And what if they found out later? She'd convinced herself the adoption was a good thing, but the way she was going about it was wrong. With a weary sigh, she tossed the remainder of her sandwich in the trash. She'd given her word to Mia. She couldn't betray her confidence. There was no going back now.

A little before three that afternoon, Sérgio and Lydia Tomaselli appeared like silent specters in Jo's doorway, Sérgio's large frame blocking the light. Jo almost jumped out of her skin, then quickly composed herself. She stood and greeted them before ushering them inside. "Can I get either of you a coffee or some water?"

Sérgio pulled his bushy black brows together and glanced at his wife, before shaking his head. "No, thank you. We're fine."

"I'm so sorry for your loss," Jo said. "If there's anything at all I can do to help, please let me know."

"Thank you," Sérgio replied. "We realize you're inundated today, and we appreciate you taking the time to see us."

Jo gave a small nod of acknowledgment. She was fighting to keep from shaking. Expensively dressed and accessorized, Noah's parents were every bit the striking couple Noah and Mia had made, but their eyes were filled with unspeakable grief, a depth of grief Jo was only too familiar with.

Lydia sniffled into the crumpled tissue in her hand, the

rings on her fingers glinting under the fluorescent light. "I just can't believe he's gone."

Her husband wrapped a protective arm around her shoulders as he addressed Jo. "We'd like to hear from you about the altercation you broke up between Mia and Noah—the day before he disappeared."

"Well, let's see." Jo interlaced her fingers on the desk in front of her to keep from trembling. "I was on my way to the staff break room when I heard shouts and some kind of commotion coming from the student locker area. I headed over there and elbowed my way through the students to see what was going on." She paused and furrowed her brow. "Mia was beating her fists on Noah's chest. When I say beating, it was more a frustrated pummeling than anything remotely close to hurting him."

"How did Noah respond?" Sérgio asked.

"He didn't lay a hand on Mia," Jo assured him. "In fact, he tried to step out of her reach more than once, but the crowd was pressing in around them. He seemed more embarrassed by the incident than anything else."

Sérgio pursed his lips, digesting this. "Do you have any idea why Mia was so angry with him?"

Jo took a moment to consider how best to soften the blow of her answer. "She seemed to be under the impression that he'd been cheating on her."

Lydia let out a few muffled sobs and leaned her head into her husband's shoulder.

Jo squeezed her fingers together. However difficult this was for her, it paled in comparison to the excruciating pain Noah's parents were enduring.

"What exactly did Mia say?" Sérgio asked, his voice more gravelly than before as he fought to keep his emotion in check. "Did she mention … a teacher, or an older woman?"

"No, nothing like that. She accused Noah of lying and

implied that he'd been cheating on her for several months." Jo hesitated and bit her lip. "I'm sorry, I don't know if there was any truth to her accusations or not. I'm only repeating what she said."

Sérgio nodded gravely. "I understand, and I appreciate your honesty. As you can imagine, this has been a devastating shock for us, none of it makes any sense. Noah's never been depressed a day in his life, and he never mentioned wanting to end his relationship with Mia. He was besotted with that girl, despite our reservations."

Jo frowned. "Can I be so bold as to ask why you had reservations?"

Sérgio rubbed a hand over his jaw. "Mia wasn't always the best influence on our son. He started drinking after he met her. It's been a sore subject in our house."

"She could be demanding, too," Lydia piped up. "Expensive gifts, eating out—that kind of thing. It put a lot of pressure on Noah."

Sérgio threw a darting glance at his wife. "Lydia and I felt they were too young to be so serious, but we'd sort of accepted the fact that they were one of those high school sweetheart couples who would go on to get married."

Jo fixed a sympathetic smile on her lips. "I think we all kind of thought that."

An awkward silence fell over them. There would be no white wedding now—only a funeral. Mia would never become the Tomasellis' daughter-in-law, and Noah would never become a father. And for that Jo couldn't help but feel grateful, despite the tragic circumstances surrounding his death.

Sérgio coughed and cleared his throat, before getting to his feet. "Well, we won't take up any more of your time." He leaned across the desk and shook Jo's hand firmly.

Lydia gave a frail smile, her eyes glistening. "We would love it if you could attend the funeral mass."

"Yes, of course I'll be there," Jo said. "I believe all of Noah's teachers are planning on attending."

"Thank you, you're very kind," Lydia whispered through her tears. "We'll let the school know as soon as a date's been set. It's all a bit up in the air, with the coroner being involved and all."

Jo watched as Sérgio tenderly guided his wife out of the office and down the corridor, their grief evident even in their gait. She sank back down at her desk, heart thundering like hooves in her chest. Evidently, the Tomasellis knew nothing about the unborn child in Mia's womb. Her secret was safe for now.

ON TUESDAY AFTER WORK, Jo drove to the other end of town for her appointment with the adoption lawyer. She still had mixed feelings about the appropriateness of keeping the appointment days before her baby's father would be buried, but she told herself it was the right thing to do. She had already set things in motion. Preparations had to go ahead. Given everything that was going on, she felt somewhat ill-prepared for the interview. She'd intended to write up a list of burning questions to ask the lawyer, but her mind was in a complete fog and she couldn't recall any of them. Hopefully, the lawyer would be competent enough to address all the pertinent issues without much prompting on her part. She was thankful she wasn't meeting with the social worker today, she had a feeling her emotions would get the better of her, making her look like a potentially flaky mother—too unstable to raise a child.

She pulled into the parking lot outside the law offices of

Parsons & Jeffrey a full fifteen minutes before her appointment. After turning off the engine, she lifted up the flap on
her visor to expose the vanity mirror and took a moment to
comb her hair and slap on some lip gloss before reaching for
her purse. She could at least look put together on the outside
even though she was a hot mess on the inside. As she headed
toward the office, a couple around her own age walked out,
hand-in-hand. They gave her a conspiratorial smile in passing, the sparkle in their eyes letting her know they were on
their way to adopting a child of their own. Jo offered a stiff
smile in return. She'd been disappointed too many times in
the past to begin celebrating this early in the process. It wasn't
a done deal yet. She pushed open the door to the lobby and
made her way to the reception desk. A well-groomed young
woman with oversized black glasses and flawless skin greeted
her in a polished tone. "Good afternoon. How can I help you?"

"I'm Jo Murphy. I have an appointment with Derek
Parsons."

"Certainly, I'll let Mr. Parsons know you're here. Go
ahead and make yourself comfortable. Can I offer you
anything to drink?"

"No, thank you, I'm fine." Jo headed over to the tufted
lounge chairs seated in a symmetrical grouping in one
corner of the room. Picture lighting highlighted the artwork
on the walls—a curious mixture of black-and-white draw-
ings of courthouses through the centuries, and vibrant color
photographs of local wildlife and fauna.

After a couple of minutes, a tall, distinguished-looking
gentleman with salt-and-pepper hair appeared in the reception area. He approached Jo and held out a hand. "Mrs.
Murphy, delighted to meet you. I'm Derek Parsons. This way,
please." He gestured for Jo to go ahead of him. "My office is
the first door on the left."

Jo stepped into a modest-sized room with monochromatic furnishings and took a seat at the oversized desk. Derek pulled a chair out and sat down opposite her. He moved a stack of papers aside before placing a thin file in front of him and opening it. "So, I understand you and your husband have agreed to adopt a friend's baby, is that correct?"

"Yes," Jo replied, feeling a little flustered. Not a lie per se, but it was certainly stretching the truth to refer to Mia as a friend. She and Liam had agreed it would be better not to bring up the fact that Mia was still a student. She would be eighteen in a couple of weeks and graduated from high school before the baby was born, so it was a moot point as far as they were concerned.

"Well, first of all, congratulations to you both," Derek said, reaching for a pen and jotting something down. "You've done all the hard work for me." He wiggled an eyebrow and smiled expectantly as if he'd cracked a well-executed joke. Jo smiled politely back, trying to play the part of a euphoric mother-to-be, despite the mixed emotions swirling around inside her.

Derek flicked through some paperwork in the file in front of him. "As a school counselor, I'm sure you've already submitted to background checks that will satisfy the adoption placement. The next step is to have the mother—your friend—fill out the adoption placement form. You and your husband should be aware that she has thirty days after the birth to change her mind. After that, she'll be required to sign a legal document relinquishing her parental rights." He frowned at his paperwork for a moment. "Father is unknown, is that correct?"

"Yes," Jo said firmly, trying to quash the sudden wave of guilt threatening to derail her.

She thought she saw Derek hoist a brow a fraction of an inch, but he quickly moved on. "I'll go ahead and set up an adoption care caseworker from the social services department to perform an in-home study. It's merely a formality to make sure you and your husband are financially and emotionally in a position to adopt your friend's child. You'll need to have some paperwork on hand for that visit—proof of income, a doctor's clean bill of health, that kind of thing. I have a list here I'll give you."

"I'm sure I can get all that together next week," Jo said.

"Excellent." Derek tapped his pen on the file. "What's the mother's due date?"

Jo blinked, heat rising in her cheeks. "I'm not sure of the exact date. She's about nine or ten weeks along."

"Great, that gives us plenty of time. Once you find out the due date, shoot me an email. After that, I'll go ahead and get a court date on the books. You and your husband will both need to attend, and that's when we'll present your petition for adoption." He paused and tweaked a smile. "Provided neither of you turn out to be felons, the judge will approve the petition and you'll become parents."

Jo's eyes welled with tears. Just hearing those words sent a powerful wave of emotion crashing through her that was hard to control. Surely she shouldn't be allowed to experience this much joy when her friend had just died. "Thank you," she said, sniffing. "I'm sorry, this is all so overwhelming." She wasn't sure she was talking about the baby anymore, but she wasn't about to explain to a virtual stranger the nerve-jangling emotional roller coaster she'd been on for the past few days.

"No need to apologize," Derek said. "It's perfectly natural to be emotional when it comes to this point in the process and it all becomes real." He pushed a checklist across the table to Jo. "These are the items you'll need to get together for the caseworker. Do you have any other questions for me?"

"I don't think so," Jo said, slipping the checklist into her purse. "I'll get to work on this." She got to her feet and shook hands with Derek before making her way back out to the reception area. Nodding to the smiling receptionist, she exited the lobby and heaved in a deep breath of fresh air. She'd made it through the appointment with the adoption lawyer without becoming a blubbering mess. She only hoped she could get through the funeral mass for the father of her baby as smoothly.

13

*L*iam and Jo dressed for Sarah's funeral in silence, a surreal rite that seemed to Jo more a mockery of Sarah's life than an act of homage. How could Sarah, someone with so much zeal and energy, be dead? It had been ten days since her body, along with Noah's, was discovered in her car. The police had wrapped up their investigation, convinced by the cumulative evidence that Sarah and Noah had made a pact to commit suicide. The burner phones located inside the car spoke volumes about the illicit relationship that had been going on for almost five months. The texts they'd exchanged had become increasingly guilt-ridden as time went on, and the idea of committing suicide appeared to have been a joint decision, neither one coercing the other into it. The coroner declared both their deaths to be the result of carbon monoxide poisoning. The autopsies determined nothing else untoward, other than that Sarah and Noah had taken an anti-anxiety prescription beforehand, presumably to help them fall asleep more quickly as the noxious gas filled the car. It was all too horrific to process.

"Ready?" Liam asked, jolting Jo from her agonizing thoughts.

She nodded distractedly, her stomach twisting at the thought of seeing Sarah lying on a bed of tufted silk in a glossy casket—as lifeless as the Bavarian doll in the glossy European brochure still buried at the bottom of Jo's purse. A trip that would never be taken by either of them.

The service was being conducted at a local funeral parlor, restricted to family and a few close friends. Robbie didn't want it to become any more of a circus than it already was. Preparing for the worst, the police were enlisted to stave off any protesters. Robbie had received several threatening emails slamming Sarah in the intervening days, and someone had gone so far as to spray-paint *molester* over his front door. Even Barb had received some abhorrent mail sent to the Alzheimer's facility accusing her of spawning a pervert who preyed on children. In the end, Robbie decided against putting an obituary in the paper, fearing it would only elicit more abuse.

Jo and Liam ducked as they headed into the funeral parlor, trying to avoid the intrusive media camera zooming in on their movements. Jo nodded to her colleagues as she entered the room where the service was being held. Soft instrumental music played in the background. The lighting was diffused and gentle, programmed not to intrude on the grieving, but to Jo the atmosphere felt stifling, a parody of the spirited life Sarah had led. It was too still, almost as if everyone were holding their breath along with Sarah. The casket—closed to Jo's relief—sat on a wooden stand at the front of the room, bedecked with an elegant gladioli floral spray and flanked by two white columns each displaying a framed picture of Sarah. On the left she was a blushing bride on Robbie's arm, and on the right, she stood at the edge of a steep hiking trail wearing a backpack, arms thrown wide and laughing—the Sarah they all loved best.

They made their way to the front row and whispered a few words to Robbie, before shaking hands with the rest of his and Sarah's extended families including a bewildered looking Barb, seated next to a caregiver from the home. Then they slipped into the row behind Robbie and waited for the service to begin.

The officiant made his entrance through a doorway to the right of the casket and walked to the podium. "On behalf of the Gleeson and Davidson families, I would like to welcome you all to this celebration of Sarah Gleeson's life. It is only natural that we should mourn today, because in a very real sense Sarah is no longer a part of our lives. But today is also a day for memories and for all of us to pay our respects and say a fond farewell to a remarkable woman who lived life with infectious joy and brought so much happiness to others. At this time, I would like to ask Sarah's cousin, Ella, to come up and read a poem she has selected to commemorate her."

Jo watched as Sarah's cousin took her place behind the podium. She looked like she was barely out of high school. Her expression was strained and her eyes red from crying. Almost immediately, her voice began to waver, "Do not weep for me, I have gone with the wind, taken flight—"

Jo scrunched her eyes shut, blocking out the words that rang so senseless. Sarah hadn't taken flight—she had taken her life, and to what end? She had accomplished nothing other than making all these people suffer. Her friends, her family, her colleagues, not to mention Noah's friends and family. *Why, Sarah, Why?*

Liam laid a hand on her shoulder and whispered, "Are you okay?"

Jo gave a tight nod, keeping her eyes forward. She was barely holding it together. Death had robbed her of far too much in the space of a few weeks, and she had yet to come to terms with any of the losses.

When Ella sat back down, Robbie stood and walked sedately to the front of the room. He smoothed a piece of paper out on the podium and then gripped the edges, hanging on for dear life as he looked out over the faces of Sarah's friends and family. "I stand before you today a broken man." He paused, the mic picking up his ragged breathing before he continued, "I never imagined I would be the first to say good-bye. I had the privilege of being Sarah's husband for eight blissful years. Not only did she spread love and happiness to everyone around her, she was my best friend and the joyous spark who brought light to our home. I know everyone here is going to miss her incredible smile as much as I do." His voice wavered, and he pulled out a tissue and discreetly wiped at his nose as he glanced down at his notes. "Sarah, my sweetheart, may you be at peace. I will never cease to love you and I will forever treasure the far too short time we enjoyed on earth together." Robbie lifted his head and looked out over the mourners. "Thank you all for coming. Sarah would want you to know that she loved each and every one of you." He folded his paper up and returned to his seat accompanied by muffled sobs from the audience.

A young woman got up next and sang a soulful rendition of "Wind Beneath My Wings." When the officiant finally stood to close the service and invite everyone to the reception in the adjoining parlor, Jo steeled herself for the awkward interactions that would follow. This wasn't a typical funeral where you could talk effusively about the great life the deceased had led. Sarah wasn't old enough for her death to be justified. And, as she'd taken her own life, they couldn't even talk about the tragedy of her dying young. The double suicide pact was the huge elephant in the room that everyone would be forced to dance around. Jo had no doubt it would be a similar conundrum at Noah's funeral mass. Suicide wasn't exactly the kind of thing you discussed if it could be avoided—to say nothing of the illicit affair that had driven Sarah and Noah to kill themselves.

After mingling at the reception for an acceptable length of time and expressing their condolences once again to Robbie's and Sarah's extended families, Jo and Liam excused themselves, and made their way back to their car to drive to St Jude's Catholic Church in time for Noah's funeral mass.

"That was rough," Liam commented as he drove. "I've never seen a man as shattered as Robbie. He's a trooper, though. To say all those beautiful things about his wife knowing she was carrying on behind his back."

Jo stared morosely out the window. "I can't imagine this next service will be any easier, at least not for the Tomaselli family. Noah's mother was barely holding it together when she and her husband came to see me."

Liam grimaced. "Sérgio was so proud of Noah. He talked about him quite a bit during that golf tournament we played in together."

A few minutes later, they pulled into the parking lot outside St. Jude's Catholic Church. To Jo's horror, the media was stationed there in full force. Evidently, the funeral of the teenager in the illicit affair was considered more news-worthy than that of his teacher. As they walked toward the entrance, Jo glanced across at a reporter standing behind an oversized mic broadcasting live. "The scene outside St. Jude's Catholic Church this afternoon is heart wrenching as mourners pack the sanctuary to pay their last respects to rising football star and high school senior, Noah Tomaselli, who died ten days ago in a tragic suicide pact with his married lover, twenty-nine-year-old art teacher, Sarah Glee-son, on staff at Emmetville High."

Jo quickened her pace, eager to get inside and away from

the relentless media coverage that couldn't seem to get enough of what they were treating as a modern-day Romeo and Juliet tragedy. She and Liam slid into a pew toward the back. The front of the church was decorated with topiaries and opulent flower arrangements interspersed with giant easels displaying blown-up photographs documenting Noah's short life. Jo was thankful she was seated too far back to make out the details. She didn't want to be reminded of his handsome smile and dark eyes that had seduced her friend to do the unthinkable. Raising her gaze and looking around, she studied the intricate mosaics, stained glass windows, and stunning arches inside the church. It was quiet and peaceful in a different way to the funeral home. Many of the pews were packed with students. Noah's teammates were wearing varsity jackets and football jerseys. Toward the front of the church, the extended Tomaselli family occupied several rows on both sides. Jo searched the pews but couldn't see any sign of Mia. Maybe she'd decided to skip the funeral. Under the circumstances, Jo could hardly blame her. It seemed Mia's suspicions about Noah had been right all along.

The music began to play, and an altar boy appeared and lit a candle before kneeling in front of the alter and crossing himself. He exited again and a few minutes later a procession of priests made their way up the aisle followed by pallbearers wheeling a polished walnut casket gleaming under the candlelight at the end of each pew. The priests spread out and took up their positions on the dais, lighting additional candles and crossing themselves. The priest who was officiating circled the table waving a liturgical censer and then handed it to one of the attendants before facing the crowd and raising his hands. "Let us pray. Oh God, who hath set a limit to this life—"

Jo buried her face in her hands, tears leaking between her

fingers. This was all wrong. God hadn't wanted them dead. Noah and Sarah had taken their lives, cheated their families and friends out of time on earth together. But why? None of it made sense. When the prayer ended, Jo wiped her eyes, raised her head, and listened numbly as one of Noah's sisters read from the book of Lamentations.

When she finished, the officiant got to his feet again and addressed the audience. "We are gathered here today in this church to celebrate the life of Noah Antonio Tomaselli." The priest paused and adjusted his glasses before continuing. "Noah received his baptism, communion, and confirmation here in this very church and now, all too soon, his funeral mass. Although his journey here on earth has come to a close, there is still much to celebrate in the resurrection of Jesus Christ, and one day soon Noah's resurrection. For those of us left behind, we remember a fine young man, a promising athlete, and an excellent student who was deeply loved by his family here on earth. At this time, I would like to ask Noah's friends to come forward."

Jo watched, blinking back hot, salty tears as several friends and teammates took their turn at the podium to share a special memory or thought.

"He was a great guy and a big contributor to the team," Brandon Edison began, choking up. "The kind of guy everyone wanted to hang out with and everyone wanted to be like. I miss him already."

After Noah's friends had all said their piece, Sérgio Tomaselli walked to the front of the church and cleared his throat while he adjusted the microphone. "The Tomaselli family would like to express their thanks to the community for their outpouring of support at this difficult time. It is impossible to describe the depths of our grief at the tragic loss of our only son, Noah."

Lydia Tomaselli bent over in the front pew and the woman next to her laid her hand on her shoulder.

Jo dabbed at her eyes and whispered to Liam, "This is too heartbreaking."

He nodded glumly, his face creased with anguish. "I don't know what to say to his parents at the reception afterward."

"No one does," Jo replied. "All you can do is offer your condolences."

When the funeral mass finally ended, they followed the crowd of mourners out past the reporters and cameras and into the adjoining church hall where the reception was being hosted.

Along with Noah's other teachers, they lined up to pay their respects to the Tomaselli family.

"Thank you so much for coming," Lydia said squeezing Jo's hand as she wiped at her eyes with her tissue.

Liam shook Sérgio's hand. "I'm very sorry for your loss."

"Thank you," Sérgio replied gravely, already reaching out his hand to the next mourner.

They moved on down the line and shook hands with Noah's sisters and several other extended family members before breaking away and moving toward the refreshments.

Jo's eyes widened when she caught sight of Mia standing with a classmate sipping on an iced tea. She waited until the other girl moved off before approaching Mia. "I wasn't sure if you'd come or not, under the circumstances. I'm so sorry."

Mia eyed her warily. She threw back the rest of her iced tea before tossing the cup in the trash. "Guess they got what was coming to them, didn't they?"

14

***

SIX MONTHS LATER

*J*o was finding it difficult to breathe as Liam hurriedly reversed out of their driveway. Mia Allen had gone into labor, four-and-a-half weeks before her due date. The last time Jo had seen her, she was dressed in a knee-length graduation gown, and tossing her cap in the air with wild abandon. Immediately afterward, she'd moved to San Francisco, and their only communication since had been through email and texts, and the occasional phone call. Jo glanced at the clock on her phone, making a quick calculation of their arrival time. It was a five-hour drive to San Francisco. Realistically, Mia's labor would probably last a lot longer than that, but some part of Jo was terrified she would miss the main event. Mia had wanted her and Liam to be at the birthing center, to *take ownership* of their baby right away as she'd put it. As harsh as it sounded, Jo could understand her decision, given the circumstances of Noah's betrayal. Mia had been so bitter at the reception following his funeral. The birth of his child would bring it all back with a vengeance.

Jo had tried to be there for Robbie as much as possible in

the months after Sarah's death. She dragged him along to various social events, concerts, and movies, and invited him over to dinner on a regular basis. On the whole, he was coping remarkably well. He'd taken over Sarah's role as power of attorney in looking after her elderly mother's affairs, and made a habit of visiting Barb at Brookdale Meadows every Sunday afternoon. He'd returned to school the week after the funeral and carried on teaching his classes —pouring his heart into his work in an effort to dull his pain, Jo suspected. Underneath his cheery demeanor, she knew he must be lonely—Sarah had been such a bright, vivacious personality. But, as the months went by, Robbie's sense of humor resurfaced, and he soon began whistling in the corridors again. They were all trying to move on in their own way.

"This is it," Liam said, grinning across at Jo as he gripped the steering wheel. "No more lazy weekend mornings reading in bed."

Jo didn't mind. She relished the idea of being woken up early by a little person who needed her. She was more than ready to throw off the mantle of childlessness, which clung to her like an objectionable aura people backed away from. The social worker had warned them not to purchase any baby gear in advance in case the birthmother changed her mind. Jo and Liam had compromised and bought it anyway but left it in the boxes. A clipboard of receipts lay on top of the dresser in the ivory-colored nursery. She'd wondered if it might be tempting fate to keep the receipts and had considered burning them on more than one occasion. The crib, mattress, and bedding alone had set them back almost two-thousand dollars. But, to Jo it was worth every penny—a far more fruitful investment than IVF.

Among the baby items they'd packed in the car was a gift she'd selected for Mia. It was a thank you gesture of sorts, a sterling silver Tiffany knot pendant. She hadn't wanted to skimp, remembering that Mia had a penchant for expensive gifts.

"I just hope the baby's healthy," Jo said with a sigh. "I know Tory assured us that Mia was going to all her doctor appointments and eating well, but how does she know that? She's relying on what Mia told her."

"We've gone over this before, Jo," Liam said in an overly patient tone. "There's no point in worrying about things that are out of our control. If Mia used the money we sent her for other things, then so be it."

"I just hope it wasn't drugs or alcohol," Jo added. Sérgio Tomaselli's comments about Mia being a bad influence on Noah had preyed on her mind ever since. Mia had admitted to Detective Saunders she'd been drinking vodka with Noah the night he died. Jo only hoped for the baby's sake she'd given it up after that.

MID-AFTERNOON, they arrived at the Sonoma Birth Center and circled the building looking for a parking spot. The ones nearest to the entrance were reserved for expectant parents.

"Technically that's us," Liam said with a mischievous grin.

Jo rolled her eyes. "I don't think I could live with myself if I forced a heavily pregnant woman to hobble all the way across the parking lot clutching her belly."

"Since you put it that way," Liam replied, "I'll park back at the fence."

They locked the car and sprinted to the front door of the birthing center as if time was of the essence. In the foyer, sofas and love seats were nestled in intimate groupings, and a well-stocked coffee station and magazine rack lined the back wall. The gray-haired woman behind the desk smiled warmly at them as they approached. Jo wondered if all adoptive parents felt like she did, plagued with doubts, an intruder in a sacred space she hadn't earned the right to enter. She fought to quash the feelings of inadequacy that threatened to bubble up and taint her happiness. This was her time, she had made this happen, one way or another.

"Good morning!" the woman said cheerily. "I'm Janice, how can I help you?"

Liam rested an elbow on the counter. "Hi Janice. We're Jo and Liam Murphy, adoptive parents to Mia Allen's baby. She went into labor this morning."

Janice's face broke into a smile of recognition. "Yes, of course! Mia told us you'd be arriving around this time." She got to her feet and grabbed a clipboard from her desk. "If you'd like to follow me, I'll take you through to the birthing partners' area." As she walked, she glanced down at the clipboard in her hand. "Her birthing plan specifies that the baby's to be brought straight to you, Jo. Of course, Mia's entitled to change her mind, so you need to prepare yourself for that possibility. But, as it stands, it looks like you'll get to hold your baby right away."

"It's so hard to believe this is happening," Jo gushed, as Janice led them into a second waiting area.

"Trust me, it will feel real before too long." Janice pointed to a door that led out of the waiting room. "There are bathrooms that way and the cafeteria's at the end of the corridor. I'll just go and find out what Mia's status is."

Within minutes, another woman appeared in the waiting area dressed in pastel scrubs and clogs, her long, black hair pulled back in a ponytail. "Mr. and Mrs. Murphy?"

Jo and Liam stood frozen to the spot, clutching each other's hands.

"Is everything alright?" Jo squeaked out.

"Absolutely," the woman assured her. "I'm Wanda, the

midwife assistant. Mia wanted me to tell you she's glad you're here."

The words fell over Jo like a soothing balm. Tears welled up and trickled down her cheeks. Mia's words were the reassurance she needed. An affirmation that she was going to leave here a mother. Her shoulders shook as Liam gently slid his arm around her.

"I know this is overwhelming, but there's no shame in crying here. Tears of joy have anointed every square foot of this building, let me assure you," Wanda said with a chuckle.

Jo blinked away her tears. Something about her breezy manner reminded her of Sarah. She wished more than anything that her friend could be here to share her joy.

"I predict this baby won't come quickly," Wanda added. "Mia's only at two centimeters so it's going to be a long night. I'll touch base with you a little later on and give you another update." She disappeared down the hallway and Jo and Liam sank back down in their seats.

"Mind if I catch the game?" Liam nodded toward the television in the corner of the room.

"Have at it." Jo pulled out her Kindle and opened up the book she was currently reading for the third time, *What to Expect the First Year*. Liam would think it was overkill if she told him she was rereading it again, but she was desperate to do everything right. It had been a grueling journey to get to this point, and she wasn't about to take a moment of it for granted. The words danced before her eyes, her mind drifting to the moment when Mia's baby would become hers. The thought was intoxicating, the warm fuzzy feeling inside her all-consuming.

From time to time she glanced across at the screen in the corner of the room. Unlike her, Liam was fully absorbed in the basketball game. She smiled to herself. She had no doubt he'd be a good dad. Years of infertility had pushed them to the edge, but adoption had brought them together again.

She was curled up on a lounge chair half asleep when the midwife returned shortly after midnight. "We're ready for you," she announced.

Jo gripped Liam's arm, her fingernails digging into his flesh. "I think I'm going to be sick."

"No, you're not," he said, leaning in to kiss her. "You're going to be a mother, and you're going to be an incredible one."

In a daze, they followed the midwife down the corridor and into a dimly-lit bedroom with a small seating area, a changing table, a crib, and a kitchenette. "Make yourselves comfortable. I'll be right back."

Moments later, Wanda reappeared with a tiny swaddled bundle and placed it in Jo's arms. She gasped as she looked down at the miniature face. The tiny human she was holding felt so light, so fragile, so utterly dependent on her protection and care.

"Is it … a boy or a girl?" Liam asked, his eyes glassy with tears as he gazed at their newborn.

"A little girl," Wanda replied. "A healthy five pounds and twelve ounces, twenty-one inches. Do you have a name for her?"

Jo and Liam exchanged a knowing smile. Names were the easy part. They'd had ten years to narrow down their choices.

"Her name's Claire," Jo said.

Wanda nodded approvingly. "Congratulations, Mom and Dad."

Jo gently traced a fingertip over her baby's soft cheek, and then glanced at Wanda. "How's Mia doing?"

"She's resting. Once she's ready to see you, I'll take you

both in there. In the meantime, you'll have your hands full. Diapering, feeding, all that good stuff."

Jo stared at her, aghast. "Are you leaving us alone?"

Wanda chuckled. "That's the plan. This is your room for the night."

Jo took a few shallow breaths, gazing in wonder at the scrunched-up face in front of her. Claire yawned, one tiny fist popping out of her blanket as she flung it toward her head. Her face twisted into the beginning of a delayed scream. Despite the months Jo had spent reading up on parenting tips, she felt panic rising up inside her. As the scream erupted, she instinctively pulled Claire close to her chest and began to rock her. The baby's cries softened and then faded to a snuffle.

Wanda turned to Liam. "Your turn, Dad. There's a microwave and a bottle warmer, and everything else you'll need over by the changing table. Time to get your daughter's first bottle ready."

Liam blinked and stroked his jaw, casting a terrified glance at the far side of the room.

Jo laughed at his obvious discomfort. "You can do this, honey. If you can configure network systems, you can make up a bottle."

"Don't worry," Wanda added. "I'll walk you through it. Believe me, I've seen firefighters and soldiers practically have a panic attack making up the first bottle."

Liam's face relaxed a little as he accompanied Wanda over to the kitchenette.

Jo gazed lovingly at Claire's perfect face. Her little blue eyes were curious, studying Jo as though wondering if this could possibly be the person who'd carried her for nine months. Jo rubbed her palm gently over Claire's soft head of blonde fuzz. Noah's Italian genes hadn't prevailed after all. Claire looked exactly like Mia, and nothing at all like her father, for which Jo was immensely thankful. There was no chance the Tomaselli family would recognize their grandchild and try to stake a claim.

Liam appeared at Jo's side holding a bottle of formula. He laid a burp cloth over Jo's shoulder. "Why don't you sit in the rocking chair to feed her?"

"I'll leave you two alone and give you some privacy," Wanda said. "I'll pop back in shortly."

Jo walked over to the rocking chair and sat down gingerly, afraid that even the tiniest movement might disturb the fragile parcel in her arms. Halfway through the bottle, Claire fell into a deep sleep, as limp as if she'd been drugged.

When Wanda reappeared to let them know that Mia was ready for them, Jo handed Claire to Liam, and dug out the gift she'd brought for Mia.

She was sitting up in bed waiting for them, looking even more beautiful than Jo remembered her. Her sleek blonde hair was woven into a loose braid that hung over one shoulder. Her eyes shone, and her face was flushed—a little fuller than normal, but it suited her.

Jo approached her bed tentatively, blinking back tears. "Thank you, Mia. She's perfect. I don't know what else to say other than thank you from the bottom of my heart. I brought you a little something." She handed the Tiffany box to her, pleased when the girl's eyes grew wide.

"I should be thanking you," Mia replied, untying the ribbon. She removed the lid from the box and peered inside. "Oh, it's gorgeous! I love it! You have excellent taste." Her eyes wandered to Liam standing back from the bed cradling Claire.

"Do you … " Jo hesitated, searching for the right words. "Do you want to hold her?"

Mia waved a dismissive hand. "No, I'm good. What's her name?"

"Claire," Jo said. "I've always loved that name."

Mia gave a distracted nod, her eyes drifting back to the pendant.

"Are your parents here?" Jo ventured.

"It isn't exactly a family occasion. It's not like I'm making them grandparents or anything."

"I just thought … doesn't your dad live close by?"

Mia narrowed her eyes. "Chuck's not interested in meeting you if that's what you're getting at."

Jo opened and closed her mouth, taken aback by Mia's sharp tone. The girl could be incredibly callous at times, and yet she'd chosen them to be parents to her child. For that, they were indebted to her.

Jo cleared her throat and changed tactics. "What will you do after this?"

Mia shrugged. "Get a job."

"It shouldn't be too hard to find work in a big city like San Francisco," Jo said.

"I'm not staying *here*." Mia scoffed. "I'm going back."

Jo raised her brows. It surprised her to hear that Mia wouldn't welcome the chance to stay clear of her past and memories of Noah. "Most of your friends have gone off to college already."

"I know. Rob—Mr. Gleeson's been keeping me up to date on what everyone's doing."

Liam shot Jo an incredulous look.

Jo furrowed her brow in confusion. "You talked to Mr. Gleeson?"

"Oh yes," Mia stared at her, the faint hint of a smile curling on her lips. "He wrote me a long letter apologizing for what Sarah did to Noah. We've kept in touch ever since— mostly emails, the occasional letter." She dropped her gaze and picked at the blanket on her bed. "He's the only one who understands what it was like. You know—Noah having the affair and all that, and then killing himself."

Jo swallowed, unsure what to say. It made sense in a way that Robbie and Mia felt a certain empathetic connection. After all, they'd both been betrayed by their partners and lost them in the most tragic of circumstances. But it seemed inappropriate for them to be communicating. Granted, Mia no longer attended Emmetville High, but she'd been Robbie's student, nonetheless. Even more disturbing was the fact that Robbie's wife had been carrying on with Mia's boyfriend and they'd died in a suicide pact together. Jo averted her gaze and pretended to adjust her glasses. It wasn't appropriate. She'd have a quiet word with Robbie about it when she returned home. Grieving people didn't always think straight—she knew that firsthand.

She cleared her throat, searching for something to say. "It was thoughtful of him. I know he felt guilty about what Sarah did."

Mia leaned over and reached for her purse on the bedside locker. "I have the letter right here. I'm surprised he didn't tell you we'd been in touch, since you're such good friends and all." Before Jo could say another word, Mia pulled out a folded sheet, opened it up, and began to read.

Dear Mia,

Words fail me as I attempt to pen an apology that can do little to compensate you for your loss. My wife, Sarah, was entirely responsible for what happened to Noah. Regardless of whether the relationship was a mutual one or not, she abused her power as a teacher to influence a student. To some degree, I'm also to blame for not realizing what was going on and stopping it. One of my students lost his life and I must live with the guilt of that as I was married to his killer.

Jo grimaced. *Married to his killer?* Is that who Robbie really thought Sarah was?

Mia paused and glanced up to make sure she had Jo's full attention.

Jo shivered. She remembered that look in Mia's eyes, she'd seen it before—it was almost like she knew she was inflicting pain and was enjoying every minute of it.

Mia continued reading aloud.

I miss Sarah every day, but I realize now that I'm missing a woman who never existed, a fantasy woman who didn't really love me. I know you feel the same deep sense of betrayal and my heart goes out to you for the pain you're experiencing. I only hope that as time goes by, we can both find happiness again.

"He goes on for several more paragraphs, but that's the gist of it." Mia sank back on her pillow, a sly grin on her face. "He's so lonely. Maybe I should introduce him to my mother."

15

_____

The first few weeks after Jo and Liam brought Claire home were a grab bag of moments of sheer bliss and utter chaos. Jo took a leave of absence from work and was endeavoring to throw herself into motherhood wholly and unreservedly, from the night feeds that left her foggy from lack of sleep, to the endless mounds of laundry, and dirty diapers.

Liam didn't work as late anymore. Now, he had a real family to come home to and Jo could tell he cherished every minute of it. He proudly pushed Claire around the mall or through the park in her stroller on weekends, basking in the oohs and ahhs of passersby admiring the bundle of perfection that was his daughter.

Jo asked Robbie to be Claire's godparent, and he readily accepted, relishing his role and making a point of stopping by to visit after school and bring her yet another stuffed animal he couldn't resist adding to her collection.

"I wish Sarah was here to share this with me," he said one Friday afternoon as he cradled Claire in his arms.

"I do too," Jo agreed wistfully. "It breaks my heart to think she'll never know my daughter." She smiled sadly at Robbie. "It's going to be hard for you at Christmas. Why don't you spend it with us this year?"

"I thought I'd spend the day by myself out of town somewhere."

"Nonsense. You've spent enough days doing that," Jo countered. "We'd love to have you. How's everything going at school anyway? We haven't talked about it much. I've been so preoccupied with Claire."

"It was awkward at first," Robbie admitted. "Some of the staff and students wanted to do something to commemorate Sarah and Noah. But the Parent-Teacher Association was opposed to any sort of memorial plaque. The football team suggested a tribute marker next to the field for Noah, but in the end, Ed decided against it. He felt it would be better not to memorialize the event like some kind of Romeo and Juliet tragedy. He had visions of weeping teenage girls leaving floral tributes at the foot of the plaque."

"He does have a point," Jo said. "It wouldn't do to glamorize the suicide angle."

Robbie grimaced. "I've already had a couple of female students knock on my office door to tell me how sorry they are about what happened, and how romantic it all was. Probably the same vein of groupies who write letters to serial killers in prison." He got to his feet and handed Claire back to Jo. "On that depressing note, I need to get going. Tell Liam hi from me."

Jo glanced at the clock on her phone. Tory had texted her earlier to let her know that Mia was out with friends, and Jo had promised to take Claire around for a quick visit before dinner. Mia didn't want any contact, but Tory had asked to see her granddaughter from time to time, no matter how short the visit.

Jo and Tory hadn't discussed what they would tell Claire

as she grew older, they both knew the visits would have to come to an end as soon as she became verbal. They couldn't risk Mia finding out, or anyone else for that matter.

After making up a bottle and strapping Claire into her car seat, Jo set off. When she pulled up alongside the curb, Tory flung open the front door as if she'd been watching out for their arrival.

"Thanks for bringing her over. I know we won't be able to do this for much longer." She gave a sad shake of her head. "One of the neighbors is bound to pick up on it at some point. I'm just grateful I've had these opportunities to hold her." She reached out her hands for Claire and her granddaughter gurgled as Tory held her close to kiss her tiny cheek. "I brewed a pot of coffee."

"Thanks." Jo closed the front door behind her. "It's chilly out there today."

"This little girl is more beautiful every time I see her," Tory said, leading the way to the kitchen.

"She really is the spitting image of Mia," Jo said. "How's she doing anyway?"

"Good, I guess. She started work a couple of days ago. She got a part-time receptionist job in a doctor's office so, between my hours and hers, we barely see each other." Tory frowned as she cradled Claire. "I think she's been seeing someone. Seems kind of soon to me."

Jo adjusted her glasses. "Maybe it's a good thing. She's young and she needs to move past what happened."

"I just hope he's not some loser," Tory said dubiously. "She's very secretive about it."

"Well, she was hurt deeply by Noah. I suppose it's understandable that she doesn't want a microscope on her new relationship."

Tory shrugged. "She's an adult, she doesn't have to answer

to me anymore. I guess I'll just have to wait until she introduces us properly."

Jo glanced at the time on her phone. "I'm sorry, Tory, but I have to get going. We have a babysitter coming over tonight. Liam and I are going out to dinner with friends."

Tory pulled down the corners of her lips as she handed Claire back. "I'd love to babysit her, if only it wouldn't raise too many red flags."

Jo smiled sympathetically. "I'll do my best to keep you updated with the odd photo now and again. Make sure to delete them off your phone afterward so Mia doesn't come across them."

"Thanks, Jo." Tory smiled at her. "You've been so considerate throughout this whole process. I couldn't ask for a better mother for my granddaughter."

The two women embraced and then Jo draped her diaper bag over her shoulder and made her way out to the car, turning to wave as Tory closed the door.

On a whim, she decided to stop by Liam's office for a few minutes. She'd dropped in once before, a few days after they brought Claire home, and she'd promised the women in the office to bring her back again soon. Now would be as good a time as any. They wouldn't be smack dab in the middle of any important projects this late on a Friday afternoon.

Liam looked up from his desk, a wide grin breaking over his face when he spotted Jo walking toward him with Claire in her arms. "My two favorite ladies." He got to his feet and held out his hands for his daughter.

The women in the office gathered around like clucking hens admiring Claire who reveled in the attention, her head swiveling side-to-side like a baby bird, eyes wide with wonder.

"What brings you by?" Liam asked, after the women returned to their desks to pack up for the day.

"I was in the neighborhood, just running some errands," Jo answered, loathe to admit where she'd been. Liam wouldn't approve of her going behind Mia's back. "That reminds me, Robbie stopped by earlier. I invited him to spend Christmas with us."

"Great." Liam threw a quick glance over his shoulder to make sure the women in the office weren't listening. "How about I invite Amy, the new receptionist, too? She's single and on her own for the holidays."

"Do you really think that's a good idea?" Jo asked. "I mean, it's only been a few months."

Liam shrugged. "I'm not trying to set them up or anything, but you never know what could develop. She's a squared away girl—not as outgoing as Sarah, but nobody's going to replace her."

Jo grimaced inwardly. Apparently, Mia had found a replacement for Noah easily enough, but she could hardly tell Liam that without triggering some awkward questions. "I'd hate for Robbie to be blindsided and feel uncomfortable about it. Why don't you run it by him first, and then invite Amy if he's up for it?"

"Yeah, sure, I'll give him a call."

"I'll plan for four unless you tell me otherwise," Jo said, getting to her feet. "I should get going, Claire's hungry. Don't forget we have dinner plans tonight."

THE WEEKS LEADING up to Christmas went by in a haze of activity. On Christmas Eve, Jo set the table for four. When she finished with the decorations, she turned to Liam. "How does it look?"

"What?" He looked up from his phone, unsure where to direct his eye.

"The table, for dinner tomorrow." Jo pointed at it. "Does it look okay?"

"Oh yeah, looks great, honey." He frowned. "Who else is coming?"

"Robbie and Amy, remember?"

Liam groaned. "Nooo, I totally forgot to invite her."

Jo glared at him. "You are kidding me, right?"

"I'm sorry, it completely slipped my mind."

"It's not too late, why don't you give her a call now?"

"She went to San Francisco to spend the holidays with friends."

"I don't believe this!" Jo turned back to the table and made a show of clearing away one of the place settings.

"Maybe it's for the best," Liam offered. "Robbie might not be ready yet."

"That's why you were supposed to ask him about it first," Jo retorted before marching off to the kitchen to put away the extra dishes and cutlery.

SHE WAS STILL MIFFED with Liam on Christmas morning and annoyed with herself for spoiling their first Christmas with Claire by allowing ill feelings to brew between them while they opened their gifts. By the time the smell of prime rib filled the house, and she had drunk a glass of red wine, she was feeling a little more relaxed about the whole situation. Maybe they could drop a few hints about Amy to Robbie and see how he responded. If he expressed any interest, she'd set up another dinner date.

Shortly before four, Robbie arrived with an oversized, soft toy in tow for Claire. "How's my favorite girl?" he crooned, touching her button nose gently.

"What's this supposed to be?" Jo asked, laughing as Robbie handed her the ridiculous-looking stuffed animal.

"The girl in the store told me it was a monkey."

Jo arched an amused brow. "And you believed her?"

Robbie grinned and hugged Jo, before slapping Liam on the back. "Got the game on?"

"Absolutely," Liam replied.

"Why don't you boys get a drink while I put Claire down for her nap?" Jo said.

She carried her daughter upstairs and tucked her into her crib for her afternoon nap. Robbie appeared to be in good form, despite this being his first Christmas without Sarah. Inevitably, she would come up in conversation at some point in the evening, but at least he was putting a good face on it.

Once she was sure Claire was asleep, Jo turned on the baby monitor and got to work in the kitchen mashing potatoes, steaming vegetables, and whipping up fresh cream for the coffee. Her stomach rumbled at the succulent aroma that wafted into the room when she opened the oven door. The prime rib was roasted to perfection, the pepper-and-herb crust a rich brown sheen, the meat tender and juicy in the center. She reached for the potholders and lifted it out, tenting it with tinfoil and letting it rest while she prepared the gravy. Moments later, Liam and Robbie appeared in the doorway. "That smell is too tantalizing to ignore. How can we help?"

"You can take the side dishes out of the warming drawer and put them on the dining room table." Jo brushed a few strands of hair out of her face with the back of her hand. "Oh, and light the candles, please."

After Liam had done the honors and carved the roast, they heaped their plates with all the fixings and Robbie filled their wine glasses with a Pinot noir he'd brought. He raised his glass in a toast. "To Claire, the best thing to happen to us all this year."

"To Claire," Jo and Liam said in unison.

Jo took a gulp of wine, blinking back tears. It had been a wonderful year, and a terrible year. But, tonight, they were celebrating the good times.

"Jo, you outdid yourself." Robbie speared another forkful of food. "This is the best prime rib I've tasted in my twenty-nine years. And I mean that most sincerely."

"Well, thank you," Jo said, self-consciously waving away the compliment. "I'm happy you're here to share it with us."

Robbie took a sip of his wine. "Actually, I'm glad you invited me. I've been waiting for an opportunity to talk to you both about something."

Jo leaned back in her chair and looked at him expectantly, a flutter of unease in her stomach. She hoped he wasn't about to tell them he was transferring to another school—that he wanted to move out of the area and start afresh.

"The thing is," Robbie said, "I've been seeing someone."

Jo darted a look of surprise in Liam's direction. Did he know about this?

"You probably think it's too soon—-" Robbie began, but Jo cut him off.

"No, we would never judge you." She looked at him earnestly. "I know you've been lonely without Sarah. I'm glad to hear you're dating again."

"I'm happy for you too, man," Liam added. "How'd you meet her?"

Robbie twisted the stem of his wine glass between his fingers. "I suppose you could say we bonded over circumstances. She lost someone close to her too."

"Well, I think that's very sweet," Jo said, smiling. "You're both coming from a place of pain, so you can be more understanding of each other. When do we get to meet her?"

"You already have," Robbie replied, "It's Mia Allen."

16

*J*o choked on a mouthful of wine and groped for her napkin.

When she caught her breath again, she stared at Robbie unblinking, wondering if she'd misheard—if perhaps the wine had gone to her head, or the lack of sleep over the past couple of weeks was finally catching up with her. The half-regretful smile Robbie returned her told her she wasn't imagining it at all. Her thoughts tumbled over one another as the meat and the alcohol swirled around in the pit of her stomach in a nauseous spin cycle. The silence at the table was almost deafening until Claire's cry broke through.

Jo sprang into action, scooting her chair out from the table. "I'll be right back."

She tripped her way upstairs and lifted her daughter out of her crib, hugging her close to her trembling body. This was wrong, terribly wrong. Yes, Robbie and Mia were the injured parties in their partners' scandalous affair, but there was something abnormal about the two of them getting together. How could she possibly go back downstairs and smile and nod and give Robbie her blessing? Granted, Mia had turned eighteen, but only just. What was Robbie thinking? Jo paced the floor cradling Claire's head as she tried to sort through her churning emotions. He *wasn't* thinking—that was it. He was still mourning Sarah, still vulnerable, and about to make a huge mistake like so many lonely men before him. If only she'd had a quiet word with him about the inappropriateness of corresponding with Mia like she'd intended. She needed to help him see that this was a bad, no, a terrible move. She had to stop him before it went any further.

Her mind made up, she went back downstairs, a stiff smile on her face. She slipped Claire into her swing and turned the setting to low, before resuming her place at the table. Liam stared morosely at the wine glass in his hand, avoiding meeting her eyes.

"I know this comes as a shock to you both," Robbie started up again. "Believe me, neither Mia nor I intended for this to happen."

"How *did* it happen?" Jo demanded icily.

Liam shot her a warning look, but she purposefully ignored him.

Robbie rubbed a finger over his brow. "I wrote to Mia and apologized for what Sarah had done." He shook his head sadly. "I loved Sarah, but I blame her for what happened. Noah was her student."

"I think they both bear some blame for what happened," Jo responded, feeling a sudden need to defend Sarah. "Maybe it was Noah's idea."

"Yes, but only one of them was an adult," Robbie said. "Anyway, Mia wrote back and thanked me, pouring out her heart in return. We soon realized we understood each other in a way that no one else could—we'd been lied to, made to look like fools. We'd both suffered the death of a partner, but we also suffered the shame of what they did—we felt like criminals in a way. When Mia moved back here after her job in San Francisco didn't work out, we met for coffee once or twice." Robbie's voice trailed off. "That's ... how it began."

Jo averted her gaze from Robbie's woebegone expression. His fledgling relationship was already based on a foundation of lies, and he was clueless. Mia hadn't gone to San Francisco to work, she'd gone there to have her dead boyfriend's baby in secret, the baby who was now sucking peacefully on her pacifier, her cheeks puffing in and out like a miniature blowfish.

"It's a bit awkward and all, but I'm happy for you," Liam said.

"What are you talking about?" Jo exclaimed. "It's completely inappropriate on so many levels."

Liam shrugged. "I don't see why. It's not like Robbie's old enough to be her father."

Jo pressed her lips in a tight line of disapproval. "It's not about their ages. It's about the circumstances. How do you think the Tomaselli family is going to feel?"

Robbie nodded in agreement. "Mia and I talked about that at length. That's why we kept our relationship under the radar to begin with. If it wasn't going to go anywhere, we didn't want to cause any unnecessary pain. But, as the weeks went by, we came to realize that we care for each other deeply."

Jo took a calming breath and tried another tactic. "Don't you think you might be confusing your feelings for her with empathy?"

Robbie shook his head. "I don't think so. What I feel for Mia is much stronger than that."

"I still think it would be better for you to date other

people," Jo responded. "This all seems too convenient, maybe you're just falling into each other's laps because you share some common history."

Liam furrowed his brow and gave Jo a subtle shake of his head, but she rolled her eyes at him. "I'm not going to hold back and pretend I'm okay with this, Liam."

"I understand it's gonna take some time to get used to the idea," Robbie said. "I'm just asking you both as my close friends to open up your minds to the possibility that sometimes … sometimes beautiful things come out of life's tragedies."

Jo bit back a retort. She couldn't argue with that. Claire was living proof of it. She squirmed in her seat, her mind racing. Maybe the real reason she was uncomfortable with the idea of Mia and Robbie getting together was because she was terrified Mia would tell Robbie that Claire was her daughter. But, even if she did, it wasn't as if she could ask for Claire back. Mia had willingly relinquished her parental rights.

But something about Mia had always disturbed her. She didn't entirely trust her crooked grin. She reminded her of a cobra that lulled its prey into a sense of complacency, then spat a cocktail of toxins at it in a deadly strike. Jo reached for her glass and took a hasty gulp of wine. She was being hysterical. Maybe she should sleep on the situation and think it through before she said something she might regret.

"Jo?" Robbie prompted.

"Well, it's a lot to take in," she said with a resigned sigh, "and I won't deny that I have my doubts. But at the end of the day, I'll support you if that's your decision."

"I appreciate that," he replied. "I realize not everyone will be so understanding."

Jo got to her feet. "How about some cheesecake and coffee?"

"Good idea," Liam said, a palpable note of relief in his voice. "I'll clear the table while you serve up dessert. Robbie, you're on Claire Bear duty."

Jo and Liam retreated to the kitchen and exchanged an appraising look with one another.

"He's not thinking straight, you know he isn't," Jo whispered. "We have to talk him out of this before it gets out of hand. He could lose his job over this."

"He's obviously thought it through and discussed it at length with Mia already," Liam said, scraping the plates into the garbage disposal. "I don't think he would have broached the subject with us if he wasn't committed to the relationship."

"They're going to have to move away," Jo hissed. "Remember the vitriolic hate mail Robbie got before the funeral?"

"Yeah, but it all died down pretty quickly afterward. Not everyone will react as strongly as you did—you were a close friend of Sarah's. Anyway, it's sort of beautiful like he said, if you think about it—a phoenix from the ashes kind of thing."

"Beautiful?" Jo echoed in disdain as she dished out the cheesecake. "More like a twisted fairytale."

"Shh, keep your voice down."

Jo gave a disgruntled humph. "He can't hear me over the garbage disposal."

"I'm not hypocritical enough to deny him a chance at happiness when our own happiness was born out of a difficult situation," Liam said.

Jo glanced through to the dining room where Robbie was playing peek-a-boo with Claire as she swung back and forth. Maybe Liam had a point and she was looking at this all wrong, letting her distrust of Mia's motives color the situation. Maybe it was the universe's way of trying to grow something fresh and new out of the tragedy that had ended two lives all too soon. She wondered how Tory would react when she found out who her daughter had been secretly dating. She'd been concerned enough about Mia hooking up with a loser on her rebound from Noah, how would she feel about the idea of her dating her former teacher? The very teacher Mia had jokingly talked about introducing to her mother.

Jo carried the tray into the dining nook and set the plates around the table. Liam followed behind her with three mugs of coffee.

"Dig in!" Jo said, reaching for her fork. "There's lots more where this came from."

"Mmm, delicious," Robbie said. He winked at Jo. "I heartily approve this cheesecake!"

"I can't take any credit for it," Jo replied. "My only contribution was to pick it up and ferry it home. Life with a baby is hectic enough without adding a cheesecake made from scratch to my agenda."

For the remainder of the evening, they avoided the topic of Mia and stuck to small talk as they sipped on their coffees. As they were gathering up the mugs and preparing to retreat to the sitting room to watch a movie, Robbie's phone beeped with a text message. He retrieved it from his pocket and glanced at the screen.

"It's Mia," he said apologetically. "She told her mother about us over Christmas dinner, but apparently it didn't go too well. I need to drive over there and smooth things out."

"Good luck with that," Liam said with a grimace.

"Let us know if we can do anything to help," Jo added, hoping she didn't sound as insincere as she felt. She secretly hoped Tory could convince them to end the relationship before it went any further.

"Thanks again," Robbie said. "I had a wonderful evening, and I appreciate your support."

No sooner had the front door closed behind him than Jo's phone buzzed on the kitchen counter. She walked over to it and picked it up while Liam lifted Claire out of her swing. Her stomach knotted. It was Tory. Frowning, she quickly made her way down the hall to the family room to take the call in private.

"Hey, Tory."

"Sorry to disturb you on Christmas evening, I didn't know who else to call," Tory babbled. "I'm just so upset … "

"Not a problem," Jo assured her. "We already finished dinner. Liam's getting Claire cleaned up and ready for bed."

"So, can you talk?"

"Yes, absolutely." Jo clenched the phone tightly in her hand bracing herself for what was coming next.

"Remember I told you Mia was seeing someone?" Tory's tone vibrated with the urgency of a panicked mother.

"Yes," Jo said, struggling to hold her own voice steady. She knew what Tory was about to tell her, but she hadn't decided yet how she was going to respond. She was trusting the counselor in her to take over and say the right things. To empathize, to neutralize the emotion, to reassure Tory that this could be resolved—even though she wasn't sure it could.

"It's Robbie Gleeson."

There was silence for a moment as Tory waited for Jo to react.

"I know," she replied quietly. "He was here for dinner and he told us."

"What … did you say to him?" Tory probed.

"I questioned the wisdom of it. I pointed out that he and Mia have both been through a very traumatic experience and might be mistaking empathy for deeper feelings for each other."

"She's only eighteen. He's taking advantage of her," Tory

ranted into the phone. "Just like Sarah took advantage of Noah. It's disgusting. I don't trust that man. He's a predator."

Jo closed her eyes and swallowed. "I understand how it seems that way. But I know Robbie. He's not like that."

"Maybe you don't know him as well as you think you do," Tory retorted. "Mia's pregnant again."

---

17

*E*verything progressed rapidly after Tory's bombshell announcement. Apparently, even Robbie hadn't known before Christmas that Mia was pregnant. But once he found out, he stepped up to the plate and one week later got down on bended knee and proposed. Mia had accepted and now sported a hefty rock on her left hand, paid for, Jo suspected, by the generous allowance from Barb's estate. It nagged at her that Mia had suddenly become a beneficiary of Sarah's rightful inheritance.

No matter how Jo felt about the whirlwind relationship, there was no going back now. Mia and Robbie were engaged and planning a wedding, and Jo, albeit reservedly, was a part of it. Robbie had even asked Liam to be his best man and he'd graciously accepted. Like it or not, on Valentine's Day, Robbie and Mia would be married. Jo couldn't help wondering if Mia had deliberately gotten pregnant to seal the deal. She still didn't trust the girl, or her motives, and the thought of inviting her into their circle as Sarah's replacement nauseated her. Some of the staff at the school had secretly expressed their reservations about Robbie's new relationship to Jo, but, at the end of the day, a baby could melt most people's defenses, and most of the teachers had adjusted to the situation and were genuinely happy for Robbie.

Mia, for her part, was already acting as though Jo was her new best friend. She'd invited her over to see her wedding dress this morning, and Jo hadn't been able to think of a good reason to get out of it.

She stood on the front step, shifting Claire from one hip to the other, as she waited for Mia to answer the door. Jo had no desire to spend even five minutes fawning over Mia's wedding dress, but she'd accepted the fact that there would be a lot of things she would have to do that she didn't really want to now that Mia was marrying Robbie. She wholly sympathized with Tory having to suck up the situation. Tory had admitted she wasn't happy about it, but she was putting on a good front, for Mia's sake. It annoyed Jo no end how much Tory seemed to be under Mia's thumb, unable to stand up to her own daughter—even allowing her to address her as Tory.

The front door swung wide and Mia peered out, a wily smile tugging at her lips. "Come on in. I've been dying for you to get here."

She threw a disinterested look at Claire before flouncing off down the hallway. "I'm so excited to show you my dress. Tory's the only other person who's seen it so far, and of course she likes it—she was with me when I picked it out."

"How are you feeling?" Jo asked, as she followed her down the narrow hallway to a small bedroom.

"Ugh," Mia responded, "You're lucky you never had to endure the woes of pregnancy. I'm sick as a dog most mornings." She gave a careless laugh. "I guess it's a good thing. I don't want to put on any weight before the wedding."

Jo frowned. "I think it's better for the baby if you gain a little."

Mia waved a dismissive hand. "Plenty of time for that after the wedding. I don't want to look like an albino whale in my pictures."

She unzipped the plastic garment bag hanging from a hook in the closet and carefully eased out her wedding dress, holding it up for Jo to gush over. "Well, what do you think?"

Jo gently bounced Claire in her arms while she studied the dress. It was a strapless chiffon and lace ensemble cinched at the waist with a broad white ribbon, designed to show off Mia's toned, slim shoulders and long blonde hair. The first thought that struck Jo was that it wouldn't have suited Sarah's fuller figure. Jo and Liam hadn't attended Robbie's and Sarah's wedding, but their wedding portrait in a cut glass frame sat on the hall table in their foyer and Jo had seen it many times. She'd always thought Sarah looked radiant in her plunging halter dress with a full beaded skirt.

Jo forced out a suitable response. "It's beautiful, I'm sure you'll look fabulous in it."

Mia smirked. "I want to blow Robbie away when he sees me walking down the aisle."

Jo turned away and pretended to fuss with Claire. Her heart wasn't in this. She didn't want Robbie to be blown away by his young bride. She wanted him to secretly wish it was Sarah walking toward him again. Why had she killed herself? It was all so unfair.

"I have homemade banana nut muffins in the oven," Mia said. "Robbie loves my muffins. Oh, and I was hoping you would read over my vows, Jo, and help me make them shine."

She bit back her resentment at being called Jo by her former student. It was just another minor detail about the whole situation that gnawed at her. But, like so many other things, she'd have to let it go. It wasn't as if Mia could call her

Mrs. Murphy forever, especially not now that she was marrying Robbie.

Grimacing, Jo followed Mia into the kitchen, wondering how her relationship with the girl had morphed from one of counseling her on college choices, to helping her write her wedding vows to Robbie Gleeson.

Mia made them each a coffee and set the mugs down on the table. She smiled conspiratorially as she slipped into the chair next to Jo and rubbed her belly. "It's so fun to think that Claire's going to have a little brother or sister, isn't it? It's like our little secret."

Jo's smile froze on her face. "You can't go around saying things like that."

Mia gave a hard laugh that grated like claws on Jo's scalp. "I'm only saying it to you, silly." She arched a devious brow. "I wonder if they'll look alike, you know—if people will notice."

Heat prickled along the back of Jo's shoulders. Not for the first time she wondered if she'd done the right thing in adopting Mia's baby. It was almost as though Mia enjoyed reminding her of what she owed her from time to time, wielding it like a weapon when she wanted to intimidate her. "I can't stay long, Mia. I have to get back for Claire's nap. Let me take a quick look at your vows before I go."

Mia sipped her coffee and shrugged. "Come to think of it, I need to work on them a little more first. We can do it some other time. First, I need to come up with some names for the baby. Robbie and I can't seem to agree on any."

To Jo's relief, Claire began to wail and rub her eyes right on cue. Jo hurriedly got to her feet. "Thanks for the coffee, Mia."

"You didn't even get a muffin yet," she protested, glancing at the timer on the oven.

"Next time," Jo said, making a beeline for the front door.

. . .

BEFORE SHE KNEW IT, the day of Robbie's and Mia's wedding rolled around. Liam appeared to have accepted the new arrangement without reservation and had thrown himself into his role as best man, but Jo was still ambivalent about the union. Her mood was subdued as she dressed Claire in the embroidered champagne-colored satin dress with matching shoes that Mia had insisted on buying, and then telling her she'd dropped a small fortune on—Robbie's money of course. She added a satin headband with an over-sized rosette and then propped Claire up on the couch to take a picture of her. She really was a beautiful child, but Jo was beginning to wish she didn't resemble Mia quite as much as she did. She hated to admit it, but it made her uneasy. What if people noticed as she grew older? She'd never dreamt that Mia would end up in her inner circle with a baby of her own close to Claire's age.

Liam walked into the room adjusting his tie, dressed in a double-breasted navy suit.

"You look very handsome," Jo said. "Do you have your speech in your pocket?" Her voice was tinged with an under-tone of anxiety. She and Liam had worked long and hard on his speech, but it still felt unsatisfactory. So many times, as they'd pored over it, they wanted to make mention of a story that included Sarah. By the time they edited everything out of the speech that didn't reference her, it felt wrung out and devoid of any heartfelt richness. Robbie and Mia had so little history together, and what they did have was pretty much a taboo subject. Still, Jo managed to push aside her lingering doubts long enough to include a few generic sentiments to support Robbie on his special day.

"I'll see you at the church," Liam said, leaning over to kiss Jo on the lips. He swung Claire up and spun her around. "And I'll see you shortly too, angel girl."

A few minutes after Liam departed, Jo strapped Claire

into her car seat and drove to the church. She missed Sarah more each day. It was worse now that Mia and Robbie were officially together. She'd visited Barb several times over the past few months hoping to trigger some memory of Sarah they could reminisce over together, but to no avail. Barb was captivated by Claire but had no clue who Jo was. Robbie sent her a wedding invitation, as a courtesy. But she was no longer in a position to leave the Alzheimer's home, not even for short trips. Tory had invited Jo to sit next to her in the church and she'd somewhat reluctantly agreed. She didn't really want a front row seat in case her facial expression slipped at a crucial time when the photographer was snapping photos or the videographer was panning the faces of the guests. But she'd relented, knowing that Tory didn't want to sit beside her ex-husband, Chuck, who was coming down from San Francisco to give Mia away.

"He already walked away when she was three years old," Tory fumed. "I don't understand why Mia wants him to give her away now."

Jo secretly agreed with the sentiment. Mia hadn't spoken very highly of her father when Claire was born. If she wanted to keep with the tradition of being handed off, she should have asked Tory to walk her down the aisle—the parent who'd been there for her all these years.

When she arrived at the church, Jo chatted with some of the other guests before making her way up to the front to take her seat next to Tory.

Liam gave her a tense smile from where he and Robbie stood facing the congregation in their matching suits and boutonnieres.

When the melodic strains of the "Butterfly Waltz" filled the church, a rustling swept through the pews as everyone stood and turned to face the aisle. Holding a wriggling Claire in her arms, Jo watched a resplendent Mia proceed down the aisle, her hand tucked into her father's arm. Tall and broad-shouldered, Chuck Allen's handsome features were ruddy and lined, either with the cares of the years, or possibly an alcohol addiction. The reception would reveal all, no doubt. He certainly hadn't aged as gracefully as Tory—they looked decades apart.

As Mia approached the front row, Tory's fingernails dug into Jo's arm. "She looks gorgeous," she whispered.

"Stunning," Jo agreed, but she wasn't looking at Mia. She was staring down at her daughter, Mia's miniature double.

When Robbie and Mia faced one another to offer their vows, Jo shifted uncomfortably in the pew, wrestling with her emotions. Everything in the church was beautiful, from the flowers to the outfits to the music, everything except the ugly feelings inside her—resentment, bitterness, and a heavy dose of regret. Why had she never noticed that something was going on between Sarah and Noah? She might have been able to intervene and encourage Sarah to break off the relationship, or not begin it at all. Had she unwittingly played some small role in what happened by not being more observant of what was going on in her friend's life? She'd been so wrapped up in her own problems, so self-absorbed in her battle to conceive that she might have missed the little clues that things weren't as they seemed. Maybe she'd missed Sarah's cry for help. *We've all been there.* Had she been trying to tell Jo something? Was she secretly unhappy with Robbie?

She blinked, tuning in again briefly to hear Mia say, " … you are my best friend, and this is the happiest day of my life … "

Sarah had been Robbie's best friend once. This might be the happiest day of Mia's life, but the fact that it existed at all was wrong. Jo bent over her daughter to hide her face from the videographer's probing lens as he swept over the congregation. When Claire began to fuss, Jo leaned over and whispered to Tory that she was going to take her outside, and then gratefully retreated down the aisle and out through the double doors.

She sucked in a deep breath of fresh air, thankful not to have to witness any more of the nauseating ceremony. She didn't want to feel this way, but she was having a physiological reaction watching Robbie promise himself to her former student, the biological mother of her baby who was now carrying Robbie's child. Jo walked Claire back to their car, opened the trunk, and got out the stroller. After two brisk circuits around the parking lots, Claire fell asleep. Jo gingerly lifted her back out of her stroller, placed her in her car seat and then climbed in to wait for the ceremony to end.

Before long, Mia and Robbie emerged in the arched doorway, their guests spilling out after them. Jo texted Liam to say she was in the car with Claire. To her surprise, she observed Tory and Chuck engaged in conversation at the side of the church. Jo had been under the impression that they weren't on speaking terms, but maybe unbeknownst to her they'd resolved to set aside their differences for the day. She watched discreetly as the photographer snapped some more photos, before the happy couple climbed into their limousine and headed off to the reception.

Jo gritted her teeth and turned the key in the ignition. Only a few more hours to endure and then this show would be over. Maybe she should reconsider going back to school in the New Year. Maybe she and Liam should move out of the area entirely now that Mia was here to stay.

18

SIX MONTHS LATER

"So, here we are again," Jo said, looking across at Liam. "Relegated to the waiting room to cheer Mia on as she gives birth. Only this time I don't want to be here."

"I absolutely want you both there," Mia had simpered to Jo just last week. "It wouldn't feel right without you. You've been my supporters since I first told you I was pregnant with Claire—my *annoying little problem*." She gave a caustic laugh. "I want you to share my happiness this time. After all, you know what it's like to love my baby."

My baby. The words sent a chill through Jo despite the heat of the hospital. Surely, she hadn't imagined the creepy undertone in Mia's voice. The more time she spent with the girl, the less she liked the cold vein that ran through her. She was a peculiar person, flinging barbed compliments around with a macabre delight that was disconcerting. Jo's instincts and her training told her something wasn't right about Mia, but she couldn't put her finger on what it was.

"I'm really happy for Robbie," Liam said, glancing up from

his phone. "The past two years have gone from being his worst to his best. There's nothing quite like having a child to renew your hope."

Jo smiled across at him. He was an amazing dad, not that she'd ever doubted he would be. This had been a really special time for them with Claire, and they'd grown closer as a couple because of her. She didn't want to allow Robbie's and Mia's relationship to drive a wedge between them. They'd settled into a routine of socializing with them once a week, or, if Jo could find an excuse to stretch it, closer to once every two weeks. She was trying to mix more with the other teachers and avoid too much interaction with Robbie now that she was back at school, but she wasn't always successful. Inevitably, he would corner her in the staff break room at some point and the conversation would turn to Mia and the baby.

Jo looked up, startled when a nurse appeared in the doorway, a broad smile on her face. "The baby's here! Come on through!"

Jo and Liam got to their feet and followed the nurse along the corridor to Mia's room where she was propped up against a mountain of pillows, her blonde hair flowing like a golden waterfall over a backdrop of crisp linens. Robbie sat on a stool next to the bed leaning over the tiny bundle in her arms. Jo grimaced. The perfect pose for the evil queen and her subjects. She sucked in an icy breath, shocked at the hideousness of her own thoughts.

"Congratulations, you two!" Liam said, setting the enormous bundle of balloons he and Jo had brought on the bedside table.

"Yes, congratulations," Jo added, the words dry as sawdust as they fell from her lips, sorely lacking the cheery ring Liam had nailed.

Nobody seemed to notice. All eyes were glued to the brand-new life in the room.

"It's a girl," Robbie choked out, his face glowing with pride.

"Isn't that wonderful?" Mia gushed. "I'll be able to use all Claire's hand-me-downs."

Jo tried to mold her lips into a smile. Was Mia insinuating that Claire would be their only child? While the fertility goddess herself continued to make babies with her best friend's husband. Jo sensed the heat rising in her cheeks even as she inwardly reprimanded herself for her pettiness. She had to stop letting her bitterness fester. It was accomplishing nothing other than marring her relationship with Robbie and his new wife—and yes, Mia was his wife and she'd just given birth to his child. A fact she needed to accept. Determined to pull herself together, Jo pulled out her phone and broadened her smile. "I need a picture to show Claire. I'm sure they're going to be best friends. Snuggle up!"

Robbie and Mia beamed at her, pulling their heads together above their newborn daughter. Jo snapped a few shots and then moved in to take a close-up of the baby's face. "What's her name, or are you still wrestling over it?"

Robbie and Mia exchanged a quick look. "Her name is Olivia Sara Gleeson," Mia announced in a fawning tone. "We wanted to do something to honor Sarah without making it too obvious to those who don't approve of our relationship. So, this was our compromise. Give her Sara as her middle name and change up the spelling—we're dropping the "h" on the end."

"It's … beautiful," Jo heard herself respond, her heart pounding erratically in her chest. It didn't feel like the name was honoring Sarah, it felt more like it was mocking her—as if Robbie had found a version 2.0.

They took turns holding Olivia, and despite her animosity toward Mia, Jo couldn't help but be moved by the sweet newborn smell of Olivia's skin and the soft blonde fuzz on her tiny head. It brought back with heart-wrenching clarity those precious early days with Claire and stirred up Jo's longing to have another child.

On the drive home through town, she was subdued, watching out the passenger window as they whizzed by buildings and people.

"You okay, honey?" Liam shot her a sideways glance. "Are you feeling nostalgic for those early newborn days? It got to me too. Claire's so big in comparison, and already trying to walk. But think of the nonstop diaper changes and the sleepless nights. We should be grateful for where we're at. Don't get me wrong, I'm not saying I wouldn't do it all again."

"Actually, I'm thinking about what Robbie and Mia named the baby," Jo said quietly. "I kind of resent that they used a variation of Sarah's name, but at the same time I'm asking myself if I would resent it more if they'd ignored her entirely." She let out a long sigh. "I don't know if it's me being overly sensitive or if Mia enjoys causing me pain. Like practically asking me for Claire's hand-me-downs, assuming I'll never need them again."

Liam raised his brows. "I doubt she meant it that way. You're reading too much into everything. Mia's young and she blurts out a lot of stuff without thinking it through. I can't imagine she's deliberately trying to be insensitive."

"I'm not so sure. I think she knows exactly what she's doing, and it creeps me out, like that sly grin she gives after saying something to needle me. It's almost as though she enjoys reminding me that I owe her." Jo sighed. "I miss Sarah so much."

"Let it go. You need to accept the fact that Sarah's gone, and Robbie's moved on. He has a family now and he deserves to be as happy as we are."

They pulled into their driveway and Jo was instantly distracted from her somber thoughts when the babysitter came to the door with Claire on her hip. Her blue eyes lit up, her little hands reaching out for Jo. "Mama! Mama!"

Jo took her and snuggled her close while Liam fished out some cash for Bethany, their fifteen-year-old next-door neighbor, who was almost as besotted with Claire as they were. "How was she?" Jo asked.

"An angel as always," Bethany raved. "Did Mia have her baby?"

"Yes, a little girl," Liam answered.

"Oh, how precious! What's her name?"

Liam shot Jo a quick look. "Olivia."

"Pretty! Tell them congrats from me, and if they ever need a sitter, I'm up for it." Bethany waved good-bye and disappeared through the side gate to her house.

Once Claire was down for the night, Jo and Liam snuggled together on the couch in front of a football game Liam had set to record. Jo pulled out her phone and clicked distractedly through her apps. She opened up the photos she'd taken at the hospital and examined them. Robbie looked thrilled and proud, chest thrust out with a protective arm around his family. Mia wore a self-satisfied smirk on her full lips. Olivia looked flawless, a china doll, just like Claire when she was born. On a whim, Jo opened up her album of Claire's first days and scrolled through to a picture of her cherub face, curious eyes staring into the camera. She was so like Olivia it was uncanny.

Excusing herself to go to the bathroom, Jo exited the room and made her way down the hall to the office. She powered up her computer and downloaded the pictures from her phone, then pulled up the photo of Olivia and one of Claire when she was only a few hours old. She enlarged them side-by-side on the computer screen and studied them. A foreboding feeling crept through her like a ghostly vapor. The pictures could easily be mistaken for the same baby. Jo pressed her fingertips to her temples as she contemplated them. But why wouldn't they look alike? They were half-sisters after all.

Jo was still sitting in front of the screen when Liam walked into the room. "There you are. What are you doing?"

"Nothing much," Jo said, trying in vain to minimize the photos before he could see them.

"Are those Claire's baby pictures?" He put an arm around Jo's shoulders. "I knew holding a newborn would put you in the mood again. She was such a beautiful baby."

"This isn't Claire." Jo pointed at the picture to the right of the screen. "It's Olivia. The one on the left is Claire. They look almost identical, don't they?"

Liam leaned in and studied the photos. "Well, they are half-sisters." He straightened up and laughed. "All babies look the same to me when they're born, wrinkled and red." He stretched his arms above his head and yawned. "Ready for bed?"

"I'll be up in a few minutes," Jo replied. "Just need to finish up something for school."

After Liam's footsteps faded up the stairs, Jo opened up her browser and typed in *can half-sisters look like twins*? She scrolled through the articles finding nothing remarkable other than that half siblings with the same mother shared slightly more genetic information than half siblings with the same father. Somewhat reassured, she closed up her computer and went to bed.

Sleep eluded her however, and she wrestled with unsettling thoughts. She tossed and turned, spooling the bedclothes around her, a wild conjecture brewing in her head. It was probably stupid, but Jo knew herself well enough to realize that she wouldn't be able to rest until she could be certain.

Was it possible Robbie was Claire's father?

19

A few weeks after Olivia's birth, Jo, Liam, and Claire arrived at Robbie's and Mia's house for dinner. In fact, they arrived with the dinner. Remembering those early days of upheaval as they'd adjusted to being new parents, Jo had offered to pick up a Chinese take away. They also brought along a couple of bottles of red wine. It was another one of those ridiculous things that made their friendship seem out of place at times, but Mia was still too young to drink when they went out. At home however, she participated freely, a little too freely for Jo's liking, but so far, she'd managed to keep that thought to herself. Mia had opted not to nurse Olivia, and Jo had a sneaking suspicion it had more to do with her drinking than anything else. It appeared to run in the family—Mia's father had consumed his fair share at her wedding reception.

Jo's palms were sweating as she exchanged pleasantries with Mia while watching Claire toddle back and forth across the floor carrying one stuffed toy after another from the basket in the corner over to Jo and jabbing it in the eye before promptly dropping it at her feet and waddling off to pick out another one. Jo wasn't concentrating on a word Mia was saying. She was pretending to be distracted by Claire, making sure she didn't trip and hurt herself. In reality, she was thinking about the Ziploc bags and the plastic disposable gloves she'd stashed in her purse before she left the house. She'd resolved to do it tonight. She assured herself she wasn't betraying anybody. She didn't have to disclose her findings to anyone and she certainly had no intention of doing so if her worst fears were realized. She wasn't about to make known publicly anything that might threaten her and Liam's legal claim to Claire. But, for her own sanity, she had to know for sure if she was Robbie's child or not. She'd told herself repeatedly since comparing the photographs that it was highly unlikely—a flawed theory that made no sense. Robbie and Mia weren't together at the time Claire was conceived. Not while Sarah and Noah were carrying on. It was preposterous to think all four of them had been engaged in some kind of seedy partner-swapping. But, after studying more recent pictures of the two girls, Jo had decided she simply had to put the matter to rest once and for all, and armed herself with the supplies she'd need to retrieve some of Robbie's DNA.

Over dinner, she observed with revulsion that Mia was drinking more than ever. She strongly suspected she hadn't abstained during her pregnancy with Olivia, as she'd claimed. The more Jo got to know Mia, the less she trusted what lurked beneath that beautiful face.

"Who would have thought babies could be so expensive?" Mia moaned, holding her glass aloft with her slim fingers, her diamond glittering under the dining room light. She directed a wide-eyed gaze at Robbie. "I mean, I still have to look pretty, too, don't I? Nails, hair—all that good stuff. It costs money to keep a girl looking hot."

A flicker of irritation crossed Robbie's face. "We do all

right. Nobody's going hungry in this house." He stretched a smile across his face for Liam's and Jo's benefit.

"I'm certainly not skipping any meals." Liam patted his stomach. "Claire likes to feed me her snacks and then stand back and laugh when I groan and rub my belly."

Everyone laughed, but the tension in the room didn't dissipate entirely. Jo knew that, along with her drinking, Mia's spending habits must be giving Robbie cause for concern.

When Robbie and Liam got up to clear away the dishes, and Mia retired to the couch to give Olivia her bottle, Jo excused herself to go to the bathroom. She made a point of bringing Claire with her. An errant toddler would be her excuse if she was caught in Mia's and Robbie's bathroom. She padded up the stairs, balancing Claire on her hip, and opened and closed the guest bathroom door before quietly tiptoeing into Mia's and Robbie's bedroom and through to the adjoining master bathroom. Heart thundering in her chest, she set Claire down and pushed the door closed behind them. She quickly donned the plastic gloves from her purse and then opened one of the vanity mirrors above the sinks. She reached for the prescription bottles and read the labels. Zofran and Lorazepam, both prescribed to Mia. She pulled out her phone and took a quick picture of the labels to look them up later on, and then put them back on the shelf and peered behind the second vanity mirror; Vaseline, Chapstick, Q-tips, not what she was after.

Next, she slid open the top drawer on the vanity. It was overflowing with expensive brand name cosmetics. Mia was going to run Robbie into the ground if he wasn't careful, even with Barb's annual allowance. Jo opened and shut another couple of drawers until she finally found what she was looking for—Robbie's toiletries, complete with a hairbrush. Gingerly, she extracted several hairs from the brush and deposited them in a Ziploc bag. She wasn't sure she'd got any with the root like the kit had stipulated, so she grabbed Robbie's toothbrush and dropped it into another bag before sealing it shut along the seam. Hopefully between the two, they would have enough to work with. With any luck he'd think Mia had tossed the toothbrush out. She stuffed everything back into her purse and snatched up a bewildered Claire who'd been following her lead opening and closing drawers while gabbling unintelligibly about the contents. After listening to make sure no one was coming, Jo hurried back through the master bedroom and down the stairs.

Liam, Robbie and Mia were all sitting around the table laughing about something as Robbie dished out scoops of ice cream. Olivia was nodding off in her bouncer in the corner of the room.

Robbie glanced up as Jo approached. "What flavor are you having, Jo? On offer tonight, we have chocolate mud pie or chocolate chip. My apologies for the heavy-on-the-chocolate theme. My wife doesn't consider it ice cream if it doesn't have chocolate in it." He winked at her and chuckled.

Jo stiffened, imagining in that moment that he looked like Claire, the way her mouth curled up and her dimples appeared when something struck her as funny. She shook the thought free even as she clutched her daughter tighter. Maybe she was losing her grip on reality. "In that case, I'll have something with chocolate in it, please," she responded, tagging on a smile.

The others laughed approvingly at the banter as she rejoined them at the table.

Claire's face lit up when Liam leaned over and spooned a sliver of ice cream between her lips. She let out a delighted *ooh!* and everyone dissolved into laughter again, the wine having eased any lingering tension between them.

Jo picked up her spoon, feeling like a heel for sitting at

Robbie's table after surreptitiously slipping several of his hairs and his toothbrush into her purse. Was she a rotten friend for harboring despicable suspicions about Robbie? He'd always been such a good-hearted sort—too naive for his own good perhaps. But maybe it was all an act and he was more devious than she'd imagined. She could still throw the bag away and forget all about it, not risk undermining their relationship. She probably should throw it away—Liam would tell her to. She took another sip of her wine hoping to dull her conscience. She would sleep on it. If she still felt guilty about it in the morning, she would get rid of the evidence. But, if the guilt had dissipated, she would send the samples off for analysis and settle the issue of Claire's paternity before it drove her mad.

WHEN THEY ARRIVED home at the end of the night, Jo asked Liam to put Claire to bed. As soon as he disappeared upstairs, she carefully placed the Ziplocs from her purse into the envelope from the DNA testing website, along with the requisite paperwork and Claire's sample. She hid the envelope at the bottom of her purse and then pulled up the pictures of the medication from Mia's vanity to research them on her phone. The first one, Zofran, was fairly innocuous—an anti-nausea drug often prescribed during pregnancy, also used to treat nausea and vomiting in cancer patients after chemotherapy. Next, she typed in Lorazepam, and scanned through the description. An anti-anxiety medication that acted on the brain and central nervous system to produce a calming effect. Jo furrowed her brow. It sounded familiar for some reason. What did Mia have to be anxious about? Her drinking? Or was the drinking just another way to ease her anxiety about something else?

. . .

ON HER WAY TO work on Monday morning, Jo dropped the package with the hair samples and toothbrush in the mail. According to the website, she could expect the results in four to five business days. In the meantime, there was nothing she could do but try and stop obsessing about it.

Determined to put the quandary out of her mind, she threw herself into her work in her office. Later that morning, there was a sharp rap on the door. Ed stepped inside and closed the door behind him, a strained expression on his face. "Robbie asked me to tell you that Sarah's mother passed away last night."

"Oh, no!" Jo exclaimed. "What happened?"

"She died in her sleep." Ed twitched his nostrils, an annoying little habit he had. "The way we all want to go. A blessing in a way."

"But she was only sixty-two." Jo adjusted her glasses trying to take it in. "She was perfectly healthy last time I saw her."

Ed gave a vague nod. "I'm sure they'll do an autopsy, but Alzheimer's takes you in the end—stroke, infection, or whatever. I've been down this road already with my father. He passed away after battling it for only three years."

"I'm sorry," Jo said. "Thanks for letting me know. I'll pop round to Robbie's after work."

After Ed exited her office, she sent a quick text to Liam to bring him up to speed, and then texted Robbie to express her sympathy and let him know she would stop by later.

Shortly after three o'clock, she climbed into her car and drove to Robbie's house. She had until five to pick up Claire from daycare, so that gave her at least an hour to spend with Robbie. He'd been good to Barb, and Jo suspected her passing would conjure up painful memories of Sarah. It crossed her mind that Robbie stood to inherit Sarah's mother's estate now. She had no idea what it was worth, but she presumed it was substantial—several hundred-thousand dollars. Mia, no doubt, would be glad to get her grubby little hands on it. Jo pressed her lips together. It was uncanny how everything fell into that girl's lap.

"Thanks for coming, Jo," Robbie said, ushering her inside. "It's all been a bit of a shock. She went so suddenly in the end."

"Where's Mia?" Jo asked, as she sat down at the kitchen table with Robbie. He looked almost as pale and haggard as he had when Sarah died.

"She took Olivia over to her mother's. I think she's irritated with me for being so upset about Barb's passing."

"Was Barb sick recently?" Jo asked.

Robbie frowned. "No, she was in good shape the last time I visited her."

"I assume they'll do an autopsy."

"Only if I insist on it." Robbie sighed. "To be honest with you, I don't want to make this any more difficult than it has to be."

Jo grimaced. "It must be bringing back memories of Sarah. I know it can't be easy for you."

Robbie rubbed his hands over his face. "Barb was my last connection to her. But I can't expect Mia to be understanding of that."

Jo gave a grim nod. Understanding was not in Mia's vocabulary. "I'm sorry. If I can help with any of the funeral arrangements, let me know."

"Thanks. It'll be a very small affair." A haunted look crossed his face. "Sarah was her only child."

"It meant a lot to Sarah that you were so good to Barb. And at least you got to spend one last Sunday afternoon with her."

Robbie exhaled a frustrated breath. "That's the thing I feel so bad about. Mia insisted I spend it assembling some furniture she wanted me to put together. She left Olivia here with me and went to visit Barb in my place."

20

In the days following, Jo's turmoil only increased. Along with the nagging suspicion that the father of her daughter was Robbie Gleeson, she couldn't shake the notion that Mia might have had something to do with Barb's sudden death. As improbable as it was, the idea that the Mia everyone thought they knew was nothing like the real Mia was beginning to be bolstered by everything Jo was finding out about her.

To allay her growing fears, she spent several hours in her office one afternoon reading back through Mia's school records, hoping to form a clearer picture of her, but she gleaned nothing new from her research. She recalled that Mia had always had a cold-hearted streak—the glee she displayed at taunting others, her seeming indifference to Noah's death. Lydia Tomaselli had commented on her obsession with money, and Jo had observed firsthand her expensive tastes. Lying seemed to come naturally to her. Then, there was her drinking. Even Robbie admitted it was becoming a problem. Jo had witnessed him trying to talk Mia out of another drink, but he'd shriveled when she turned on him.

"What?" she demanded. "Are you afraid I might let something slip and embarrass you?" The self-satisfied smile on her lips and way she said it sent a chill through Jo. It sounded a lot more like a threat than a heavy-handed attempt at humor. What exactly was she threatening to let slip? Jo was becoming increasingly worried for Robbie. She could see the writing on the wall. Things were not going to end well unless Mia got help.

On Thursday, Jo picked Claire up from daycare and drove home, stopping at the bottom of her driveway to open the mailbox. Her heart raced a little faster as she rolled down the window. Would today be the day the paternity test results arrived? Bracing herself, she pulled down the lid and peered inside. To her surprise, it was empty. She frowned in puzzlement. It wasn't a public holiday. Surely there should be something inside, even if it was only circulars. She closed the mailbox and turned into the driveway, activating the garage door opener. As the door yawned open, she sucked in a sharp breath. Liam's car was parked inside. Why on earth was he home so early? More importantly, had he already retrieved the mail?

Tension built in Jo's shoulders as she unbuckled Claire and lifted her out of her car seat. The DNA testing website had assured discretion in its packaging, but Liam might ask her what was in the envelope. She opened the door to the mudroom and called out, "Hey, honey! We're home." She unzipped Claire's coat and shrugged off her own, then hung them both up and walked into the kitchen. Claire toddled straight over to her toy kitchen and began chattering to herself as she reached for a plastic cup. A watery-eyed Liam was sitting at the table with a steaming mug of tea in his hands. "Hi," he croaked. "I came home early. I must be coming down with something."

"Oh no," Jo soothed, scanning the room in vain for the mail. "Why don't you lie down for a bit?"

"I'll just go to bed early tonight. I might lay down on the couch for a while and watch TV or something. I hope Claire doesn't catch whatever I have."

Hearing her name, she toddled over to the table and held out her arms to be lifted up. Jo set her in her high chair and placed some cut-up chicken on the tray table, which Claire proceeded to examine piece-by-piece, systematically sucking on each one and then dropping the rejected chunks onto the floor and peering down at them with satisfaction.

Liam reached over and lifted a pile of mail from the chair next to him, leafing half-heartedly through it. "How was your day?"

"Oh, you know," Jo said, staring intently at the mail as if she could somehow x-ray it. "Just the usual fires to put out, sullen teenagers, irate parents, and everything in between."

Liam picked up a letter from the top of the pile and tore open the envelope. "Bills, bills and more bills," he said, tossing it down. He blew his nose and glanced at the next envelope before setting it aside. "How many credit card offers do they think we need?"

Jo held her breath as he reached for another envelope. She was frantically calculating in her mind if today could actually be the day the results arrived. Her throat began to close over as Liam ripped open the envelope in his hand without as much as glancing at the name on it. He pulled out a folded sheet and opened it, sneezing once in the process. His eyes rapidly crisscrossed the page, a deep frown forming on his forehead. After an agonizing wait, he glanced up at Jo, an incredulous look on his face. "What's this?"

"I … don't know," she said, holding out her hand for the

sheet. He passed it to her and she stared at it, the words blurring in front of her eyes before the letters came together.

Probability of paternity is 99 9%.

She re-read the words to make sure she hadn't got it backwards. No, there was no mistaking the results. Robbie Gleeson was Claire's father.

"Jo?" Liam's voice was thin, as if signaling from a distant planet. "What is this? Does this have something to do with Claire?" His tone had an edge to it now, anger, disappointment, a sense of betrayal perhaps.

"Yes," Jo replied resignedly. "It has everything to do with Claire. I don't trust Mia. I haven't trusted her for some time, and it seems I had good reason not to."

"What are you talking about? Whose DNA did you send in to be tested?" Liam blinked, his face contorting as he struggled to connect the dots. "It couldn't have been Noah's, so … who's was it?"

Jo swallowed hard. She was still coming to terms with the shock herself. Robbie was their baby's father. She held the proof in her hands. Which meant he'd been lying to them all along. Robbie and Mia had been sleeping together at the same time that Sarah and Noah were carrying on their secret affair. How could Robbie do this to them? He'd seemed so gutted when he told them about Noah and Sarah being found in the car, so broken at Sarah's funeral, so lonely in the months that followed. Had it all been an act?

"Jo!" Liam rasped. "I asked you whose DNA it was?"

"Robbie's! It was Robbie's. Claire's his child."

Liam mopped his sweating forehead with a tissue and shook his head. "No, that's not possible."

"Don't you remember those two photos of Claire and Olivia as newborns that I had side-by-side on my computer?" Jo asked. "Something told me they were more than just half-sisters. Maybe it was some maternal instinct, I don't know. But I had to be certain. It's been haunting me."

Liam rubbed his brow, his face stricken. "But … that means … "

"Yes," Jo said. "Robbie and Mia were together when Sarah and Noah were carrying on their affair."

Liam shook his head incredulously. "That's disgusting. Not to mention illegal. Why would they do that? Revenge? Do you think they knew about Sarah and Noah all along?"

Jo placed her elbows on the table and sank her head into her hands, contemplating the question. "Maybe that's what Robbie was talking about when he said that grief brought him and Mia together. Maybe he wasn't referring to Noah's and Sarah's deaths. Maybe he was talking about finding out that they were having an affair."

Liam frowned. "So why was Mia so angry with Noah that day when you had to intervene? If she and Robbie were already together, why would she care what Noah was doing?"

"I'm beginning to think her outburst was all show," Jo said. "It's almost as if she wanted to make sure to throw Noah under the bus when she had a crowd of spectators."

Liam blew his nose and leaned back in his chair. "My head's so fuzzy I can't think straight."

"I'm confused too," Jo replied. "But one thing's clear—Robbie's been lying to us as well. I can't even begin to tell you how disappointed I am in him. I trusted him. All this time, he led us to believe he was the injured party. That's the only reason I showed him some grace when he got together with Mia." She drummed her fingers on the table. "It makes me wonder what else he might have lied about."

"What do you mean?"

"Maybe he knew Mia was pregnant the first time too."

"I doubt it. She didn't want anyone to find out." Liam was

silent for a moment. "Mia might not even know that Claire is Robbie's daughter."

Jo grimaced. "I bet she does. I bet she knew all along."

"We have to tell Robbie," Liam said.

"No!" Jo cried out. "We can't say anything to him. What if he wants custody of Claire?"

"He can't do that. We're her parents now!"

"But if he didn't know at the time that Claire was his daughter, he might have rights we're not aware of. If he gets the right lawyer, there's no telling what he could accomplish. And now he has the means with the inheritance from Barb's estate. Liam, you have to *promise* me you won't say anything to him."

Claire began to whine, and Jo lifted her down from her high chair and let her waddle back to her toy kitchen.

Liam stared at the stack of unopened mail. "What about Mia? Are you going to confront her?"

"I haven't decided yet." Jo rubbed her fingertips around her eye sockets. "There are so many things about that girl that never added up." She watched as Claire shoved all the cups and plates into the plastic dishwasher in her toy kitchen and then tried in vain to close the door. "Something else has been bothering me too. Mia was the last one to see Barb alive."

Liam hefted a brow. "What are you suggesting, Jo?"

"I'm not suggesting anything, yet. I'm just saying it's kind of odd that the one and only time Mia goes to Brookdale Meadows without Robbie, is the night Barb dies."

"You can't say things like that. That's Robbie's wife you're practically accusing of murder."

"I'm not accusing her, it's just … another odd coincidence." Jo glanced across at Claire, who was happily scooping everything back out of the dishwasher and onto the floor. "I think I should address the issue of Claire's paternity with Mia."

"Then you'd better be prepared to face the consequences," Liam responded. "There's a chance she'll go straight to Robbie and tell him everything."

Jo MUSED over her options the following day until the bell rang signaling the end of classes. Resolved to have it out with Mia no matter the fallout, she got in her car and drove straight to her house before she could change her mind. She would confront her about everything—the lying, the drinking, and of course, Claire's paternity. She couldn't carry on as usual now that she knew the truth. Robbie had an after-school chemistry study hour, so she'd have plenty of time to talk to Mia without any fear of him walking in on them.

Mia answered the door, narrowing her eyes suspiciously at Jo's grim expression. Judging by the way she was balancing against the door frame, Jo guessed she'd been drinking. Frustration brewed inside her. It was only three-thirty in the afternoon, and Mia was alone in the house with a young baby. She was completely irresponsible.

"Didn't know we were getting together today," Mia slurred.

"You must have forgotten," Jo replied firmly, brushing past her into the hallway.

Mia followed her to the kitchen and threw herself into a chair. An empty wine bottle sat on the counter by the sink and another half bottle sat on the table next to a glass with ruby dregs in the bottom of it. "Wanna join me?" Mia asked, twisting her lips into a smirk.

Jo shook her head in disgust. "Were you drinking while you were pregnant?"

Mia slumped back in her chair eying Jo from beneath

perfectly arched brows. "Which baby are we talking about? I expect you care a whole lot more about yours than mine."

"I care about both of them," Jo said indignantly. "And I care about you too, Mia. You're still a teenager and you're turning into an alcoholic."

Mia slapped her palm down on the table causing the empty glass to wobble precariously. "Now that's just plain rude. You're in my house and you're insulting me."

"I'm your friend. I'm trying to help you. Robbie's trying to help you. We're all trying to help you."

Mia rolled her eyes. "See that's funny because I always thought you were just trying to help yourself, Jo. You helped yourself to my baby, after all."

Jo stared at her aghast. "What are you talking about? You came to me and asked for my help."

Mia jabbed a finger in Jo's direction. "I asked for your help *to get rid of it. You* talked me into keeping it because you were so desperate for a baby, even though you knew it was wrong not to tell Noah." Mia half rose out of her chair and stuck her face up close to Jo's, her breath hot against her skin. "Pretty convenient he ended up dead, so you never had to."

21

*B*efore Jo could stop her, Mia reached for the bottle on the table and clumsily refilled her glass. She got to her feet and took a large swig of wine, a contemptuous smile forming on her lips.

Fighting to restrain herself from saying something she might regret, Jo snatched up the wine bottle and stomped over to the sink, emptying the remnants into the drain. "You can't look after a newborn in this state. It's dangerous." She set the empty bottle next to the other one and turned to face Mia. "I'm going to let your sickening insinuation about Noah's death go for now as you're obviously too drunk to realize what you're saying."

Mia tinkled a laugh that scraped like glass shards over Jo's nerves. "Come on, admit it, you must have felt at least a little relieved when you heard your baby's daddy was dead." She ran a fingertip slowly around the rim of her glass. "You can tell me, I don't care. He was screwing around with your friend, Sarah, the whole time anyway."

"You mean while you were screwing around with

Robbie?" The words erupted from Jo's lips before she could contain them. She clapped her mouth shut and gripped the edge of the counter, berating herself inwardly. This wasn't how she'd intended to bring up the topic.

Mia took a sip of wine studying Jo with a conniving look, seemingly unfazed by her accusation. "You should be careful about sticking your nose in where it doesn't belong. What did you really come here for anyway?" She swirled her wine around waiting for Jo to speak, biding her time until the words that were dancing on the tip of Jo's tongue spilled out.

"Claire *is* Robbie's daughter, isn't she?"

Mia twitched one amused brow upward. "Whatever would make you say such a thing?"

"Perhaps the fact that they look exactly the same in their baby pictures. It's your turn to fess up, Mia. They could be twins. Claire doesn't look anything like the Tomaselli family."

Mia shrugged. "So, she takes after me."

"She doesn't have a single Italian gene in her blood! You and Robbie were sleeping together at the same time Noah and Sarah were. Why? To get revenge? Is this all some twisted game to you?"

"I don't know what you're talking about. Are you jealous just because I have a daughter now too?" Mia staggered back to the table and plopped herself down on a chair.

"Don't be ridiculous. Look at yourself! You're hammered out of your mind and you've got a young baby sleeping upstairs. How are you supposed to look after Olivia like this?"

Mira glared at her. "Is that a threat? Are you going to call CPS on me? Is that what this is about? You're not happy with only one of my daughters, you want to take the other one too?"

"You're not thinking rationally, Mia. I'm not trying to

take Olivia away from you. I'm trying to find out why you lied to me about who Claire's father is. Why didn't you just tell me the truth? It can't be easy living with the lies. Maybe that's what the drinking's all about." Jo removed the glass from Mia's shaking hands and set it out of reach on the other side of the table. "Is that why you're taking anti-anxiety medication too?"

A malevolent shadow crossed Mia's face. "Been nosing around in my house, have you? That's called trespassing. I should call the cops on you. They might be interested to hear how relieved you were that Noah Tomaselli killed himself, so you could keep his baby." She thumped a fist on the table jiggling the glass on the other end, then pushed her chair out from the table and stood unsteadily. "Get out of my house, now!"

"At least let me make you some coffee first," Jo entreated her.

"I said get out!" Mia screamed in her face. "Get out, or I'm calling the cops!"

"Okay, I'll leave. Do you want me to take Olivia with me until Robbie gets home from work?"

Mia shoved Jo in the chest, startling her and causing her to step backward to keep from stumbling. "Don't you dare touch my baby. You'll never get your hands on her. And don't dig around in my affairs anymore or you'll regret it."

Without another word, Jo picked up her purse and walked down the hallway to the front door, feeling Mia's eyes drilling into her with every step. She glanced back over her shoulder to see Mia's lips curve into a cool smile of satisfaction. Jo shivered as she let herself out and hurried to her car. She was more certain than ever there was something seriously wrong with Mia. As soon as she closed the door, she called Robbie's cell phone. *Come on, come on, please pick up.*

After several rings, the call went to voicemail. Jo dialed again, closing her eyes as the phone rang.

"Jo, what's up?" Robbie said.

"Sorry to interrupt you. Mia's really drunk, Robbie. I don't think she can make it up the stairs if Olivia wakes up. I'm afraid to leave. I think you should come home now."

There was silence for a moment and then Robbie said. "Can you wait there for a few minutes?"

"Sure, I'm right outside in my car."

"Thanks, Jo. I feel bad you got dragged into this. I need to get Mia some help. Her drinking's gotten completely out of control. I'll be there in a few."

True to his word, Robbie peeled into his driveway less than ten minutes later, and screeched to a halt. Heart pounding, Jo climbed out of her car and walked to the front door to meet him. She'd tried to think of a good excuse to give him as to why she'd been visiting Mia in the first place, but everything sounded like the lame lie it was. She dreaded to think how she would respond if Mia told Robbie the truth. "I didn't want to get in the middle of things," she said, "but I was afraid for Olivia's sake."

"You did the right thing," he replied, sticking his key in the door. "I might need you to stay and help with Olivia for a few minutes."

Reluctantly, Jo followed him back inside. From upstairs she could already hear Olivia's faint cries. "I'll go get her. You take care of Mia."

Robbie strode toward the kitchen while Jo hurried up the stairs. She went into the nursery and walked over to the crib. The stench reached her first. "Poor baby," she soothed. She carried Olivia over to the changing table and set about changing her diaper. To her horror, Olivia had a nasty diaper rash. The diaper she was wearing was bloated and obviously hadn't been changed all day. Jo rummaged around for some cream and applied it liberally before carefully placing a fresh diaper on Olivia. She picked the baby up, wiped a few damp, blonde strands of hair from her forehead and carried her downstairs.

Mia's raised voice drifted toward her from the kitchen. "Don't tell me what I can and cannot do. I'm not your student any longer. I'm your wife, or did you forget that part?"

Jo hesitated at the bottom of the stairs, not wanting to make her presence known in the midst of a heated argument.

"Of course, I haven't forgotten you're my wife. Don't you realize how ridiculous you sound when you say things like that?"

"So now you think I'm ridiculous?"

"You need to calm down, Mia."

Olivia started to squawk in Jo's arms. Despite her reluctance to intrude, Jo made her way into the kitchen. "I'll make up her bottle," she said, walking over to the counter where the formula was sitting, avoiding looking either Robbie or Mia in the eye.

"I suppose you're the one who called Robbie and told him to come home early. Counselor Jo to the rescue yet again!" The knife-edge tone of Mia's voice caused the hairs on the back of Jo's neck to rise.

She turned around, cradling Olivia in her left arm. "I just wanted to make sure Olivia was safe."

Mia let out a scornful laugh. "I'm sure you did. We wouldn't want anything to happen to Claire's little sister now, would we?"

Jo shot Robbie a sharp glance. He gave her an apologetic shrug in return. "Let's leave Jo out of this," he admonished Mia. "She's looking out for our best interests."

"That's a joke," Mia snapped back. She folded her arms in

front of her and glared at Jo. "She's only ever looked out for her own interests, haven't you, Jo?"

"That's enough!" Robbie said, reaching for Mia by the arm. "You're drunk! You need to go upstairs and sleep this off."

Mia shook herself free, her messy bun falling loose, blonde hair tumbling over her shoulders. Her eyes flashed with menace. She looked like a wild woman, an unharnessed beauty who had become something ugly and deranged. "Tell him, Jo. Tell him why you came to see me. I think he should hear it from you."

Jo's arms began to shake. She clutched Olivia tighter, half-afraid she might drop her. "Robbie's right, you should go and lie down. I'll feed Olivia and change her again before I leave."

"No!" Mia marched over and plucked Olivia from Jo's arms. "You already took one of my babies. You're not getting this one."

Jo's gaze locked with Robbie's. Surely he must have picked up on it this time, or had he dismissed it as drunken drivel? She was sure the fear bubbling up inside her was visible on her face. Her own deception was coming back to haunt her. She couldn't hide the truth from him if Mia was determined to tell him. Jo snatched a breath, reminding herself that she and Liam had tried to do something good, to make something beautiful out of a difficult situation.

"She doesn't have the guts, so I'll tell you. Claire's my daughter," Mia announced with a triumphant edge to her voice. "Can you believe my high school counselor talked me into giving her my baby? That's an abuse of power, don't you think?"

"That's enough," Robbie said in a tone of disgust. "You're drunk."

"Not that drunk," Mia drawled. "I can clearly remember

Jo holding Claire moments after she was born. Isn't that right, Jo?"

The confusion on Robbie's face was slowly being replaced by a look of horror. He stared at Mia open-mouthed and then turned to Jo. "What's she talking about?"

A sickly sweat prickled over Jo's forehead. She gripped the edge of the counter tighter. This wasn't supposed to come out like this—or at all. Mia had agreed to a closed adoption, had insisted on it. Would she stop at telling Robbie that she was Claire's birth mother? Or was she building up to telling him that Claire was his biological child? Surely he would wonder.

"It's true," Jo replied, fighting to hold her voice steady. "It was a closed adoption. Mia didn't want anyone to know she was pregnant."

Robbie paled. He sat down at the table and stared at the floor for a long moment before he spoke again. "Why didn't you tell me, Mia?"

"Do you think I'm stupid?" she retorted. "You wouldn't have wanted me if you'd known I was pregnant with Noah's baby."

Robbie shook his head slowly as if trying to process it all. "I thought you moved to San Francisco for a job after Noah died."

Jo released the shallow breath she'd been holding. Mia hadn't dropped the biggest bombshell of all on Robbie, at least for now. But she was unstable. There was no knowing when she would unload it on him. It was all a game to her. But Jo wasn't willing to play along anymore, despite her threats. It was time to tell Robbie the whole truth, and face the consequences. She would fight for Claire in the courts if she had to. "You've started now, Mia. You might as well finish and tell him everything."

Mia narrowed her eyes, searing Jo with a caustic glare. "I don't know what you're talking about."

Jo joined Robbie at the table. She folded her hands in front of her and took a deep steadying breath. "Claire is your biological daughter."

Robbie's eyes widened. He blinked rapidly and then rubbed a hand slowly over his jaw. For a moment, Jo thought he looked almost contrite, as if he might be about to confess that he'd been having an affair with Mia long before Sarah and Noah had died, but then in a sudden burst of anger he shoved his chair out from the table. "You betrayed me, Mia. You kept the pregnancy from me, told me you went to San Francisco to work. Now, you're lying to me about who the father of the baby is. You're no better than Sarah. You're a bigger liar than she ever was."

"Calm down, Robbie, please," Jo urged.

He turned and glared at her. "You stabbed me in the back too. You and Liam adopted my child without telling me."

"No, that's not true," Jo protested. "We thought all along it was Noah's baby. I only confronted Mia about it this afternoon."

Robbie eyed her skeptically. "How did you find out?"

"I … figured it out. I compared Olivia's newborn pictures to Claire's. They look like twins." Jo hesitated, her hands shaking. "I always wondered why Claire didn't look anything like the Tomaselli family."

Robbie dropped his head into his hands. "You should have told me Mia was pregnant before."

Jo got to her feet, barely able to constrain her fury. "And you should have told me you were sleeping with her! That was you parked outside Mia's house the night she argued with Noah and stormed out of school, wasn't it? You took Sarah's car so it wouldn't look suspicious. I ached for what you were going through after Sarah died, never suspecting for one moment that you were cheating on her too."

Robbie tightened his lips. He glanced across at Mia, his eyes dark and rippling like the surface of a troubled lake. "It was one time. Believe me, I'm not proud of myself. I blame myself for not confessing what I'd done to Sarah. If I had, she might never have killed herself out of guilt over her relationship with Noah."

22

*J*o and Liam sat at a corner table in The Coffee Pot, a small family-owned café within walking distance of their house. Claire was wedged into a wooden highchair, methodically picking apart a blueberry muffin. At least half of it was falling to the floor in a shower of crumbs in her bumbling attempts to direct it to her mouth, but for once, Jo wasn't focused on cleaning up after her. She was still reeling from yesterday's revelation that Robbie was Claire's biological father, even though she'd half suspected it. More importantly, she was shocked, and baffled that all this time Robbie had let her believe he was the innocent party in Sarah's affair. How could Jo have been so wrong about her two best friends? The more she thought about it, the more she began questioning everything. If Noah and Sarah had concealed their relationship from their partners, what were the odds of Robbie and Mia getting together at the same time? Astronomical. Some might say impossibly long. Was there something more to it all? Something she was overlooking?

"I don't know what to think about Robbie and Mia anymore," Jo said, picking up her latte and taking a sip.

"It's a twisted situation," Liam agreed. "Seems they were both spinning lies to suit their own purposes. You were right. Mia's turned out to be a master manipulator. As for Robbie, he'll always be my friend, but I've lost all respect for him."

"There's got to be more to the story," Jo said. "I'm starting to question *everything* about Sarah's and Noah's relationship."

"What do you mean?"

"We don't even know if they were really in a relationship at all."

Liam looked baffled. "Of course they were. Their phone records proved it. Why else would they have committed suicide?"

Jo looked at Liam intently. "Those were burner phones. Anyone could have sent those messages."

Liam handed Claire a blueberry that had rolled across the table. "What are you getting at?"

"I'm not sure. I know it sounds crazy, but it's just that Mia is so devious. I wonder sometimes if she had a hand in it somehow."

"Now *that's* crazy thinking," Liam retorted.

"Maybe so," Jo mused. "But I've never been convinced Sarah killed herself. It's just not who she is … was."

Liam frowned. "The police investigated every angle. It was an open and shut case. Nothing was tampered with. There were no other fingerprints on the hosepipe, other than Noah's. The phones confirmed their relationship, and don't forget there was a suicide note."

"I never really bought the suicide note either. It was too vague, not like Sarah at all, and it was odd that the rest of the writing on the page was illegible, almost as if someone deliberately destroyed it so you couldn't read it in context. Maybe because it wasn't a suicide note at all."

Liam scratched his neck. "I think it's a stretch to suggest Sarah and Noah weren't involved with one another. It's not unusual when relationships aren't going well for partners to look elsewhere."

"But it *is* unusual for the wronged partners to end up in each other's beds. Not to mention the illegality of Mia and Noah being minors, and the huge risk Robbie and Sarah were taking—assuming Sarah actually did have a relationship with Noah." Jo tapped her nails on the side of her cup peering at Liam over the rim as she held it to her lips. "There *is* one way we might be able to find out if Mia had a hand in it."

"What's that?" Liam asked warily.

Jo flicked a glance over the nearby tables and then lowered her voice. "You could search her computer. Make a copy of her hard drive or whatever it is you do to retrieve information. There might be something incriminating on there."

"That's illegal, Jo," Liam said.

"And what if we find out that she did something illegal?" She leaned closer and whispered, "I looked at Mia's prescriptions in her bathroom. One of them is Lorazepam. I knew it sounded familiar for some reason. It's the same anti-anxiety drug that Noah and Sarah took before they committed suicide. Don't you think that's a bit of a coincidence? Maybe she found out that Noah was sleeping with Sarah and threatened to tell everyone—maybe she drove Noah to kill Sarah and then take his own life."

Liam widened his eyes and dragged a hand through his hair. "Do you realize what you're implying? I don't want to get involved in this."

"We are involved, whether you like it or not." Jo set down her mug and wiped some crumbs from Claire's mouth. "Robbie might be too, if he's figured out what she did. He could be protecting her. There might be evidence on his computer too—emails, or something. You could access his computer at school. I need to be sure, Liam. You know how I am when I get something in my head. I can't keep going on like this, wondering if Mia had something to do with it. It's all too convenient."

Liam said nothing as he fished Claire's sippy cup out of the diaper bag and handed it to her.

"Please, Liam. You've got to admit there's something's off about this whole situation."

He let out a heavy sigh. "Okay, I'll take a look at Robbie's school computer. But that's as far as it goes. If there's nothing incriminating on it, you have to drop this." He looked at Claire, his face softening. "If Robbie decides to pursue custody, we'll fight him in court. But I can't imagine he will."

"We don't know that," Jo said.

Liam grimaced. "I can't access his computer right away. I'll have to make it look like I'm at the school for routine network maintenance."

"Maybe you can think of some emergency," Jo said, draining the last of her coffee. "We shouldn't wait any longer. Mia's putting Olivia's life at risk with her drinking. I suspect the strain of whatever she's hiding is getting to be too much for her."

THE FOLLOWING MONDAY, Jo's phone pinged as a text came through. She glanced across at it, still tapping away on her keyboard. Her fingers froze in position. It was Mia.

Call me. We need to talk.

Jo's stomach churned as she considered what to do. She had no desire to engage again with a drunken Mia, at least not until she'd ruled out any possibility that she was involved in Noah's and Sarah's deaths. But Mia might want to talk to her about Claire. Jo and Liam were on the same page about any challenge to their parental rights—they would fight all the way to the Supreme Court to keep their daughter if it came down to it.

Jo picked up her phone, typing and deleting several lines of text before finally hitting send.

What do you want to talk about? I'll only agree to meet if you haven't been drinking.

A few minutes later, Mia typed back a response.

It's about Robbie. Can you meet me in the park near the school after work? I haven't touched a drop today. I swear on Olivia's life.

Jo reread the text, her thoughts plummeting into a bottomless well of despair. Robbie must be intending to pursue custody. How could he do such a thing after seeing how much she and Liam loved Claire? Was he really prepared to tear their family apart and possibly his own in the process? She gritted her teeth as she sent a reply.

I'll be there at three-fifteen. No more lies and no more games.

She got the thumbs up emoji in response. Jo curled her lip. She didn't relish the thought of meeting Mia, even sober, although she had her doubts that would be the case. But if Mia was planning to forewarn her about Robbie's intentions, it was important to hear her out. She and Liam would have to hire a lawyer and find out what their rights were. At least this way they'd have time to prepare before they were hit with a lawsuit.

As luck would have it, Jo found herself in a last-minute meeting with a particularly vulnerable sophomore whose parents were getting divorced and moving away from the area, forcing her to change schools and leave her friends behind—an unfathomable act of tyranny from the girl's point of view that merited a spate of cutting. Jo had no choice but to patiently talk her off the ledge—anything less would have been irresponsible. It was already three-twenty by the time she pulled out of the school parking lot and after three-thirty by the time she reached the bench where Mia was sitting, pushing Olivia's stroller back-and-forth.

"Sorry I'm late," Jo panted. "My meeting ran over."

Mia batted her eyelashes. "I'm used to it with Robbie."

Jo eyed her furtively. "I'm relieved to hear you haven't been drinking today."

Mia twisted her lips, staring at the stroller. "Robbie went through the house and found my stash of wine and confiscated everything. It's worse than living with Tory."

"He's only trying to help you. He cares about you."

Mia turned and looked at Jo, her face pinched. "I don't think he does. He's losing interest."

"What makes you think that?"

"He spends all his time in front of the TV when he comes home. He used to want to talk to me, now he just wants to be left alone, unless he's giving out to me or telling me what to do."

"That might have something to do with the fact that you're always drunk when he comes home."

"I've been under a lot of pressure," Mia said, her voice almost plaintive.

"It's hard with a newborn," Jo admitted. "But it's not a reason to start drinking."

"I don't mean that kind of pressure." Mia twisted her wedding band on her finger. "The truth is, I'm afraid of Robbie."

Jo hesitated before responding, wrestling with her tendency to immediately rush to Robbie's defense. Was this another one of Mia's attempts to manipulate the situation in her favor? Or was there a darker side to Robbie? Jo took a shallow breath. All her instincts told her to tread cautiously. "Why are you afraid of him?"

"He flies into rages. You saw how angry he got yesterday,

how he yanked my arm. That's assault." Mia's eyes bored into Jo's. "He gets so angry sometimes I think he's going to … to kill me."

Jo let out a gasp. "Don't be absurd. You can hardly blame him for getting angry about what we told him. My husband would have reacted the same way if someone had dropped a bombshell like that on him. It takes a lot to get Robbie riled up."

Mia arched a challenging brow. "He comes across as easygoing, but it's all an act. He's very intense when we're alone—very controlling. Especially if I don't do exactly what he wants me to do."

Jo thought for a moment, trying to recall any incidents when Robbie had got angry or intense about something. It didn't seem to fit his character. Sarah had hinted at problems between them but she'd never mentioned anything about Robbie having an anger problem. On the other hand, Mia had proven she was an accomplished actress, but Jo thought better of pointing that out. Instead, she said, "Give me an example of what you're talking about, other than yesterday. How's he controlling?"

"He doesn't want Tory babysitting anymore, and he doesn't want me taking Olivia over to her house either."

"I thought Robbie liked your mom."

"I thought so too," Mia replied, her tone conspiratorial. "But ever since Barb died and he got control of her money, he doesn't want Tory involved in anything to do with Olivia. He says we can afford to hire a babysitter if we want to go out."

Jo furrowed her brow. "Do you know how much money was in Barb's estate?"

"A little over four million."

Jo's jaw dropped. "What? Are you sure?"

"Yeah, I saw the paperwork. Why?"

"No reason. It's just that I always assumed it was a few hundred thousand dollars." Jo's heart was racing. People killed for a lot less than that. She leaned forward and peered into the stroller at a sleeping Olivia, so innocent of the lies and intrigue that surrounded her young life. Was it possible Sarah had been killed for the money she stood to inherit? And what had really happened to her mother? "Speaking of Barb, I've been meaning to ask you," Jo said casually. "Was she in good form that Sunday afternoon you went to visit her?"

Mia shrugged. "Yeah, I mean, she didn't know who I was, but then she never could remember my name."

"Why did you go that day instead of Robbie?"

A smug smile crept over Mia's lips. "He asked me to, he wanted to surprise me with something. While I was gone, he assembled some furniture for me that's been sitting in the garage in boxes since Olivia was born."

Jo swallowed a painful knot in her throat. Sweat prickled along the back of her neck. Robbie had made a point of telling her that Mia insisted he stay behind. Yet again, one of them was lying. The problem was that they took turns doing it and it was becoming increasingly difficult to sift through their deception and find out what was really going on.

23

*J*o couldn't focus on the juvenile probation report she was trying to read on one of her troubled students. It was clear she would have to make a difficult call to his parents at some point, but at the moment she was more preoccupied with the crime she was about to commit. Liam was due to arrive at the school at six o'clock, purportedly to undertake some maintenance work on the servers. The school janitor didn't arrive until eight so that should give them more than enough time to accomplish their task.

It was highly unlikely any of the teachers would be working late in their offices on a Friday. Nonetheless, Jo wouldn't be able to rest until she watched the last of her colleagues leave the building. She'd enlisted one of the other moms at Claire's daycare to pick her up and drop her off with the babysitter next door. Jo had every intention of being here with Liam when he searched Robbie's computer, partly because she wanted to know at once if he found anything, and partly to act as lookout in case any of the staff returned unexpectedly.

When the final bell rang signaling the end of classes, the corridors quickly filled with the usual sounds of Friday mayhem. The extra buzz of adrenaline associated with the weekend was palpable as students made a beeline through the main exit to freedom. Jo kept her office door closed, hoping to dissuade any last-minute crises from materializing in her office. The students thronged past, backpacks slung haphazardly over their shoulders, pushing and shoving each other jovially—thankfully none of them throwing as much as a backward glance in her direction.

A couple of teachers knocked on the glass inset in Jo's door and waved good-bye in passing. She smiled and waved in return, immediately focusing her attention back on her computer screen. Once the sound of footsteps faded, and the last stragglers had disappeared from the building, she left her computer and made her way to the staff break room to make herself a coffee. She still had a couple of hours to kill before Liam showed up. She'd left herself plenty of work to do, but now that she was alone in the building, she couldn't bring herself to tackle it. Instead, she found herself wandering along the corridor in the direction of Sarah's old classroom. On a whim, she unlocked the door using the master key on her wristband and then closed it quietly behind her. She pressed her back against the door and shut her eyes briefly, inhaling deeply. She could almost sense Sarah's spirit in the room. They'd spent countless hours in here talking and laughing as Sarah prepped for her art classes.

Jo let her gaze travel around the room, taking in the extensive art projects that covered every square inch of the walls, and even the ceiling. Much of the art on display was work done by students Sarah had taught. Jo knew from counseling many of Sarah's former students that they sorely missed her.

She began wandering around the room, tracing her fingers over the artwork, wondering how much coaching and time Sarah had poured into each picture. She could almost hear her cheering her students on, her bright smile convincing them that they could accomplish anything. How could someone who had loved life so much have committed suicide and encouraged one of her students to do the same? It was unthinkable.

Jo shook her head as she eyed the paintings. No, it was impossible. The Sarah Gleeson Jo knew would never have taken advantage of one of her students. That left only one alternative. Someone had murdered her. It seemed unlikely that it was Noah, but Jo couldn't rule out that possibility yet. Mia had been very convincing in her outburst in front of the lockers when she'd accused Noah of cheating on her. What if he'd been stalking Sarah and killed her when she rejected his advances, before killing himself?

Jo rubbed her temples. Her theory that someone had murdered Sarah was almost as preposterous as the idea that she'd committed suicide—almost, but not quite. If Liam didn't turn up anything on Robbie's computer tonight, she'd figure out a way to get a hold of Mia's laptop next. And if that didn't uncover anything, she would sit down with Lydia and Sérgio Tomaselli and try to find out if they'd noticed anything strange about Noah's behavior in the months leading up to his death. Someone had orchestrated Sarah's death. Somehow, some way, she'd get to the bottom of it all.

She walked back to the filing cabinets in the corner of the room and pulled open a drawer at random. She flicked through some old art projects, admiring the talented contributions that were lying in a drawer in the dark. It was such a shame. They were worthy of a place on someone's wall. She would talk to Ed on Monday about the possibility of returning some of this artwork to the students who had graduated. Maybe they would appreciate the pieces as a memento of a favorite teacher.

Working her way from the top of the filing cabinet to the bottom she browsed through the miscellaneous folders, losing herself for a while in a sheaf of student caricatures, trying to guess which of the students she was looking at. Her heart stopped when she pulled out a caricature of Noah Tomaselli. His broad football shoulders had been exaggerated to the padded dimensions of the Hulk, and his wide toothy grin encompassed half of his face, but there was no mistaking the handsome features lurking in the drawing. It was heartbreaking to think Noah was gone, but it was even more terrifying to think he might have killed Sarah.

Throwing a furtive look over her shoulder, Jo slipped the drawing into an empty file folder and set it aside. She would use it as an excuse to visit the Tomasellis and do some digging. Now that Noah was gone, they would treasure items like this, another piece in the composite of the life lost to them. She was about to slam the file drawer shut when she noticed something lying on the bottom tucked beneath the hanging file folders. She pushed the folders back in the drawer and squeezed her hand between them to grab what looked like a notebook of some kind. Flipping it open, she sucked in a breath when she saw the name *Sarah Gleeson* in the top right-hand corner in her friends's artistic handwriting.

She cast another sidelong look in the direction of the door, then went behind the desk and sat down in the swivel chair to look through the journal. It was unlined, more like a sketchbook. As she opened it to the first page, a small smile turned up the corners of her lips. It was a sketch of a hand raised up toward the sun, fingers outstretched. Beneath it,

Sarah had written, *When the new day dawns, dare to be grateful.* Jo turned another page, in awe once again at Sarah's artistic talent. As she flicked randomly through the book, she found herself drying her eyes at times when she was particularly moved by some of Sarah's thoughts or annotations. She'd never been a perfectionist and had often crossed out words here and there or altered quotes and added lines at awkward angles to make them fit on the page. It was more of an eclectic doodling book that she might have occupied herself with while her students were working on other things in the classroom. The pages were filled with the exuberant joy with which she had always lived life, no hint of underlying sadness or depression.

Jo closed the book and stared at it for a long moment. She didn't want to put it back in the dark drawer. It felt too much like putting a live body in the morgue. But there was no one to give it to now that Barb was dead. Robbie wouldn't want it. After a moment's hesitation, Jo slipped it inside the file folder along with the caricature drawing of Noah. She closed up the drawers and then exited the art room, locking it behind her.

She was almost back at her office when she heard footsteps approaching. She glanced at her phone, but it was only five-fifteen, too early for Liam, and far too early for the janitor. Her breath stuck in her throat when Robbie came striding into view. She took a hesitant step backward, for one terrible moment envisioning him lashing out at her in anger like Mia had described. The school suddenly seemed more dangerous in its desolation. He slowed his pace when he caught sight of her, his expression somewhat discomposed. "Hey, Jo, just leaving?"

"Uh ... pretty close," she stammered. "I thought I'd catch up on some reports I've been putting off. It's hard to find a quiet time during the day to keep up with all the paperwork. What are you doing back? Forget something?" She was talking excessively, she only hoped Robbie wouldn't pick up on her guilt-ridden tone.

"Yeah, I meant to bring the chemistry quiz I gave my students home with me. I need to grade it before Monday." He glanced down at his feet before giving Jo a shamefaced look. "Look, I want to apologize. This has all been a terrible shock and my reaction the other day was totally out of line. I just want you to know that I'd never do anything to separate you and Liam from Claire. I don't want you to worry about that." He shook his head sadly. "I can't say it doesn't sadden me in one sense knowing that Claire and Olivia won't grow up as sisters, but I'm thankful you and Liam adopted her and not some strangers. I couldn't ask for better parents for my daughter."

Jo fidgeted with the file folder in her hands. "I appreciate that, Robbie. It must be very difficult for you to come to terms with. I'm not going to sugarcoat things, though. Liam and I are still cut up about what you did, and the lies you told."

Robbie's shoulders sagged. "It was wrong of me. It was immoral and illegal, and I realize you could report me to the authorities. You have the proof, after all—my biological daughter. The only thing I can say in my defense is that Sarah and I were drifting apart. I suspected she was seeing someone else, although she never admitted to it. And Mia, as you know, can be very persuasive. I was weak, feeling rejected by Sarah, and I gave in to temptation—it was just that one time, I swear."

"I never got the sense from Sarah that you two were drifting apart," Jo replied frostily. "She was excited about taking that trip to Europe with you."

"That was a sore spot between us. I didn't want to go but she insisted on booking it." Robbie swallowed hard. "Did you know the Tomasellis had arranged to send Noah to Italy to visit relatives as a graduation present? I think Sarah was planning to hook up with him there."

24

*J*o stood rooted to the spot, digesting Robbie's words in silence. Empty words. She had no way of proving or disproving them now that Sarah was gone. It was possible Noah's family had been planning on sending him to Italy as a graduation present—she could ask Lydia about it. But that didn't mean Sarah's trip to Europe had anything to do with Noah other than being a convenient fit to Robbie's narrative. Why would Sarah have invited Jo and Liam along if she was planning an illicit rendezvous with Noah? It didn't make sense. Jo didn't know what to believe anymore. If Robbie wasn't the friend she thought she'd known all these years, then the only feasible alternative was that he was a sociopath, and an extremely clever one. A chemistry buff who would know exactly how to kill someone with carbon monoxide. Her heart thudded in her chest. Maybe Mia had been telling the truth when she'd said she was frightened of him. Until Jo had proof in hand, she wasn't about to challenge him. She'd give him the impression she was on his side for now.

"I'm sorry, Robbie," she said. "I had no idea Noah was

going to Europe too. And of course, I'm not going to turn you over to the authorities. What you and Mia did was wrong, but you're trying to do the right thing now. You have a young wife who needs you, and a beautiful daughter to raise. And thanks to you, Liam and I finally have a child to raise as well."

Robbie blinked back tears and then stepped forward to embrace her. Jo forced herself to respond in kind, all the while repulsed by his touch, wondering if the arms wrapped around her were the same arms that had killed her friend in cold blood. When he released her, she gestured toward her office. "I need to wrap things up and get home to Liam and Claire. Have a good weekend, Robbie."

"You too. Thanks for listening and ... understanding." He raised his hand in parting before striding off down the corridor in the direction of his office to fetch his paperwork.

Jo sank down at her desk and remained frozen in place until he returned moments later, waving again before exiting the building. She remained in her office for a full five minutes before making her way to the main entrance and peering around the parking lot. To her relief, Robbie's car was nowhere in sight. She glanced at her phone. Five fifty-five. She waited just inside the glass doors, exhaling in relief when Liam's car pulled up.

"Don't tell me you've been standing here all this time," he said, when Jo depressed the crash bar on the door and let him in.

"Robbie just left," she blurted out.

Liam threw her an alarmed look. "You should have texted me. I could have bumped into him."

"I didn't know he was coming by. He showed up to pick up some tests to grade and then he left again."

"Are you sure he's not coming back?"

"As sure as I *can* be. I'll keep an eye out in the corridor while you're on his computer."

Liam gave an uncertain nod. "All right, let's do this."

Jo led him through the deserted building to the science wing and unlocked the door to Robbie's office. Liam strode over to the desk and set down his laptop case. He unzipped a small pouch on the side and pulled out a gadget that looked like a thumb drive.

"What is that thing?" Jo called from the doorway.

"Basically, it's an input device," Liam explained. "It contains software that trawls through the hard drive and collects anything suspicious, any sensitive files that Robbie has password protected, any search terms I direct it to look for in the browser history." He sat down in front of the computer and powered it on before inserting the device. "I also installed some software on it to circumvent Robbie's password. I don't want to reset anything, or he'll realize someone was messing with his computer."

Jo peered briefly down the corridor in both directions and then made her way over to the desk to watch what Liam was doing. "We're safe, no one's coming," she reassured him when he shot her a nervous look.

The computer booted up and Jo sucked in her breath at the beautiful black and white photo of Olivia that filled the screen. If it wasn't for the fact that the photo had been taken in Robbie's family room, it could have passed for Claire. Jo was only halfway convinced by Robbie's assurances that he wouldn't seek custody of Claire. If he really was a sociopath, there would be strings attached to his promise, an unspoken agreement that he was rewarding her for not turning him over to the authorities for having a sexual relationship with an underage student.

A small black screen appeared in the top left corner of the computer monitor, rapidly filling up with text and code.

Liam leaned back in his chair, grasping the arms as he watched the software he'd installed do its work.

"Is it finding anything?" Jo asked. "I can't tell what I'm looking at."

"I won't know until I take it home and go through the files. This is only the collection process. I'm uploading everything it's retrieving to my Google account."

"Can't you take a peek at it here?" Jo persisted.

Liam's eyes traveled to the door. "Not worth the risk. The sooner we get out of here, the better."

A swishing sound signaled the software had done its job.

"That's it," Liam said, sounding relieved. He ejected the device and powered down the computer before retrieving his laptop bag. "Let's go before the janitor shows up."

They set the alarm and locked the school entrance doors before climbing into their respective cars and pulling out of the parking lot.

Bethany had already put Claire to bed by the time they got home. "She was really tired, so I thought I'd just go ahead and bathe her and put her down for the night."

"Thanks for doing that." Jo pulled out her phone to issue payment through her PayPal app. "See you Saturday as usual?"

"Looking forward to it." Bethany said.

As soon as the front door closed behind her, Jo locked eyes with Liam. "Let's see what we've got."

She followed him into the office and pulled up a chair next to him in front of the computer. Liam's fingers flew over the keys as he entered his password and logged into his Google drive to view the files he'd retrieved. "What do you want to start with? Browser history or password-protected files?"

Jo grimaced. "The files."

Liam opened up the screen and Jo quickly scanned the

folders, dismissing most of them out of hand. "Exam results, chemistry tests to be administered—these are all school-related." She read down through the list until she came to one titled *Robbie's Stuff.* "Let's see what this is all about. Probably school-related as well, but we might as well check."

Liam clicked on the file and waited for it to open. Inside, was a miscellaneous collection of JPEG's, PDF's, and documents. Liam randomly clicked on a JPEG and an image appeared on the screen—a meme of two kittens hugging each other. The caption read *your face needs my kisses.*

"Cheesy but harmless," Liam commented.

"Depends on who Robbie was thinking of sending it to," Jo responded, nauseated by the thought of Robbie carrying on like a schoolboy in an effort to seduce a seventeen-year-old. Although to hear him tell it, Mia had been the seductress. "Click on some of the others. Let's see what else is here. Maybe there's some photos of them together."

The rest of the JPEG's proved to be nothing more than funny, romantic memes, the kind of sappy images lovesick teenagers might send each other. A sad-looking dog resting his head on the couch next to a phone waiting for it to ring, two bananas hugging beneath a caption that read *I love the Peeling.*

"I can't imagine Robbie sending this kind of drivel to Sarah," Jo said. "She was far too artistic and sophisticated to appreciate it. But they are the kind of images a teenage girl might appreciate."

"Maybe." Liam sounded dubious. "But they aren't exactly incriminating."

Jo pointed to the screen. "Let's see what that PDF is all about."

Liam clicked on it and a poem appeared.

. . .

Can't get you out of my mind.
The way you walk, the way you talk,
The way you look at me and smile.
Lay your honey on my lips
With your passionate kiss.
Forever I am yours and you are mine.

"Robbie must have written it for Mia." Jo pulled a face. "It's pretty bad. He should stick to chemistry. Let's check the rest of the stuff just in case."

They spent the next few minutes opening up and reading through more bad poetry, and corny love memes.

"There's nothing in here that has anything to do with Sarah or Noah," Liam said. "We could go through his emails next, but I have a feeling it's going to be more of the same. Do you want to review his browser history?"

"What did you direct the program to retrieve?" Jo asked.

"I gave it several different topics to search for. Suicide, carbon monoxide poisoning, love trysts, how to murder someone and get away with it."

Jo shot him a sharp look, her heart thundering in her chest. This was real. They were actually trying to find out if their friend had helped cover up a murder. They were investigating Robbie, illegally looking through his computer search history, questioning everything the police had accepted as fact. Were they mad? Her gut told her to keep digging. She wouldn't give up until she had answers—it was how she was wired, how she went about everything in her life. "Pull it up and let's see what we've got."

Liam tapped his fingers lightly over the keyboard and, a couple of minutes later, several URLs appeared on the screen. "These are the results for suicide."

Jo scanned through the URLs quickly dismissing each

one. *Holly Grove adolescent treatment center* didn't mean anything. Robbie could have been looking up something to show the students. He often discussed drugs and the opioid crisis in his chemistry class. The next link was for *theatre arts and lectures in Los Angeles*. A bunch of different plays were listed and one of them had the word suicide in the title. The other links were even less relevant. "There's nothing here," Jo said. "Try *carbon monoxide poisoning*."

The only pertinent link that came up was a chemistry test—something about carbon monoxide and oxygen under pressure. Liam clicked on it and it opened up to reveal a standard test that was part of the high school curriculum.

Discouraged, Jo asked, "What else have you got?"

"*How to murder someone and get away with it*," Liam said pulling up the search file history. "Here's one, *celebrity killers*."

Jo batted at the air with her hand. "Probably some click bait title. We've all clicked on those before."

Liam tugged his fingers through his hair, stifling a yawn. "There's nothing else here other than a news story about a pro football player charged with covering up a murder."

"Try your other search term," Jo urged. "I forget what you said it was."

Liam scratched his head and then typed something on the keyboard. "Love trysts, I doubt it will bring up anything useful."

A single URL appeared on the screen, *the most shocking moments of madmen season five*.

"Robbie used to watch that show religiously," Jo said glumly. "Is that it?"

"I ran a couple of other searches, but I don't think they're relevant—too generic. Hiding bodies, police investigation, that kind of thing."

"We're here now, we might as well look. We can't afford to miss something that could be important."

By the time they'd combed through every last search Liam had retrieved from Robbie's hard drive, and gone through all his emails, it was well after midnight. Jo ran her fingers despairingly through her hair. They hadn't come up with a single incriminating piece of evidence. Other than a file of sappy memes, Robbie's computer was squeaky clean.

That left only two possibilities in Jo's mind, either Mia or Noah had murdered her friend. She wouldn't rest until she found out which of them it was.

25

———

The following Monday, Jo texted Lydia Tomaselli and asked if she could meet with her and her husband. She'd mentioned she had some art work belonging to Noah to give them, but that she also wanted to talk to them about something important. It was several hours before Lydia responded.

Sérgio's out of town but I can stop by your office after school.

Jo immediately texted back and asked if she could meet Lydia at her house instead. She couldn't risk Robbie or any of the other teachers seeing Noah's mother at the school and asking awkward questions.

Shortly before four, Jo pulled up outside the Tomaselli's spacious residence, a modern farmhouse-style house painted white with a row of decorative dormer windows. She reached for the file folder containing the caricature of Noah and then slung her purse over her shoulder before climbing out of the car. Despite having talked with hundreds of parents over the years, her nerves were beginning to get the better of her. After all, she wasn't here in her usual capacity as a counselor, a role she was good at and comfortable playing. She was here to dig around and find out from Noah's bereaved mother if her son could possibly have been involved in Sarah's murder.

Jo rang the elaborate brass doorbell and stepped back to wait while a melodic chime announced her arrival. She eyed the steps leading up to the front door flanked by ornate footed pedestals overflowing with succulents and flowering plants. Jo wasn't much of a gardener, but she appreciated the tasteful arrangements of vibrant color and greenery against the crisp white backdrop of the house. It certainly didn't look like the kind of home in which children grew up to become cold-blooded killers. But looks could be deceptive. Someone had murdered Sarah, that she was increasingly sure of.

The door opened and Lydia peered out, her eyes sunken as though her spirit had long since vacated them. She managed a wan smile as she stepped aside to usher Jo in. "It's thoughtful of you to bring by Noah's artwork," she said, leading her through to the kitchen.

"It's not his artwork per se," Jo hastened to explain. "It's a caricature drawing of him that one of his classmates did. But it's quite good and I thought you might appreciate having it."

Lydia gestured for Jo to take a seat at the table and then sat down next to her. "I cherish everything I can find that smells of him or looks like him or even reminds me of him in some way. It's still so hard to make sense of what happened. And yet I feel like everyone expects me to accept it and move on."

Jo nodded sympathetically, her mind flitting to the box of tiny baby clothes and blankets at the back of her closet that were her only tangible link left to the children she'd lost. "You can never really move on. It doesn't necessarily get better, you just learn to live with it being different."

Lydia sighed. "Sometimes I feel like I'm the only one mourning. Sérgio won't open up to me. It's like he's sealed his grief inside a time capsule. I'm afraid it's going to explode one day."

"It's not unusual for men to be angry and not want to talk about it when they lose a child. And Noah's death was very traumatic."

Lydia tilted her head to one side. "Yes, it was. I think that's always been the hardest part for Sérgio—accepting that our son committed suicide."

"Actually, Lydia, that's what I wanted to talk to you about."

A perturbed frown formed on her forehead, but she waited for Jo to continue.

"I wanted to ask you if you'd noticed anything strange about Noah's behavior in the months leading up to his death."

Lydia clasped her hands on the table in front of her and thought for a moment. "I've asked myself that same question many times. I'd hate to think I missed the signs. But there's nothing that comes to mind. He was always outgoing and social, a ray of sunshine in the house. He was very fond of Mia, of course, to a fault. He followed her lead a little more than we would have liked. She wasn't always the best influence—the drinking, for example. I think her outburst in school the day he disappeared embarrassed him, but he didn't believe it was over between them."

"What makes you think that?" Jo asked.

"Well, Mia asked Noah to meet her the following evening. He thought she was going to apologize to him for accusing him of cheating." Lydia shook her head. "That was the last we saw of him."

"Do you have any idea what they talked about? Did he text you or anything afterward?"

Lydia looked uncomfortable. "No, I never heard from him again. Mia said she tried to smooth things out between them, but he was too drunk. Apparently, they'd been drinking vodka. Eventually, she got out of his car and drove away."

Jo nodded thoughtfully. It was pretty much what Mia had told the police at the time. "Did you have any idea that Noah and Sarah Gleeson were in a relationship? Were there any clues at all?"

"None. I shudder at the thought. I knew he liked her as a teacher, but Noah wasn't like that—" Her voice trailed off on a despairing note. "At least, I didn't think he was. I'm more angry at Sarah Gleeson though. As his teacher, she betrayed his trust."

"That wasn't the Sarah I knew. I was a good friend of hers." Jo leaned forward in her seat. "Lydia, I realize this is hard, but do you think there's any possibility Noah was stalking Sarah?"

Lydia's eyebrows shot upward. Her lashes fluttered as she blinked in confusion. "What? Of course not. And I resent you insinuating such a thing. If that's why you're here, then maybe you should go."

"I'm sorry," Jo said gently, reaching for the file folder. "I'm genuinely searching for answers. I'm just as bewildered as you are as to why Sarah and Noah would have committed suicide. The truth is, I'm not convinced they did."

Lydia's pale lips parted in shock. "I ... don't understand. What do you mean? Are you saying you think someone killed them?"

"All the evidence points to the contrary, but evidence can be planted. The suicide pact theory doesn't fit with either of their personalities, especially not after listening to you describe Noah. It's all wrong."

Lydia nodded absentmindedly, gazing at a spot in the far corner of the room. "That's how my husband feels. He thinks it's a little too convenient that Mia and Robbie fell in love while Noah and Sarah were supposedly carrying on behind their backs."

"I suppose it's possible, but I'm not a big believer in coincidence—*true* coincidences are rare." Jo flipped open the file folder and pulled out the caricature drawing of Noah. "I recognized his smile right away," she said, sliding the sheet over to Lydia.

Lydia picked it up and studied it, her eyes taking in every pencil stroke. She pressed a hand to her mouth, her eyes growing watery. "This captures so much about him, even though it's only a caricature." She smiled at Jo. "Thank you for bringing me this. It means a lot. I know you lost a friend too. If there's anything you need to help you get to the truth, please let me know—funds or whatever. I don't know what else to do. I mean, even the police are convinced it was suicide."

"There is one thing." Jo held her gaze. "It might be worthwhile hiring a private investigator."

Lydia frowned. "What for?"

Jo hesitated. She didn't want to cast any aspersions on Robbie until she was sure he was covering something up. But she didn't have the same qualms when it came to Mia. "I can't explain it exactly, but there are things about Mia that don't add up. I don't trust her."

"Like what?" Lydia asked doubtfully.

Jo hesitated, her breath coming in sharp jabs. "For one, she takes an anti-anxiety medication called Lorazepam. It's the same drug the autopsies detected. What if she had a hand in Sarah's and Noah's deaths? What if she drove them to it, threatened to expose them or something?"

Lydia stared at her, aghast, for a long moment. "I can't believe she would go that far, but there's always been something about that girl that nagged at me. I want to know the truth, however awful it is. Sérgio has connections. I'll make a few calls. Leave it to me."

A few minutes later, Jo left the Tomaselli residence with Lydia's promise of help ringing in her ears. Buoyed by her success, she set her sights on one more target—Mia's mother, Tory.

26

*J*o sent Tory a quick text asking if she was at work or at home and telling her she needed to speak to her urgently. Tory responded almost immediately.

Home. What's wrong?

Jo typed back a quick response before starting up the car.

Be there in 10

Tory's face was creased with worry when she opened the door to Jo and showed her inside. "Is everything all right? Is this about Mia?"

"Possibly," Jo replied. "I'm hoping you can help me answer that."

Tory took her into the family room and sat down on the couch next to her. "I'm glad you're here," she blurted out. "I'm really worried about Mia. She's drinking more than ever—something's definitely eating at her." Her eyes clouded over. "To tell you the truth, I think she's scared of Robbie."

Jo frowned. "How do you know that?"

"She's mentioned it several times, but I didn't take her seriously at first. I thought he was getting angry with her about her drinking, and I didn't blame him. He has Olivia to think of. But Mia insists Robbie flew into rages even before she began drinking. She says he's very controlling about everything, especially ... money."

Jo raised her brows. Robbie had never given her the impression he cared much about money when Sarah was alive. But, now that she thought about it, he had expressed concern about Mia's spending habits on a few occasions.

"Mia hasn't always been truthful with me," Tory went on. "But this time I believe her. I think she's genuinely afraid of him."

"Robbie hasn't always been honest with me either," Jo conceded. "It's hard to figure out what exactly's going on between them. I'm questioning everything about their relationship. It all seems to be based on lies."

"What do you mean?" Tory asked, picking at her fingers nervously.

"Don't you think it's a little strange that they got together at the same time their partners were having an affair?"

"Well, perhaps a little, but in a way it made sense," Tory said, sounding uncertain. "They each knew what the other was going through."

"Maybe that's what they wanted us to believe. I'm beginning to wonder if it's possible one of them had something to do with what happened to Sarah and Noah." Jo let out a heavy breath and leaned back on the couch. "I know it sounds shocking, but I keep coming back to the idea."

Tory chewed on her lip, a shrewd look in her eye. "That could be why Mia's afraid of Robbie. Maybe she found out something. He might be threatening her to keep her quiet."

Jo held Tory's gaze for a long moment. Mia could just as easily be holding Robbie hostage. She didn't want to accuse Mia without any evidence, but she wasn't going to lie to Tory either. "I don't know what to think, other than that one of them knows more than they're letting on."

Tory frowned. "You don't really think Mia had any part in it, do you? She's manipulative and a good liar, but she's more self-destructive than anything else."

Jo grimaced. Mia was such a good liar that there was no telling what all she was capable of. But she couldn't risk alienating Tory by pointing that out. "Her conscience is plaguing her about something."

Tory rubbed her temples slowly. "If she knows what Robbie did, she might be in danger."

Jo blinked, sensing an opportunity. "I can't help her unless I can uncover some evidence that proves Robbie was involved. If you could get a hold of Mia's laptop, my husband Liam can check if there's anything incriminating on it—emails from Robbie hinting at what he was planning, or threatening her if she goes to the police, anything of that nature."

Tory thought for a moment. "Is that legal?"

"No, but neither is covering up murder. If it turns out Robbie did something, and Mia knows about it but is too afraid to say anything, then she's culpable too. The best thing we can do is find out what's really going on and then urge her to come forward with the truth."

"I'm not sure how to get my hands on her laptop," Tory said. "Robbie doesn't want me to babysit Olivia anymore, so I don't go over there very often these days."

"Do you still have a key to the house?" Jo asked.

"Well, yes." Tory tugged at her earring nervously. "Are you asking me to steal her laptop?"

"Borrow would be a better term. I only need it for about a half hour. Liam and I could meet you at a nearby café. What's Mia's schedule like?"

"She goes to the gym at lunchtime—she says she isn't

drinking anymore since Robbie threw out her secret stash, but who knows?"

"Does she take Olivia with her to the gym, or will the babysitter be at the house?" Jo asked.

"She takes her. There's childcare there."

Jo nodded, assessing their limited time frame. "Can you get the laptop tomorrow at lunchtime?"

"I suppose I could try." Tory tugged at her hair. "If Mia's hiding the fact that Robbie killed those poor people, I'll never forgive her."

"There's no sense jumping to conclusions yet," Jo said, getting to her feet. "Let's wait and see what Mia's laptop reveals. Liam and I will meet you at The Mill coffee shop tomorrow. You know where that is, right?"

Tory gave a nervous nod.

"Text us once you're on your way. And whatever you do, don't mention our conversation to Mia," Jo warned her. "You could be putting us all in danger if she warns Robbie we're on to him."

27

*J*o and Liam were already seated at a table in the back of The Mill when Tory arrived shortly after one o'clock the following afternoon. She quickened her pace when she spotted them, weaving her way through the packed tables. As she sat down, she placed a black laptop bag on the table and slid it toward Liam. "She's at the gym." Her voice was husky with fear. "This better not take long. She never did like me touching her stuff even when she lived with me."

"I don't need much time," Liam assured her. "I'll jump right on it."

"Her password's Olivia44," Tory added.

Liam gave an approving nod. "Good, makes my job that much easier."

Jo and Tory went up to the counter to order coffees while Liam got to work. By the time they arrived back at the table, the hacking program was already running.

"That went smoothly," Jo remarked, glancing at the screen.

Liam's gaze swerved between her and Tory. "Sort of. I had

to circumvent the password. Are you sure this is Mia's laptop and not Robbie's? There's no email program on it so I can't tell."

Tory's eyes widened. "What? I thought ... it looks like the one she uses."

Liam shrugged. "I might as well sweep the hard drive now that we have it."

Tory's fingertips fluttered nervously over her brow. "What if Robbie finds out? He could have me arrested. I'm scared of what he might do—"

Jo laid a hand on her arm. "Don't worry about it. Liam will make sure he doesn't detect a thing. And if he does, I'll take full responsibility."

Tory interlaced her shaking fingers around her paper coffee cup. "How long is this going to take?"

"Only a few minutes," Liam assured her. "The software's very efficient."

Despite his assurances, time seemed to drag on as they made small talk and sipped on their coffees. Jo found herself glancing at the door more than once, half afraid she might spot Robbie or Mia, or both of them, walking in. At last, a familiar whooshing sound signaled that the program had run its course.

"All done!" Liam announced. "I'll take a quick look at the results."

"Start with the browser searches this time," Jo said.

Liam tapped on the keyboard. "Okay, I'm pulling up a list of URLs."

Jo and Tory exchanged anxious glances as he silently scanned the screen for several long minutes. Eventually, he peered over the lid of the laptop at them. "I think I've got something."

They scooted their seats around to the other side of the table and leaned in to take a look. "There are several searches about carbon monoxide poisoning," Liam said, pointing at the screen. "What's really revealing is that these dates indicate they were all carried out in the span of roughly four weeks prior to Sarah's and Noah's deaths."

Jo stared at the screen, blood flushing her face as she read through the links. *Carbon monoxide kills in minutes, painless suicide, death by carbon monoxide, how to kill yourself using car exhaust fumes.* She read the dates on each of the links. A tight feeling gripped her gut. Liam was right—all the searches had been conducted prior to Sarah's and Noah's deaths. This was not the action of a bereaved partner searching for answers. This was the work of a killer laying out a sadistic plan.

Tory's lip trembled. "Mia must have found out what he did. That's why she's been drinking so heavily." She slumped down in her seat, dropping her head into her hands. "I'm shaking. I can't take this in. I knew I should never have trusted a teacher who would take advantage of a seventeen-year-old. He must have murdered his wife so he could be with Mia. What other explanation is there?"

"That's for the police to decide," Jo responded grimly. It didn't look good for Robbie, but there was still the possibility that Mia had conducted the searches. Still, it wouldn't be wise to point that out to Tory. She was far too easily influenced by Mia and Jo was afraid she might tip her off. "We don't know anything for sure yet. But we need to let the police know about this."

Tory passed a hand over her brow. "Are you going to give them the laptop?"

"No, put it back where you found it." Liam ejected his device and pocketed it. "I have everything I need right here."

"Are you going straight to the police?" Tory asked.

Jo and Liam exchanged a quick glance.

"One of us has to," Liam said.

Jo gave a terse nod. "I'll do it."

Liam handed her the memory stick lookalike. "Hopefully, it's enough to reopen the investigation."

Tory slid the laptop back into the sleeve and got to her feet. "How can I ever forgive myself for letting my daughter marry that monster?"

"It's not your fault," Jo reassured her. "If it turns out it wasn't suicide, then even the police were fooled."

"What if the Tomasellis think Mia was in on it?" Tory said. "They'll hire the best lawyers and go after her."

"There's no point in getting ahead of ourselves," Jo replied. "We'll turn everything over to the police and let them investigate. I'll call you as soon as I hear anything."

They exited the café and headed to their respective cars. Jo texted Ed and explained that she had an emergency and wouldn't be coming in that afternoon. Her heart felt like it was being squeezed inside a fist as she drove to the police station. She hadn't wanted to frighten Tory prematurely, but there was no getting around the fact that someone had conducted searches on carbon monoxide suicide on the laptop prior to Noah's and Sarah's deaths. It was damning evidence. It remained to be seen if either Robbie or Mia would admit to anything.

Jo pulled up outside the police station and walked up the steps, her legs threatening to buckle beneath her. She went inside and asked for Officer Bowman.

"Take a seat, please. I'll let her know you're here," the receptionist said.

Jo sank down on the caramel-colored plastic seat in the waiting area. Her palms were clammy with sweat. How could she share her findings with the officer without implicating Liam in an illegal search? Tory had a key to Mia's and Robbie's house, and Liam was Robbie's computer tech, so perhaps that made it legitimate. Jo had no idea whether the evidence would be permissible in court or not, but it would surely be enough to prompt the police into reopening the case and interviewing everyone again.

"Mrs. Murphy?" Officer Bowman appeared in the hallway and gestured to Jo to follow her into her office.

Jo sank down in the chair opposite her and placed the device with the files on the desk between them.

Officer Bowman glanced at it and then raised a questioning brow. "What can I help you with today?"

"I'm here about the double suicide case last year—Sarah Gleeson and Noah Tomaselli."

"Hard one to forget," the officer commented drily.

"The thing is, I'm not convinced Noah and Sarah committed suicide.

Officer Bowman's demeanor changed from mildly bored to moderately alert. "What makes you say that?"

"I never really believed it. I've never known two people less likely to commit suicide," Jo began. "They had everything to live for. They were both upbeat people and well-liked by their peers."

"By all appearances," Officer Bowman responded. "Sometimes things look very different beneath the surface. Sarah Gleeson was having an illicit affair with an underage student. She would have gone to prison if they'd been discovered. That's a fairly weighty consideration to factor in to the suicide."

Jo sat up straighter in her chair. "I was one of Sarah's best friends. She never once hinted to me that she was having an affair with Noah Tomaselli."

Officer Bowman shrugged. "People go to great lengths to hide affairs from friends and family. The evidence was right there on their phones."

"Burner phones that anyone could have placed in the car with them," Jo said, testily.

"Technically, that's true," Officer Bowman conceded. "But

someone would have had to go to considerable trouble to send texts between the two phones for several months prior."

"Someone who was highly organized and analytical, a sociopath, perhaps. Don't you think it's just a little too much of a coincidence that Robbie and Mia found solace in each other's arms while their partners were supposedly carrying on this illicit affair?"

"Look, I sympathize with you that you lost your best friend and a promising student," Officer Bowman said. "But unless you have evidence to support your theory, there's nothing more I can do." Her eyes darted to the thumb drive. "*Do* you have evidence?"

Jo pushed the device toward her. "The browser history on the laptop in their house indicates multiple searches for carbon monoxide poisoning, *how to kill yourself with the car exhaust fumes*, that kind of thing—all conducted in the weeks prior to Noah's and Sarah's deaths."

Officer Bowman frowned and reached for the thumb drive. "Where'd you get this?" she asked, as she inserted it into her computer.

"We had access to it. My husband's a computer tech," Jo replied, glossing over the particulars. "I asked him to trawl through the browser history. I've always had my suspicions about Sarah's and Noah's deaths."

The officer studied her screen for several minutes, fingers tapping on the keyboard as she scrolled through the list of URLs. When she'd finished, she sighed and leaned back in her chair. "I admit it's disturbing, but we can't use this as it was obtained illegally."

"Can't you get a search warrant and retrieve the information yourselves?" Jo countered.

"A judge won't grant a search warrant if we don't have probable cause. Unless you have something more than this to show me, that's not gonna happen."

Jo's heart sank. She'd been certain the police would at least agree to re-interview the key witnesses. Maybe they'd be able to get Mia or Robbie to admit to something that would justify a search warrant. Jo had nothing else to offer them. It wasn't as if either Mia or Robbie had confessed anything to her. Her mind cast around in desperation for something to bolster her case. *Sarah's journal?* If nothing else, it proved she hadn't been suicidal leading up to her death. Jo dug it out of her purse and thrust it at the officer. "Read through these pages and tell me this is the work of a woman who would take advantage of a minor and then talk him into committing suicide with her."

Officer Bowman reached for the journal with a skeptical air. She flipped through it, barely stopping to admire the artwork, let alone read the motivating quotes. Just when Jo had begun to despair of anything coming of her visit, the officer's demeanor changed. "What happened here?" She turned the journal around and pushed it back across the table to Jo.

Jo frowned. She hadn't noticed there was a page missing toward the center of the journal. She quickly flicked through the rest of the book, but everything else was intact.

Officer Bowman pinned a penetrating gaze on her. "Where did you get this?"

"It was in Sarah's classroom, lying under some artwork."

The officer got to her feet abruptly. "Wait here. I need to check something."

As soon as she exited the room, Jo pulled out her phone and texted Liam.

Evidence is inadmissible—obtained illegally. They can't get a search warrant without probable cause. Not looking good. :(

Liam texted her back almost immediately. *That sucks. They should at least interview Robbie and Mia. Search history is highly suspect.*

Before Jo had a chance to respond, Officer Bowman strode back into the room carrying a small plastic bag. She opened up Sarah's journal to the spot where the page had been ripped out, and then placed the plastic bag next to it.

Jo's eyes widened in disbelief. Her eardrums rang with the thud of her quickening pulse. The missing page was in the plastic bag. A perfect match. Badly damaged, but she could still make out a few words, *shame, regret, never look back.*

Officer Bowman looked grim. "The so-called suicide note."

Jo shook her head, the sickening realization flooding her. "It was never intended to be a suicide note. It was a quote that went with the drawing, the one that's been destroyed— deliberately destroyed I'm willing to wager. Someone planted it to make her death look like suicide."

Officer Bowman tapped her fingernails on the desk. "This changes things. I'll apply for a search warrant for the laptop. I can't promise anything, but I've seen enough to convince me we need to take a second look." She ejected the thumb drive and placed it in another evidence bag. "I'll hold on to this, at least until our tech team can get access to the laptop. In the meantime, I need you to carry on as usual around Mia and Robbie. I don't want their suspicions aroused."

Jo got to her feet. "I can do that."

"You'll need to make yourself available in the event we have to interview you again," Officer Bowman added. "If this turns out to be a murder inquiry, your testimony will be required in court."

Jo nodded. "Mia and Robbie have both been lying to me from the beginning about their relationship. I don't know what to believe anymore, but I should mention that Mia told me recently she was scared of Robbie. She's been drinking a lot. I'm not sure if it's due to a guilty conscience, or to take the edge off her fear. She's already on anti-anxiety medication—coincidentally, the same medication that Sarah and Noah took prior to their deaths. It's called Lorazepam."

"Have you ever known Robbie Gleeson to be violent?" Officer Bowman asked.

"No," Jo admitted. "He comes across as pretty mellow and easy-going by nature. If anything, Mia's the one who tends to fly off the handle. Everything's a game for her. She has a cruel streak, and I think she enjoys hurting others."

Officer Bowman looked pensive for a moment and then reached for her walkie talkie. "We need to move quickly. It's very possible Robbie Gleeson is the one who should be afraid."

28

*L*ater that evening, Liam and Jo were at the store picking up groceries, when Jo received a call. "It's Robbie," she hissed, as if he might overhear her. "What should I do?"

"Don't forget what Officer Bowman said," Liam cautioned her. "Take the call. We have to act normal."

Heart drumming in her chest, Jo slid the bar across the screen and pressed the phone to her ear ."Hey, Robbie."

"Jo," he choked out, his voice cracking. "Mia's been arrested."

"Arrested! What are you talking about?" Jo asked, struggling to compose herself. "What for? Has she been drinking again?"

"No! Nothing like that. She's been arrested on suspicion of murder."

Jo let out a spontaneous gasp. Hearing Robbie say the words out loud made it seem real for the first time. Mia was officially a suspect in Sarah's murder. Had Officer Bowman made a connection between Mia and the suicide note? Jo took a moment to steady her voice. "Murder? I don't understand."

"I don't either," Robbie said, starting to sob over the phone. "The police think she had something to do with Noah's and Sarah's suicide. It doesn't make any sense. I know what we did was wrong, but Mia would never … this is so crazy. I can't believe this is happening."

"Calm down, Robbie," Jo soothed, her eyes locking with Liam's. "There must be some kind of misunderstanding. Why would the police suddenly arrest Mia?"

"I don't know, I don't know anything. They said some new evidence came to light, but they wouldn't tell me anything. Can you come over, please? I feel like I'm going crazy."

Jo hesitated. She moved the phone away from her ear and mouthed to Liam, "He wants us to go to his place."

Liam lifted the palms of his hands in an expression of helplessness and gave a reluctant nod.

"All right, Robbie," Jo said. "Give us some time to drop Claire off with the babysitter and then we'll head your way."

She ended the call and grimaced. "I'm nervous about going over there, but I didn't know what else to tell him."

"You did the right thing," Liam said. "It would have looked odd if we'd refused. What I don't understand is why they arrested Mia and not him."

Jo frowned. "I told Officer Bowman about Mia's prescription for Lorazepam. And she had access to Sarah's journal in the art room. They might be going to question her about the suicide note."

"Yeah, and they probably don't have a warrant for the laptop yet. They won't arrest Robbie unless they have good reason." Liam let out a heavy sigh. "He must have known something—suspected at least. They'll get him for concealing evidence."

"I'll call Officer Bowman and let her know Robbie's asked us to go over there," Jo said, scrolling through her contacts. "Why don't you text Bethany and ask her if we can drop Claire off early."

Jo spent several minutes bringing Officer Bowman up to speed, and then lifted Claire out of the shopping cart. "She wants us to act supportive and see if Robbie spills any useful information. We're not to tell him anything. She's sending a patrol car to the sub-division as a precautionary measure. Let's go. Leave the groceries."

They abandoned their cart and hurried out to the parking lot, ignoring the curious stares of the other customers. On the way, Jo made a quick call to Tory. "I just heard about Mia's arrest. I'm so sorry."

"I'm at the police station," Tory replied, her voice shaking. "Mia's confessed to luring Noah to the garage where the bodies were found, but she insists she was terrified for her life. She says Robbie threatened her. He gave her no choice but to do exactly what he said."

Jo swallowed hard, digesting this new information. She'd been right that Mia was hiding something. But it still didn't mean Robbie was involved. Of course Mia would try and pin the blame on him. Jo's thoughts raced down myriad pathways. It remained to be seen what had really gone down in that garage that fateful night. A lover's tryst gone wrong? Maybe Noah and Mia had conspired to kill Sarah and then Mia had taken her revenge on Noah. Whatever had transpired, surely the truth would have to come out now. "How did Mia lure Noah to the garage?"

"She met him the night after their blowup. They were drinking vodka in his car and eating Chinese that she'd picked up on the way." Tory let out a heart wrenching sob. "She says Robbie crushed up some pills from her prescription and told her to add them to Noah's curry. Mixed with the vodka, it knocked him out."

Jo clapped a hand to her mouth. She couldn't believe what she was hearing. It was so cold, so evil. Was Robbie really capable of such a despicable act? "Go on," she whispered into the phone.

Tory sniveled. "Mia took Noah's car to the garage where Robbie was waiting and then drove back to her car. She swears she had nothing to do with what happened afterward. She thought Robbie was just going to scare Noah, tell him to back off. Supposedly, Noah had discovered them kissing in Robbie's classroom and was threatening to go to the police."

Jo kneaded her brow. "So, Mia's blaming Robbie for killing Noah, but what about Sarah?"

Tory choked back another sob. "Mia had no idea Robbie was planning to get rid of his wife too. She said he was waiting for her in the garage with Sarah in her car. She was in the driver's seat and she looked like she was sleeping. Mia was too afraid to ask any questions—she just wanted to get out of there as quickly as possible." Tory began to whimper. "I'm so scared, Jo. Robbie set Mia up as an accessory to murder."

Jo grimaced. Or else Mia had been in on the scheme from the beginning. One thing was clear. Noah and Sarah hadn't committed suicide that night. They'd been murdered in cold blood. "Robbie called a few minutes ago," Jo said. "He wants us to go over to his place."

"Don't go!" Tory said, a beat of fear in her voice. "I'm telling you, he's dangerous."

"Liam's going with me, and there'll be a patrol car cruising the sub-division," Jo assured her. "We're dropping Claire off with the babysitter. Where's Olivia?"

"She's here with me at the station," Tory replied. "I know it's not ideal, but I'm not leaving her with Robbie."

"We'll help you all we can," Jo reassured her. "I'll let you know what he has to say for himself."

Less than an hour later, they arrived at Robbie's place. He opened the door to them, looking like he hadn't slept in days. Tufts of dirty blond hair accentuated his bedraggled, unshaven appearance, and his motions were jittery as if he'd been drinking coffee since early morning.

"I just can't take it in," he said, once they were seated in the family room. "This is crazy. How could Mia murder two people? She had nothing to do with it."

Jo shot Liam a quick look. Evidently Robbie wasn't aware that Mia had already confessed to driving Noah to the garage, purportedly at Robbie's behest.

"Did Mia ever hint that she might have had a hand in Noah's death?" Jo asked.

Robbie shook his head vehemently. "Never. She was as stunned and heartbroken as I was at Sarah's death."

Jo shifted uncomfortably on the couch. Somehow, she doubted that. Mia certainly hadn't seemed too put out at Noah's funeral. She'd said something about Noah and Sarah getting what was coming to them. As for Robbie, he and Mia had already slept together by then. Robbie maintained it was only one time, but Jo couldn't trust anything that came out of his mouth anymore.

He rubbed trembling fingers back and forth across his brow. "It's the drinking. She must have blurted out something stupid that made someone question the circumstances of Noah's death." He lifted his eyes and stared at Jo, a crazed look in his eyes. "Or maybe the Tomasellis went to the police with their baseless suspicions. They always insisted Noah wouldn't have committed suicide."

Jo felt heat rising to her cheeks. Had Robbie found out that she'd talked to Lydia? She averted her gaze, her mind flailing around for something to say.

"It might have been Tory who went to the police," Liam said, bailing her out. "She had an axe to grind with you. You stopped her from visiting her only grandchild."

Robbie gave a worried nod. "I wondered about that. She's not a good influence on Mia. I didn't want her around when I wasn't home—I didn't want her babysitting Olivia anymore either. I suppose this could be her twisted way of taking revenge."

"What do you mean, she's not a good influence on Mia?" Liam prodded.

"She was jealous of anyone who took Mia's attention away from her," Robbie replied. "She kept trying to poison our relationship. She was far too wrapped up in Mia's life."

"What did she do that made you think she was jealous?" Jo asked.

Robbie rubbed his hands on his thighs and sighed, a forlorn expression on his face. "Tory was always coming between us, pointing out my flaws, undermining me, saying I was too controlling, trying to convince Mia I wasn't a good father to Olivia. She wanted Mia to move back in with her."

Jo frowned, trying to reconcile the Tory she had gotten to know with the picture of Tory that Robbie was painting. Mia had said she was afraid of Robbie. Perhaps that's why Tory had suggested Mia move back in with her. Any good mother would do the same. Jo would have to be careful what she said. She couldn't risk alerting Robbie to the fact that she was questioning everything he told her at this point. "I know you don't want to believe it, but have you considered the possibility that Mia might have had something to do with Noah's death?"

Robbie looked at her, ragged emotion in his eyes. "I don't want to believe my wife's lying to me. I've been down that road once already with Sarah."

Jo bristled at the comment. "You lied to Sarah too."

Robbie heaved out a weary breath. "It's not like you think. I never told you this before, but I received an anonymous note—months before I got together with Mia—letting me know that Sarah was carrying on with Noah behind my back. At first, I dismissed it as a sick joke, but then Mia received a similar note, along with a picture of Sarah and Noah alone in the art room in each other's arms. Mia approached me one day after school and showed it to me. I confronted Sarah, and Mia confronted Noah, but they both denied it. Sarah made up some lame excuse about Noah being upset about something and needing a hug."

Jo churned it over in her head. It *could* have been an innocent hug. Not entirely appropriate in today's environment, but Sarah had a bigger heart than sense sometimes. Maybe that's what Sarah had meant about spouses getting the wrong end of the stick. But someone had taken that picture. Someone had been watching them. Had Mia set them up?

Robbie dragged his fingernails over his scalp. "Sarah was furious with me for doubting her. That's when she began distancing herself. She planned that trip to Europe, even though I told her I didn't want to go." He sighed. "Noah was pushing Mia away too. He told her he was going to Europe that summer and was going to meet up with Sarah in Italy. What were we supposed to think? Mia and I were thrown together, just two hurt people trying to comfort each other."

Jo and Liam exchanged skeptical looks.

"Why didn't you tell us all this before?" Liam demanded.

Robbie wiped the back of his hand across his eyes. "I didn't want to make Sarah look any worse in your eyes. I loved her to the end. I thought she didn't love me anymore." He stared down at the carpet in front of him, tears streaming down his cheeks.

"I'm sorry, Robbie," Jo said, frozen in her seat. His tears

seemed genuine, but she couldn't bring herself to touch him. Not if there was any chance he was Sarah's killer.

An uncomfortable silence followed until Jo's phone rang. "It's Tory," she said.

A look of confusion flitted across Robbie's brow. "Why's she calling you?"

"I'm … not sure," Jo replied, her finger hovering over the screen.

"You'd better answer it. She might need you to watch Olivia. I'm waiting for a call to go into the station to see Mia."

Jo nodded and slid the bar across the screen. "Hi Tory."

"Are you with him?" she asked in a hushed tone.

"Yes. Liam's here too."

"Olivia's had enough of this place. I'll have to take her home, unless you can look after her, so I can be here for Mia."

"Of course," Jo replied. "Bring her over to our place. We'll be home in about thirty minutes."

"Thanks. I don't know what I'd do without you."

Jo ended the call and glanced at Robbie. "You were right. She needs me to look after Olivia. Maybe I can pick up some clothes for her while I'm here."

Robbie gave a distracted nod. "If you don't mind getting what you need from the nursery. I can't think straight."

"Don't worry about it. I'll be right back."

Upstairs, she busied herself packing a bag for Olivia. She had no idea how long she would be looking after her, but the tiny clothes didn't take up much space, so she packed plenty just in case. She glanced approvingly around the nursery before she left. Mia had done a wonderful job decorating the room with rustic shelving, floor-length drapes and an expensive crib. The glider rocker and beanbag footstool were custom-upholstered and coordinated with the drapes. By Jo's reckoning, the nursery must have put Robbie out five times what Claire's nursery had cost. It was certainly convenient that Sarah's mother had passed away when she did. Almost as convenient as Sarah passing away to open the door for Mia in the first place. But maybe things didn't really fall into Mia's lap. Maybe it was all the result of a carefully orchestrated plan to take what she wanted. Most things in life you had to go after, as Jo knew only too well. She closed the nursery door behind her, her mind spinning from the horror of what was unfolding.

Just as she reached the top of the stairs, the doorbell rang. She descended the stairs in time to see Robbie open the door to two police officers.

"Robbie Gleeson, you are under arrest for the murder of Noah Tomaselli and Sarah Gleeson. You have the right to remain silent. If you do say anything, it can be used against you in a court of law ..."

29

*J*o and Liam argued the whole way back to their house. Neither of them wanted to believe that Robbie had murdered Sarah, but the alternatives didn't quite pan out either.

"Mia couldn't have acted alone," Liam insisted repeatedly. "A seventeen-year-old girl couldn't have killed two people without help. Robbie must have been involved."

"What if Noah helped her kill Sarah?" Jo argued. "Maybe Mia told him she wouldn't get back together with him unless he got rid of her."

Liam threw her a horrified look. "The kid's dead! I can't believe you're tossing Noah under the bus like that!"

"I'm not. I'm just thinking through all the possible angles. Mia's a very accomplished liar and a masterful manipulator."

"As much as I hate to say it, I think Robbie was involved," Liam said. "It would take a man's help to get Noah out of his car and put him in the passenger seat of Sarah's car. Noah was a big guy."

"Mia could have pulled it off somehow. That girl could do anything she put her mind to."

"She's petite," Liam pointed out. "She might have been able to haul Noah out of his car, but there would have been drag marks on the garage floor. The police would have noticed something like that."

"You might be underestimating her strength," Jo said, unwilling to concede the point. "I can't believe Robbie's a cold-blooded killer—not unless he looks me straight in the eye and admits it."

Liam sighed. "This isn't getting us anywhere. We need to let the police do their job."

"I don't have much faith in them. They didn't do their job properly the first time. What makes you think they'll get it right this time?"

"They have new evidence now that leads in a different direction. They're investigating murder, not suicide."

Jo fell silent, unconvinced. Even after going over in her mind a thousand times the various combinations of possible suspects who could have been responsible for Noah's and Sarah's deaths, she still felt like she was missing something. She had no problem believing Mia was involved in some capacity, but it was hard to accept that Robbie could have participated in something so heinous. Still, Liam did have a point that it would have been difficult for Mia to act alone. Robbie hadn't been honest with them about his relationship with Mia from the beginning. He could be lying about a lot of other things too, like who he really was behind closed doors.

Tory was waiting for them when they pulled up at their house. She climbed out of her car with a crying Olivia in her arms. "She's exhausted. I tried feeding her, but she's not interested."

Jo took the baby from Tory and rocked her gently to soothe her while Liam went next door to pick up Claire. "Have you talked to Mia at all since she was arrested?"

Tory shook her head. "Only her lawyer. If Robbie confesses, her lawyer's optimistic the charges against her will be dropped because she was locked in an abusive relationship."

"The police are taking her claims seriously," Jo said. "They arrested Robbie just before we left his house."

Tory's eyes widened. "I'm relieved to hear that."

"I can't imagine what this is going to do to Noah's parents," Jo said.

"It's killing me," Tory sighed, smoothing a hand over her brow. "There's no point in me heading back to the station. They told me I won't be able to see Mia until tomorrow."

"Come in and I'll make some tea," Jo suggested. "You look exhausted."

Olivia fell asleep almost right away after Jo tucked her into the bassinet she'd set up in the guest room. Tory went to the bathroom to freshen up while Jo put the kettle on. Liam was playing with Claire in the family room. Every so often, Jo could hear Claire's giggles and it warmed her heart that such innocence still existed, when everything around her had become such a sordid mess.

Her phone buzzed, and she fumbled in her pocket to retrieve it. She frowned at the unknown number. "Hello?" she said in a guarded tone.

"Jo, it's Lydia Tomaselli. I just heard the news about Mia's arrest."

Jo frowned. "How did you find out?"

"I told you, Sérgio has friends in the police force," Lydia said with a tremor in her voice. "I wondered if you knew anything more. I know you're friendly with her and Robbie."

Jo hesitated before responding. Evidently Lydia hadn't heard yet that Robbie had also been arrested, or that Mia was accusing him of orchestrating the crime. "I don't know too much myself," she said.

"It's shocking to think Mia was involved in Noah's death," Lydia choked out, the anguish in her voice making her almost incoherent. "Why didn't she just break it off with him if she wanted to be with Robbie? She always was a bit of a money-grubber, but I tried to believe the best of her. I suppose she really did want to get her hands on the money all along."

"What money?" Jo asked, confused by the direction the conversation was taking.

"Sarah's mother's estate," Lydia answered.

"Mia may be materialistic," Jo said, "but to be fair, she didn't know about the money until after she married Robbie."

Lydia let out a scoffing laugh. "I highly doubt that. I'd be surprised if her father hadn't told her."

Jo frowned, growing more baffled by the minute. "How would he have known about it? Chuck Allen lives in San Francisco."

"He does now," Lydia replied. "But he used to work at Brookdale Meadows where Sarah's mother lived."

Jo blinked, trying to assemble her thoughts as she made the connection. "Doing what?"

"He was their accountant, until he got fired. Some kind of fraud allegation, I think."

Jo's pulse was doing double time. She tried to figure out what it meant, if anything. If Mia knew all along that Sarah's mother was wealthy, did that mean Mia had planned to seduce Robbie and get rid of Sarah? Jo shivered as another thought struck her. Mia might even have written those anonymous notes to drive a wedge between Robbie and Sarah before she made her move. "Have you told the police about this?"

"I ... no. I didn't think it was relevant until now, I suppose."

"Lydia, I need you to get off the phone and call Officer Bowman right away. Tell her exactly what you told me. It could be important. Mia's trying to pin the murders on Robbie. The police arrested him a short while ago. If what you're saying is true, it gives Mia a compelling motive to get rid of Noah and Sarah."

Jo hung up the phone and hurried into the family room to tell Liam what she'd learned.

He let out a low whistle, looking thunderstruck. "So, it was all about money for Mia."

Jo grimaced. "It's beginning to sound like it. I'm going down to the police station to talk to Officer Bowman. If she's not available, maybe I can talk to Robbie's lawyer."

Liam looked dubious. "What about Olivia?"

Jo gave him a teasing smile. "You can make up a bottle. You learned before I did, remember?"

Liam blew out his cheeks like balloons. "So much responsibility. I'll do my best, but don't be long. I don't know how I'll cope if they both start crying at the same time."

"Tory will know what to do." She lowered her voice. "Tell her I had to run down to the station to answer a few questions about Robbie. Don't say anything else until we know more."

For the second time that day, Jo found herself sitting in the hard-plastic chairs in the reception area of the police station. Officer Bowman was tied up on a conference call, but the receptionist told her Robbie's lawyer would come out to speak to her as soon as he had a chance.

Half an hour went by before a stocky, balding man in an expensive suit appeared. He strode over to Jo and shook hands with her. "You must be Jo. I'm Paul Garcia, Robbie's attorney. He told me I could speak freely with you. He's grateful you came."

Jo swallowed a sudden lump in her throat. "How is he?"

"Shaken up. The detective's pushing hard for a confession. He had motive and opportunity—his late wife's estate was substantial—and the detective makes a compelling case that Mia is too slight to have accomplished everything herself on the night of the murders. The evidence on the laptop doesn't help either. Not to mention the fact that he's a chemistry teacher. Of the two of them, he's the one most likely to be able to pull off murder by carbon monoxide poisoning."

"I don't agree that Robbie has a motive," Jo protested. "In all the years I've known him, he never cared about money, but Mia's obsessed with it. She makes it difficult for him to keep up with all her demands."

"Do you have any evidence of that?"

"I'm sure Robbie does. He says she spends every penny he makes, and then some." Jo paused, frowning. "And there's something else. It always struck me as odd that Sarah's mother died the evening Mia visited her. They never conducted an autopsy. Isn't it possible Mia gave her something?"

"All circumstantial," Paul countered. "It won't hold up in court. We need something solid."

"I do have another lead that might be worth following up on," Jo said. "I found out this afternoon that Mia's father worked for several years at the Alzheimer's facility where Sarah's mother lived. He was their accountant until he was fired for some kind of fraud. If he knew about Barb's estate, he might have told Mia about it."

Paul pulled a notebook out of his jacket pocket and jotted something down. "Do you know his name and where he lives, by chance?"

Jo pulled out her phone. "I can share his contact information with you. Mia lived with him for a few months. What's your number?"

Before he could respond, Jo's phone buzzed with a text notification from Liam.

Tory watching girls. Emergency at the office

Jo sent him a thumbs up emoji in return and smiled apologetically at Paul. "Sorry about that."

He recited his phone number and Jo plugged it into her phone and forwarded the contact information to him.

"I'll pass this along to the detective in charge," Paul said. "It's probably a long shot. But it's a lead they should follow up, nonetheless."

"Is Mia still claiming that Robbie coerced her into driving Noah to the garage?"

Paul gave a curt nod. "At first, she said she didn't see Sarah there that night, but she finally broke down and admitted that Sarah's car was already in the garage when she got there. She assumed Robbie had drugged her too, but she didn't know why, and she was too scared to ask."

"That's a stretch," Jo retorted. "Mia's not afraid to ask anything."

Paul grimaced. "She's been pretty convincing so far. Now she wants to press charges against Robbie for statutory rape as well as unlawful coercion to commit a kidnapping."

Jo squeezed her eyes shut momentarily. The situation was going from bad to worse. Even if Robbie wasn't charged with murder, Mia was going to make sure he didn't walk away from this a free man.

Paul glanced at his watch. "I need to get back to the interview room. I'll try and give you a call later with an update."

"Wait!" Jo laid a hand on his arm. "Can you tell Robbie that Liam and I are looking after Olivia and that ... that we're here for him?"

The lawyer gave a curt nod before disappearing back down the corridor.

Jo wasn't entirely sure why she'd asked him to let Robbie

know he had their support. Even if he hadn't been involved in Sarah's murder, he'd betrayed their trust and friendship with his lies. But in her heart, she still harbored some compassion for him. She only hoped he wasn't the monster Mia was making him out to be. As Jo turned to leave, Officer Bowman came striding into view. "I'm glad I caught you," she said. "I had a call from Lydia Tomaselli."

Jo raised her brows hopefully. "Did she tell you that Mia's father used to work at Brookdale Meadows where Sarah's mother lived?"

Officer Bowman nodded, her eyes sharp and alert. "I just talked to the director of the home. Mia's father was fired for forging a resident's signature on a will leaving several hundred thousand dollars to a Lance Patterson. Turns out Lance Patterson is an alias for Chuck Allen."

30

Jo stared at Officer Bowman, thunderstruck. "If Chuck knew about Barb's estate, then he might have been in on it with Mia."

"It's an avenue worth exploring. We're bringing him in for questioning. But it doesn't rule out the possibility that Robbie was involved on some level."

Jo gave a half-hearted nod of acknowledgement. She still baulked at the idea that Robbie was a heartless killer who had premeditated Sarah's murder for money and lust. She would much rather believe that Mia's father had been the other half of the evil duo that had taken the lives of two innocent people.

Her phone rang and she answered it immediately when Lydia's number popped up again. "Hi, I'm here with Officer Bow—"

Lydia cut her off before she could say another word. "Put me on speaker."

Jo shot Officer Bowman a look of alarm as she pressed the speaker button. "What's wrong?"

"I just heard back from the investigator I hired to dig into

Mia's background," Lydia blurted out. "Turns out the Allen family has been hiding more than one dark secret."

Jo's gaze locked with Officer Bowman's.

"Go on," the officer said.

"The PI sent me a copy of Chuck Allen's marriage certificate. His wife's name wasn't Tory, it was Natalie."

"I … don't understand," Jo said. "Was he married before?"

"No," Lydia replied, her voice falling away. "Natalie's dead."

An icy gasp escaped Jo's lips.

Officer Bowman frowned. "Then who's Tory Allen?"

"Turns out she's actually Mia's older sister. She was twelve when Mia was born."

A sinister tingling crept over Jo's shoulders. "Tory's alone at my house with the girls."

"You need to get them right away," Lydia said.

"Why? Do you think the girls might be in danger?" Officer Bowman asked, her fingers wrapping around her walkie talkie.

"Yes … maybe. It's just that the PI said Natalie's death was suspicious." Lydia's words tumbled out faster. "She was alone in the house with Mia, who was thirteen at the time. Tory found their mother at the bottom of the stairs when she came home from work. She said Mia was asleep in her bed and knew nothing about it." Lydia took a shaky breath. "The PI said the police suspected a coverup, but there wasn't enough evidence to prove it was anything other than an accident. If Tory covered for Mia before, she might do it again, or worse. Mia has some kind of hold over her."

Before she'd even finished speaking, Officer Bowman was talking into her walkie-talkie, dispatching officers to Jo's house.

Jo tried calling Liam, and when he didn't pick up, she frantically messaged him to go home ASAP.

"You can ride with me," Officer Bowman said, already striding toward the door.

Sirens cut through the air like a knife, piercing Jo's heart with terror. With every mile they covered, her dread multiplied. She'd only ever wanted to be the best mother possible to Claire, but she'd left her in the care of someone who possibly had blood on her hands, someone who'd covered up her own mother's murder at the hands of her sociopathic sister. Jo cursed Liam inwardly for leaving Tory alone with the girls. They'd never left Claire alone with anyone other than Bethany before. *Bethany!* She'd be home from school by now. Jo pulled out her phone and dialed. The phone rang several times and then went to voice mail. Biting back her frustration, Jo sent a quick text asking her to run next door and check on the girls. She chewed on her fingernail, waiting desperately for a response. Bile rose from her stomach. The drive was taking forever. Weren't police cruisers supposed to fly through traffic? All the cop shows she'd ever watched had squad cars racing at unimaginable speeds through neighborhoods.

At long last, Officer Bowman turned down Jo's street. Jo peered anxiously out the window as they approached her house, shrouded in darkness. Her heart sank. Two squad cars were parked outside, engines running and lights flashing, but Tory's car was nowhere in sight. "She's taken the girls!" Jo cried.

"Can you describe her vehicle?" Officer Bowman asked.

"It's a green Subaru ... I don't remember the model."

Officer Bowman's walkie talkie crackled once more as she relayed the information. She gave a quick description of Tory, and then called in additional officers to pursue the vehicle.

A moment later, they pulled up to the curb, and rushed to

Jo's front door, accompanied by four other officers from the parked squad cars.

"Stand back!" Officer Bowman ordered Jo. "We can't be sure she isn't inside. Do you have your key?"

Jo fumbled in her pocket and handed over her front door key.

"Police!" Officer Bowman yelled, before turning the key in the lock. She pushed the door open slowly, gun drawn, and then dropped to her knees and yelled, "Call an ambulance!"

Jo's heart lurched. She screamed and stumbled forward. "Claire! Where's my baby?"

A heavyweight officer barred her way.

Officer Bowman called out to her. "It's not a kid. It's a young woman with shoulder-length brown hair."

"Bethany!" Jo gasped. "That's our babysitter. Is she alive?"

"She's breathing," Officer Bowman confirmed. "Looks like she sustained blunt force trauma to the head."

Jo turned as another vehicle screeched to a halt on the side of the street. "Liam!" She ran down the driveway to meet him, tears pouring down her face.

He grabbed her by the arms, his face drained of color. "What's going on?"

"Tory's taken the girls!" She sobbed for a moment before collecting herself enough to fill him in on everything. "She's dangerous, Liam. She attacked Bethany."

He clenched his jaw. "Let's hope for her sake the police get to her before I do."

Before Jo could respond, an ambulance pulled onto the street, sirens blaring. For the next several minutes, everyone's attention was focused on Bethany as the medics secured her to a stretcher and placed her in the back of the ambulance.

Jo buried her head in Liam's chest. "How could Tory have

fooled me like that? I'm supposed to be a good mother, and I didn't suspect for a minute that she was lying to us all along too. All that talk about raising Mia as a single mother. She's such a good actress."

"You mustn't blame yourself," Liam soothed. "She played on your emotions. She had everyone fooled—us, the school, the police."

Officer Bowman walked over to them, her lips gathered in a tight line. "We've got a hit on a green Subaru heading north on the freeway. The driver matches Tory's description. Officers are in pursuit."

"Thank God!" Jo wiped the tears from her eyes with the back of her hand. "She doesn't even have car seats for them."

"Once we apprehend her, we'll take the girls to the hospital to have them checked out as a precautionary measure," Officer Bowman said. "You might want to head there now."

Jo exchanged a stricken look with Liam. It hadn't even occurred to her that the babies might need medical attention. She'd never forgive Tory if she'd drugged them or harmed them in any way.

Liam squeezed her hand. "Let's go. We can check on Bethany while we're there."

They turned into the emergency room parking lot just as an ambulance pulled up. Jo and Liam leapt out of their car and raced to meet it. The back doors opened, and a medic stepped out holding a bewildered-looking Claire, her head swiveling to look at the flashing lights. When she caught sight of Jo, her face lit up with a bright smile. "Mama!" she squealed, bouncing up and down on the medic's hip.

Without a second's hesitation, Jo snatched her into her arms and held her close, burying her face in her soft curls. Liam wrapped his arms around them both, choking back a sob.

"Ma'am, sir," the medic said quietly. "We'll need to take your daughters inside and have them checked out."

Jo blinked through her tears as a second medic stepped out of the ambulance carrying a whimpering Olivia. Jo gave Liam a subtle shake of her head, warning him not to correct the misconception. Olivia needed them to be her advocate. Right now, they were all she had.

Once inside, a swarm of medical staff took over. Jo's fears were soon put to rest when both girls turned out to be uninjured and, to all appearances, none the worse after their ordeal. Jo explained to the ER doctor on duty who Olivia was, and after consulting with Officer Bowman, she got Robbie's permission to take Olivia home for the night.

Before they left, they paid Bethany a quick visit. To Jo's relief, she was sitting up in bed and conversing animatedly with a nurse. Bethany's mother was seated next to her and smiled tentatively when she saw them.

Jo let go of Claire's hand and wrapped her arms around Bethany. "I'm so sorry she hurt you. I shouldn't have asked you to go next door. I never dreamt she'd be violent toward you."

"It's not your fault," Bethany said. "I just wish I could have stopped her from taking the girls."

"You delayed her," Liam replied. "If you hadn't, she might have had enough time to disappear. You went above and beyond the call of any babysitter."

Bethany smiled at the girls. "I'd do anything for those two precious peanuts."

Jo's phone beeped with a text notification. She pulled it out of her pocket and read the message out loud. "It's from Officer Bowman. *Tory in custody. Willing to testify against Mia if you drop kidnapping charges.*"

31

*T*hings moved rapidly after Tory's arrest. In return for immunity, she signed a statement saying that Mia had convinced her to take the girls and flee to San Francisco with them. Chuck Allen was brought in for questioning and a search warrant issued for his house, where enough incriminating evidence regarding Barb's estate was pulled from his computer to arrest him on suspicion of conspiracy to murder. To secure a plea deal, he confessed at his hearing, and Robbie was subsequently cleared of all charges relating to Sarah's and Noah's deaths. However, as Jo had feared, his attorney advised him he would likely serve time for soliciting sex with a minor.

Jo and Liam took off work to attend court for Mia's trial. She entered a plea of not guilty, doggedly sticking to her story that she had done nothing more than drive Noah to the garage. The only amendment to her original testimony was that she was now pinning the blame for the murders squarely on her father.

Chuck Allen's testimony painted a very different picture. According to his version of events, Mia had come to him with a plan that went one step further than his failed attempt to write himself into an elderly resident's will at Brookdale Meadows. Together, the two plotted to divest Sarah's mother, Barb, of her considerable inheritance. Knowing the estate had been willed to her only child, they came up with a plan to get rid of Sarah, paving the way for Mia to marry Robbie. They even cooked up a scheme to lay a trail of incriminating text messages between two burner phones over a five-month period, during which time Mia got to work seducing Robbie.

Despite Chuck's compelling testimony, during which the spectators sat spellbound, and the media scribbled frantically, the prosecutor had his work cut out for him to prove that Mia had been a willing accomplice in the double murder plot. The evidence against her was all circumstantial, including the browser history on the laptop which, the prosecution argued, belonged to Robbie.

The prosecutor paced in front of Mia, glancing from time to time at the jury to make sure they were tracking. "You testified that your only role in the crime was to drive a drugged and inebriated Noah Tomaselli on the evening of April 02 to the garage at 427 Lennondale where your father was waiting. However, your father testifies that earlier in the evening you also drove Sarah Gleeson to the same garage."

"That's a lie," Mia retorted, jutting out her chin. "He abducted her and brought her there himself."

The prosecutor splayed his palms. "And yet there's no evidence of a struggle. Sarah Gleeson had no DNA under her fingernails. There was no bruising on her body, no contusions to indicate she'd been hit over the head and knocked out. In fact, the only evidence is the contents of her stomach —coffee and an anti-anxiety drug, Lorazepam, the same prescription found in your bathroom cabinet. Furthermore, we have CCTV footage of a woman exiting a coffee house next to Target earlier that day with two paper cups of coffee and walking over to Sarah's car. Did you or did you not meet with Sarah Gleeson that afternoon during which time you gave her a drugged coffee before driving her to the garage where your father was waiting?"

"Absolutely not," Mia scoffed. "I often pick up a coffee for my sister after school and take it around to her work."

Jo glanced across to where Tory was sitting, head bowed. Despite everything Tory had done, Jo couldn't help feeling sorry for her. She was still being used by her conniving sister. Jo's assessment of her had been accurate—she was weak and easily influenced.

The prosecutor reviewed his files and cleared his throat. "In your original statement you said that you drove Noah to the garage so that Robbie Gleeson could scare him into not reporting your illicit relationship to the authorities. Robbie Gleeson, you asserted, was afraid of losing his job. Now you're claiming you drove Noah to the garage and left him with your father. What did you think your father was going to do to him?"

"Objection!" the defense lawyer shouted.

"Overruled," the judge replied. "Let the defendant answer the question."

Mia shrugged. "I asked him to rough Noah up a little so he'd tell me who he was seeing."

"And by rough him up a little, did you mean poison him with carbon monoxide?"

Mia narrowed her eyes, her face flushing. "I had nothing to do with that."

"Objection!" Her defense lawyer shouted.

"Sustained," the judge rejoined.

"No further questions, Your Honor," the prosecutor said, returning to his seat.

"Do you wish to cross-examine the witness?" the judge asked, looking pointedly at Mia's defense lawyer.

Jo held her breath as the defense took the floor.

"I realize this is a difficult subject for you, Mia," the defense lawyer began, "But can you please describe to the court your relationship with your father growing up?"

Mia cocked her head to one side, her blonde hair falling over her shoulder. She lifted a hand and brushed away what Jo strongly suspected was a crocodile tear. "It was extremely abusive. He was an alcoholic and very controlling. If we didn't do what he wanted, he would punish us, beat us and stuff." She gulped back a sob. "He was a ... a big man. I was scared of him."

"And what about your relationship with Noah Tomaselli?"

"We were high school sweethearts." Mia's face crumpled. "He was the love of my life until Sarah Gleeson seduced him."

"Objection!" the prosecutor called out.

"Sustained."

The defense lawyer softened his voice. "How did your relationship with Robbie Gleeson, your chemistry teacher, begin?"

"I went to him privately to tell him about the anonymous note I got. He was very sympathetic at first—he said he'd received one too. He kept pursuing me after that, asking me if I was okay, which of course I wasn't. I was devastated. It started with Robbie putting an arm around my shoulders. I ... I thought he was just trying to comfort me." Mia burst into tears. "Now I realize he was grooming me. And then later on, when I tried to get out of the relationship, he threatened me and my baby." She sniffed hard and looked piteously in Jo's direction. "He's a violent man just like my father. That's the reason I wanted to give my baby up for adoption."

Jo sat frozen in her seat hanging on every word as the defense continued to question Mia. Her performance was brilliant, evocative, powerful, masterful, but at the end of the day it was a performance. Jo knew that now, but would the jury recognize it?

When the defense lawyer finally resumed his seat, the prosecutor stood.

"I would now like to call Tory Allen to the witness stand."

Tory stood unsteadily and made her way to the stand. Her hand shook as she held it up in front of the court and swore to tell the whole truth and nothing but the truth.

"Miss Allen, can you please tell the court where you work."

Tory squeezed her hands nervously in her lap. "I clean offices at a variety of locations."

"And one of those locations is 2160 Bellfield, is it not?"

Tory nodded. "Yes."

"Can you tell us what type of business operates at that address?"

"It's … it's a fertility clinic."

Jo glanced up sharply, the address suddenly registering in her head. She and Liam had used that clinic.

"Did you at any time access confidential patient information?"

Tory's shoulders heaved. "Mia wanted me to photocopy Jo and Liam Murphy's file for her."

"I see. And how did you access the information?"

Tory shrugged. "It's not hard to open a locked file drawer. My father showed me how."

The prosecutor raised a brow. "Quite the criminal mastermind family."

"Objection! Your Honor, this is speculative and leading the jury."

"Quite," the judge agreed. "Please refrain from leading commentary going forward."

"Did Mia tell you why she wanted the information?" the prosecutor continued.

"She said … " Tory cast a hesitant glance around the courtroom.

"Miss Allen?" the prosecutor prompted.

"She said she'd found a way to make sure Robbie's best friends would support him when he told them about her. She said Jo was a crazy cow who would do anything for a baby."

Jo pressed a hand to her mouth. *No!* The courtroom began to spin around her. Was it possible? Had the adoption been Mia's idea all along?

"So, your sister premeditated giving up her baby for adoption to the Murphys," the prosecutor said, hanging on the word *premeditated* for maximum effect.

"You could say that," Tory agreed. "She wanted to make them think it was their idea."

"Did your sister also premeditate the murders of Sarah Gleeson and Noah Tomaselli?"

"Objection! The witness is being asked to speculate again."

"Your Honor, I believe what Miss Allen has to say is relevant."

"Very well, answer the question, Miss Allen."

"I overheard Mia and my father talking about one of the residents at Brookdale Meadows—Barb Anderson. Mia said she had a plan to get rid of her daughter, Sarah, and seduce Robbie." Tory brushed a lock of hair from her face. "She said she'd cut our father into the deal if he helped her."

The prosecutor nodded thoughtfully. "Which he did, as he has already testified to. Miss Allen, can you please tell us why your parents divorced?"

Her eyes darted nervously around the room before settling on the prosecutor. "My mother had a small settlement from a car accident that she kept in an account for our education. When Mia was born, she checked the account and discovered it had been drained down to practically nothing." Tory drew in a hard breath before continuing. "Our father denied touching the money, but she knew it was him. Not long after, she learned he'd run up gambling debts. The final straw was when he was fired from his job at Brookdale Meadows for forging a signature on a resident's will."

"Was he ever prosecuted for that?"

"No, the board of directors wanted to keep it quiet. It would have been bad for business if it had come out that their accountant had attempted to alter one of the resident's wills."

The prosecutor nodded thoughtfully. "Miss Allen, would you say your father is a pathological liar?"

"Yes." Her voice was wistful, and her expression theatrically pitiful.

Jo grimaced, trying not to feel sorry for her.

The prosecutor shuffled a couple of papers in front of him and then turned back to Tory. "And what about your sister, Mia Allen? Would you say she's also a pathological liar?"

Tory's eyes drifted over the gallery seated in front of her, coming to rest on Mia. She held her sister's gaze for a long moment.

After pulling out a tissue, she dabbed at her eyes before returning her attention to the prosecutor. "She's a far better one than our father."

The prosecutor raised his brows. "Can you give us an example of that, Miss Allen?"

Tory pulled back her shoulders and looked straight at the jury. "She pushed our mother down the stairs and convinced everyone it was an accident. Then she told me she'd kill me in my sleep if I didn't back up her story."

Shocked gasps rippled around the courtroom.

"Objection!" the defense lawyer yelled, his face reddening as he jumped to his feet.

The judge frowned but before he could respond the prosecutor said, "No further questions, Your Honor."

"Very well. The objection is sustained. At this time, we'll hear the closing arguments, after which the jury will retire to deliberate," the judge announced.

Jo slipped her hand into Liam's and squeezed it as they sat through the closing arguments from both sides. Other than Chuck Allen's testimony, the evidence against Mia was still mostly circumstantial. It remained to be seen if the jurors would believe her or her father. Chuck Allen was already going down for double murder. But was his testimony enough to convince a jury that his daughter had masterminded the plot, and been a willing and able accomplice in carrying out the gruesome deed?

After the judge charged the jury, they deliberated for less than three hours before returning to the courtroom.

The judge seated himself at the bench, rustling his robes and shuffling some papers before turning to the jury foreman. "Has the jury reached a verdict?"

"Yes, Your Honor. In the case of Noah Tomaselli, we the jury find the accused, Mia Allen, guilty of murder in the first degree. In the case of Sarah Gleeson, we the jury find the accused, Mia Allen, guilty of murder in the first degree."

Jo dropped her head into her shaking hands. The relief that swept through her was all-consuming. It was over at last. Justice had been served. Liam rubbed her back gently. "The jury saw straight through her," he whispered.

Jo nodded gratefully, not trusting herself to speak. Mia and her father had conducted a perfectly choreographed waltz of evil. They'd murdered two beautiful people, mown them down like developers clearing the land for their materialistic purposes. Chuck had evaded the death penalty by way of a plea deal, and Mia by way of being two weeks short of her eighteenth birthday when the murders had been carried out, but they would rot in jail for the better part of their lives.

After Mia was escorted out of the courtroom, Jo and Liam joined the other people filing out. Jo caught sight of Tory hurrying toward the steps leading out of the courthouse. "I'll be right back," she said to Liam, breaking into a jog to catch up with her.

She laid a hand on Tory's shoulder. "Wait! Do you have a minute?"

She swung around and stared at Jo, a wary glint in her eyes.

"I know Mia's been controlling you for a long time," Jo said. "I can't quite forgive you yet for abducting the girls, but I just wanted you to know you did a brave thing testifying against her."

Tory pressed her lips together. "I did it for my sister. She needs help. If she isn't stopped now, she'll only hurt more people." Before Jo could respond, she turned and slipped away. Her immunity deal meant she was a free woman. Jo wasn't sorry to see her go. Hopefully, she'd never set eyes on her again. She'd risked the girls' lives by fleeing with them. Jo had no idea what her intentions, or Mia's, were beyond that, but it could have involved blackmail, or worse—it didn't bear thinking about.

THE DAY OF THE SENTENCING, Jo got a call from Officer Bowman. "I wanted to reach out and thank you personally for everything you did to help us get to the bottom of this case. Without your help, justice might never have been served."

"Thanks, I appreciate you moving swiftly on the new evidence," Jo replied.

"Part of the reason I'm calling you is that Mia has requested to see you with her lawyer."

"Mia wants to see me?" Jo blurted out. Her pulse picked up pace. What on earth did Mia want to see her for at this juncture? Surely she wasn't going to bring a suit against her. She had no legal right to get Claire back, but that wouldn't stop someone as low as Mia from putting Jo and Liam through the process just to watch the pain of it chip away at them. She enjoyed tormenting people. And she'd already tried kidnapping Claire by enlisting her sister's help. "What does she want?" Jo asked tentatively.

"Her lawyer will explain everything," Officer Bowman said. "She's been granted visitation at the jail this afternoon at four o'clock if you can make it."

"I ... yes, I suppose so."

"Good." Officer Bowman graced her with a tight smile. "I'll let her lawyer know to expect you."

By the time Jo pulled up in the parking lot outside the jail, her throat was like sandpaper and her heart was drumming so loudly she was half afraid she might set off the security alarm when they scanned her through. She hadn't texted Liam to tell him where she was going. She didn't want to burden him with bad news until she'd confirmed it. He'd stand by her regardless—they were both committed to fighting to keep Claire at all costs.

She went through the security in a daze, placing her purse and shoes and overcoat in a tray on the conveyer belt and then walking through the scanner. With increasing trepidation, she followed a corrections officer to the visitor waiting room and sat down, feeling like a criminal herself. Maybe she deserved this. She'd tempted fate by her willingness to do almost anything to become a mother, even going as far as to keep quiet about the identity of Claire's biological father. She'd been willing to deprive Lydia and Sérgio of their rights as grandparents when she'd still believed Noah was Claire's father. She was hardly an innocent party. Her own questionable behavior had contributed to this tangled mess no matter how she sliced it.

It seemed like an eternity before Mia walked into the room, accompanied by a smartly dressed woman in a herringbone suit and black pumps. Jo swallowed hard, struck again by how truly beautiful Mia was even in her unflattering prison jumpsuit.

A satisfied smile flicked across her lips. "I wasn't sure you'd come," she said in a slow drawl, her liquid blue eyes roving over Jo like a predator eying its prey. "Despite what good friends we'd become."

Jo rubbed her hands nervously on her thighs beneath the table. "To be honest, I wasn't sure I should come."

Mia gave a sharp-edged laugh and leaned back in her chair, folding her arms in front of her. She looked remarkably relaxed, as at home in her new environment as she had been turning heads across the high school campus. "I'm glad you did. You would have missed out if you hadn't." She straightened back up and leaned across the table, looking intently into Jo's eyes. "We were good friends for a while, weren't we, Jo?"

"Robbie was my friend," Jo said stiffly. "You were his wife, and I respected that. But you seduced him, and betrayed him. You murdered Sarah and tried to frame him for it. You can't expect me to offer my continued friendship after that."

Mia wagged a finger at her. "Now, you're twisting the truth. I admit I tried to blame Robbie for what my father did." She glanced idly at her nails and then flexed out her fingers in front of her before adding with a hint of amusement, "But I didn't murder anyone. I was a lowly chauffeur in an evil plot. An abused child who couldn't stand up to her abuser."

Her lawyer cleared her throat and pulled out a leather folder. "Shall we begin?"

Sweat prickled along the back of Jo's neck. Her breathing came in small shallow pants as she waited for the lawyer to deliver the blow she fully expected was coming. The sooner it was out on the table, the sooner she could get to work recruiting the best adoption attorneys in the state to keep her daughter out of Mia Allen's clutches. As a convicted murderer, she'd never win custody, but she would revel in tormenting Jo in the process.

Mia reached across to her lawyer's leather folder and retrieved some paperwork. She straightened it in front of her and then raised her head and looked Jo directly in the eye. "I want you and Liam to adopt Olivia."

Jo's jaw dropped. She blinked, speechless, wondering if this was another twisted joke in Mia's repertoire.

"She's Claire's sister and all they have is each other now," Mia continued. "Thanks to Robbie's testimony about my drinking, I've been declared an unfit mother. And I don't want Tory raising her."

Jo blinked across the table at her. "Why not? You told her to abduct Olivia from my house."

A twisted smile formed on Mia's lips. "So she said. It's what you want to believe, isn't it—that I'm the evil sister and she's the sad, little victim?" Mia paused, and leaned across the table. "Well, that sad little victim drained our mother's account dry. And then she killed her, two days after my thirteenth birthday. I couldn't sleep for years afterward, I was terrified she was going to kill me next."

Jo shook her head slowly. "No, you're lying again. You're sick."

Mia arched a condescending brow. "I'm flattered you

think I was the brains behind it all, but you give me too much credit. Tory outfoxed us all."

Jo took a few shallow breaths. "Then why let her get away with it?"

"There's nothing to pin on her. She never gets her hands dirty." Mia slid the paperwork across the table. "Robbie signed it already of his own accord. You can check with his attorney."

Jo stared at the adoption placement form, the words swimming in and out of focus, and then glanced at the attorney, numb with shock at this stunning turnaround. Mia could have gone in the opposite direction and tried to get Claire back, hanging the case up in court for years, and forcing Jo and Liam to endure the stress and financial burden of it all. But, for whatever reason, she'd chosen the higher road.

Jo blinked back her tears. With Robbie facing charges of his own, Olivia had no one left to bat for her. "My answer is yes, gladly."

Mia turned to her lawyer and nodded. "Show her where she needs to sign."

After Jo had added her signature to the form with shaking fingers, Mia stood, a curious smile on her lips. "Have fun with those two little she-devils of mine."

She walked over to the corrections officer standing in the doorway and then turned back to Jo, arching a theatrical brow. "Oh, and be careful on the stairs."

32

*J*o smiled up at Liam sitting next to her on a park bench on a warm summer evening. He reached for her hand, his familiar fingers slipping between hers as he tilted his head down to kiss her. When they drew apart, he casually draped an arm around her shoulders. They watched in comfortable silence as Bethany pushed Claire on a swing while Olivia slept in the pram next to them. They were a family of four now, a patchwork family that had risen above the nightmare they'd lived through to build this life together.

In the end, Robbie was sentenced to three years in prison, but Jo and Liam assured him once he was released, he could visit the girls whenever he wanted to and that he'd always be included in birthdays and holiday celebrations.

"Don't tell them I'm their biological father," he said. "They can call me Uncle Robbie. I only want the best for them. I gave up the right to be their father when I made the decisions I made."

At times, Jo worried about how much of Mia was in the girls—Mia's parting words had a bad habit of echoing around inside her head late at night—but Liam always reassured her that the way they raised them would be enough to instill a sense of right and wrong to serve as their moral compass. Whether it would be enough to counter any predisposition to their mother's sociopathic ways remained to be seen. Mia had expressed no interest in ever seeing the girls again, and although she'd promised to write to them, so far nothing had materialized. Secretly, Jo hoped it never would. Mia showed no remorse for what she'd done, and Jo feared she would only grow harder behind bars. Officer Bowman had informed them she was appealing her sentence—which didn't surprise Jo in the least.

In another twist, the state was struggling to build a strong enough case to prosecute Mia for her mother's murder. Tory, their star witness, had inexplicably disappeared. Jo still wasn't sure which of the sisters had really killed their mother —but she was certain either one was capable. She could never quite shake the fear that Tory might resurface one day. She even caught herself glancing over her shoulder from time to time, shivering at the thought that Tory was out there somewhere, watching them perhaps. But it did no good to speculate.

Jo had gone to visit Sarah's grave shortly after the trial ended. She brought Sarah's art journal with her, along with a bunch of daffodils. She sat beside the tombstone in the setting sun, taking the time to go through the journal slowly and read everything that Sarah had written. It was a heartwarming celebration of life, a life that had been so cruelly taken. Jo desperately missed her, even more so now that Robbie was incarcerated. It felt as though she'd lost a limb.

Every once in a while, she drove by their house. It looked unloved and uncared for. The gardeners still came by once a week, but the flowers Sarah had planted looked jaded. The lights were on a timer and came on every evening but there was no spirit behind the drawn curtains. Barb's money should have been more than enough to take care of things, but her niece, the same Ella who had read a poem at Sarah's funeral, had filed a new lawsuit laying claim to the estate, alleging it had been illegitimately inherited by Robbie. For his part, Robbie didn't care about the money, which was one thing Jo had got right about him.

There had initially been some discussion about exhuming Barb's body, but, in the end, the extended family decided against it. The doctors at Brookdale Meadows advised them that there was a good chance Barb had passed away of complications from Alzheimer's. Mia adamantly denied having done anything to contribute to her death, and it would be an uphill battle to prove otherwise.

Jo still had her suspicions, but she'd made her peace with it. Exhuming Barb's body wouldn't change anything at this point. Justice, to the best of anyone's knowledge, was being served for Sarah.

Lydia had called Jo and let her know that she and Sérgio visited Mia in prison a few weeks after her incarceration. They wanted to look her in the face and ask her why she had helped murder their son. But they'd gotten no satisfaction from the visit. Mia had fluttered her eyelashes and stuck to her story that her only role had been to drive him to the garage.

"It was as if she was laughing at us," Lydia told Jo over the phone. "There was nothing in her eyes but darkness. It breaks my heart to think that Noah loved her to the end, never suspecting she would ever harm him."

"He had a good heart," Jo responded. "People with good hearts always believe the best of others. Naïve perhaps, but the world would be better off with more people like Noah."

"You and Liam are good people too," Lydia said. "Not everyone would have taken on Mia's children. At one point, I expected to be the grandmother of her children. After seeing what she's capable of, I'd be scared to take on that task."

"They're innocent children," Jo replied, quashing the niggling thread of fear that sometimes surfaced. They wouldn't be children forever. One day they would be thirteen—and she couldn't deny that the thought filled her with an element of dread at times. "I refuse to put the burden of what their mother did on them. They're the only beautiful thing to come out of the evil Mia intended."

After the phone call, Lydia had surprised her and Liam by sending a generous check to start an education fund for the girls. She included a short note thanking Jo for her persistence in getting to the bottom of what had happened.

Jo also had a long conversation with Ed McMillan regarding her position at Emmetville High and decided to take a couple of years off to raise the girls. "I feel my role is with them right now. So much has been taken from them. They need me."

Ed rubbed his jaw and nodded. "When you're ready to come back, your job will be waiting for you. You're an excellent counselor, highly praised by both parents and students alike. We're lucky to have you, and those girls are lucky to have you as their mother."

LIAM GOT up from the park bench and stretched, letting out a loud yawn and startling Jo out of her ponderous thoughts. "We should take the girls back to the house before it gets too late. Do you want to invite Bethany for dinner?"

Jo nodded. "Let's pick up some pizza on the way home."

She got to her feet and walked over to the swing, smiling at Claire's shrieks of delight as Bethany pushed her higher and higher.

"Ready to go?" Bethany asked, catching sight of Jo.

"Yeah, it's time to get this little madam in the bathtub. Will you join us for pizza?"

Bethany smiled. "I'd love to."

AFTER BOTH GIRLS had been scrubbed and put down for the night, Jo, Liam and Bethany gathered around the table over pepperoni pizza and Caesar salad.

"That was so much fun today," Bethany said, reaching for another piece of pizza. "I love seeing Claire's face light up when I push her on the swings. She's such a little thrill seeker, not afraid of anything."

Jo caught Liam's eye and smiled uneasily. Time would tell whether they had a daredevil or a she-devil on their hands. "The girls are lucky to have you as their babysitter, Bethany. You're so patient with them."

"And you're a wonderful mother to them," Bethany replied. "At least Mia's instincts didn't lead her astray when it came to that. She knew you'd be a good mom."

WHEN ROBBIE WAS RELEASED from prison three years later, Jo and Liam were there to pick him up.

"How are the girls?" he asked, his voice husky with emotion as he climbed into the back seat.

"Very talkative and inquisitive, and extremely smart," Liam responded as he started the engine. "Prepare to be bombarded and depleted of all energy reserves."

Jo turned around and grinned at Robbie. "We told them their Uncle Robbie is coming for a visit, and that he loves pillow fights, is a formidable tickle monster, and always keeps his pockets stuffed with candy."

Robbie let out a snort of laughter. "I think I can live up to that, although we might have to stop at a gas station to stock up on the candy."

"Already done," Jo said, rattling a plastic bag at her feet.

Robbie stared out of the window for a few minutes absorbing the sights. And then out of the blue he said, "How's Mia doing?"

Jo exchanged a quick look with Liam before responding. "Same as ever. Still working on her appeal. No word on Tory's whereabouts. Let's hope it stays that way."

"Mia wrote to me a couple of weeks before my release," Robbie said quietly.

Jo bit her lip, waiting on him to continue.

"She said she wanted me to—" His voice cracked, and he heaved a heavy sigh. "She wanted me to know that my name was … the last word on Sarah's lips. That's as close to a confession as I'm ever going to get. I know she just wanted to twist the knife, but it gives me some peace of mind to know that Mia's sentence was a just one."

They rode the rest of the way to the house in silence, a tribute of sorts to their memories of Sarah.

Jo unlocked the front door and two little girls scampered down the hallway to greet her, followed by a smiling Bethany. The girls ran straight past Jo and came to a halt in front of Robbie, staring unabashedly up at him.

Olivia pulled out her thumb and pointed at him. "What's your name?"

"He's our Uncle Robbie," Claire said indignantly.

Robbie kneeled down and winked at Olivia. "Your sister's right. I'm your Uncle Robbie and I'm … a … tickle … monster."

The girls tore off down the hallway shrieking with delight as Robbie thumped after them, arms outstretched. Bethany pulled out her phone and followed them to video their antics.

"I'm loving this already," Liam said. "I can put my feet up and watch the game while Robbie provides the evening's entertainment."

Jo smiled and slipped her arms around her husband's neck. "You know, at one point I wasn't sure we'd make it—all the heartbreak, the miscarriages."

"But we did," Liam assured her, brushing a strand of hair from her face. "And that's all that matters to those two little girls. They may have been conceived in a web of lies, but they'll be raised in the truth that they have always been loved and very much wanted."

A QUICK FAVOR

Dear Reader,

I hope you enjoyed reading *I Know What You Did* as much as I enjoyed writing it. Thank you for taking the time to check out my books and I would appreciate it from the bottom of my heart if you would leave a review, long or short, on Amazon as it makes a HUGE difference in helping new readers find the series. Thank you!

To be the first to hear about my upcoming book releases, sales, and fun giveaways, sign up for my newsletter at **www.normahinkens.com** and follow me on Twitter, Instagram and Facebook. Feel free to email me at norma@normahinkens.com with any feedback or comments. I LOVE hearing from readers. YOU are the reason I keep going through the tough times.

All my best,
Norma

WHAT TO READ NEXT

Ready for another thrilling read with shocking twists and a mind-blowing murder plot?

Check out my entire lineup of thrillers on Amazon or at www.normahinkens.com.

Do you enjoy reading across genres? I also write young adult science fiction and fantasy thrillers. You can find out more about those titles at **www.normahinkens.com.**

THE OTHER WOMAN

Start reading *The Other Woman, the next book in the **Domestic Deceptions Collection**!*

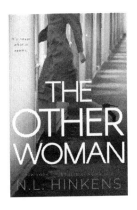

Not all secrets are what they seem.
When Bridget spots an elegantly dressed woman leaving her husband's office late one night, she fears the worst. Her marriage is already strained but things are about to take an even more shocking turn when her family is suddenly torn apart by a horrific crime they all become entangled in.

Her trust is shattered, her husband is on the run, and her son is hiding a dark secret. Bridget's life has become a dangerous lie and the clock is ticking as the police close in on a killer.

But who can she trust when all roads lead back to her husband and son?

- A gripping thriller that will leave you doubting those you love most! -

BIOGRAPHY

NYT and USA Today bestselling author Norma Hinkens writes twisty psychological suspense thrillers, as well as fast-paced science fiction and fantasy about spunky heroines and epic adventures in dangerous worlds. She's also a travel junkie, legend lover, and idea wrangler, in no particular order. She grew up in Ireland, land of storytelling and the original little green man.

Find out more about her books on her website.
www.normahinkens.com

Follow her on Facebook for funnies, giveaways, cool stuff & more!

BOOKS BY N. L. HINKENS

BROWSE THE ENTIRE CATALOG AT
www.normahinkens.com/books

VILLAINOUS VACATIONS COLLECTION

- The Cabin Below
- You Will Never Leave
- Her Last Steps

DOMESTIC DECEPTIONS COLLECTION

- Never Tell Them
- I Know What You Did
- The Other Woman

PAYBACK PASTS COLLECTION

- The Class Reunion
- The Lies She Told
- Right Behind You

TREACHEROUS TRIPS COLLECTION

- Wrong Exit
- The Invitation

NOVELLAS

- The Silent Surrogate

BOOKS BY NORMA HINKENS

I also write young adult science fiction and fantasy thrillers under Norma Hinkens.

www.normahinkens.com/books

THE UNDERGROUNDERS SERIES
POST-APOCALYPTIC

- Immurement
- Embattlement
- Judgement

THE EXPULSION PROJECT
SCIENCE FICTION

- Girl of Fire
- Girl of Stone
- Girl of Blood

THE KEEPERS CHRONICLES
EPIC FANTASY

- Opal of Light
- Onyx of Darkness
- Opus of Doom

FOLLOW NORMA

FOLLOW NORMA:

Sign up for her newsletter:
https://normahinkens.com/
Website:
https://normahinkens.com/books
Facebook:
https://www.facebook.com/NormaHinkensAuthor/
Twitter
https://twitter.com/NormaHinkens
Instagram
https://www.instagram.com/normahinkensauthor/
Pinterest:
https://www.pinterest.com/normahinkens/

Made in the USA
Middletown, DE
27 August 2023